The Narcissist's Daughter

A Meshugenah Love Story

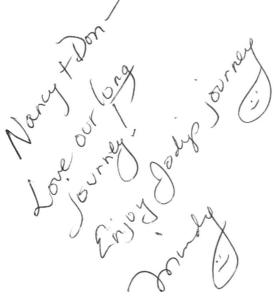

Nancy + Don
Love our long
journey!
Enjoy Jodys journey

Published by The Place for Words Press
Bedford, Massachusetts 01730

ISBN 9780983739777 (paperback)

Cover design: Monderer Design
Cover illustration: Patricia Kaegi
Author photo: Carlton Soohoo

Notes:

➤ *This is a work of fiction. Names, characters, places, and incidents are the products of the author's imagination or are used fictitiously. Any resemblance to actual events, locales, or persons, living or dead, is entirely coincidental.*

➤ *For those who may find it useful, a glossary of Yiddish words/Jewish terms used in this novel can be found at the back.*

Dedication

Dedicated to the late Jerry Christen, founder of Bedford Center for the Arts, who "saw" me before I could see myself. And to his widow, Charlotte Christen, whose fostering of my BCA creative writing classes ignited one of my greatest joys—guiding writers of all ages toward their goals.

I also dedicate this novel to my dear friend and college roommate, Shelley Rotman, gone way too soon.

Nothing

The pain gets locked inside a child, and there's a
child in us all...

And Mama it's not just irrelevant nonsense
What are you hiding? Where is your conscience?
You expect me to follow, but I'm stronger than you
and ready to feel life, ready to find out....

And it is only in ourselves we can choose to let it be
but now I'm grounded at the gate....

You don't even know me
Do you know how that feels?
It feels like I'm no one, It feels like I'm nothing....

You expect me to follow, but I'm stronger than you
and ready to feel life, ready to find out....
Not afraid to find out.

- excerpted from Kristen Hall's "Nothing"

PART ONE

Prologue
December 24, 1996

It started as an ordinary Christmas Eve. Well, ordinary for a Jewish couple with a crazy—*meshugenah*—December twenty-fourth ritual.

On that chilly day, Stewart stayed home to catch up on paperwork while our toddler took her long midday nap. My task was to return a bunch of Chanukah gifts at the mall, then purchase our secret bone-in, butt-end ham for dinner. I preferred joining our Jewish friends for Chinese food that night, but my husband insisted on sticking to our annual tradition.

So when I found myself stuck in bumper-to-bumper traffic on the highway, feeling curiously rebellious, I bailed out at the second exit, skipped the mall and headed for the groceries. What was I thinking, agreeing to go to the mall on Christmas Eve, anyway?

Just outside the door to Market Basket, I pulled my black ski hat low on my forehead and shoved my gloves into the pockets of my pea coat. I grabbed a red hand basket and raced to the meat department. When my clogs clomped too sharply on the linoleum floor for this clandestine mission, I slowed down.

At the holiday meat refrigerator, the first petite, spiral, hickory-smoked half-ham I spotted was unusually cheap. Good, since my husband would barely eat three slices and I'd just pick at one. Then, like his late parents did, we'd toss the rest in the trash. Every year, I wanted to ship the leftovers overseas to starving children. Or make ham and pea soup for the local soup kitchen I volunteered at—but then my secret would be out.

I glanced around, not that I would know anyone at this location, but I needed to be careful. Coast clear, I heaved the ham into my basket and fashioned my wool hat around its red netting until I had completely disguised the half-soccer-ball-sized piece of pig meat.

Sauntering to the pet aisle, I swung my goods as carefree as Little Red Riding Hood off to see Grandma, then casually tossed a box of Milk-Bones into the basket. I laughed when it landed like it knew its job was to hide a foolish, hat-covered ham. And thank God for that—just after picking up the pineapple and peas, I spotted Gossip-Is-My-Middle-Name Ethel Schwartz at the far end of the canned goods section. Had she seen me with the ham? My heart pounded as I imagined Mother telling everyone the shameful tale of the Yenta-from-Temple-Who-Witnessed-Jody-Buying-Treif. I immediately reversed direction, slinking behind all the other last-minute holiday shoppers, and sped the long way around to Produce, annoyed that my noisy clogs were tapping out a tune of potential doom. After seizing a zucchini for our toddler's dinner, I crept toward the under-ten-items register, glancing about repeatedly, painfully aware my basket contained contraband.

It was a short line, fortunately. After paying, I thanked the helpful young man for triple bagging my stuff as I'd requested. Didn't need it plopping onto the market floor during my exodus.

It's not that I grew up in a religious family, or anything. We didn't observe Sabbath, for instance. I guess we were what people referred to as "High Holiday Jews" who go to temple mostly at the Jewish New Year in autumn. More culturally Jewish than pious. And although my Bubbe refused to eat verboten foods like shellfish and bacon, her son—my father, the most religious of us—consumed his share of treif, and so did the rest of us. Nonetheless, that Christmas Eve afternoon, I wasn't just buying a bit of bacon bits; the act of purchasing and making *a whole ham* would make most Jews squirm, probably even secular ones. And I was sure if my mother were to learn her daughter bought a ham, she would fall over and plotz.

The ham dinner tradition, ironically, originated with Stewart's religious Jewish parents, may they rest in peace. They kept kosher three hundred and sixty four days a year, except on their wedding anniversary—December twenty-fourth, when my mother-in-law would mark the occasion by pulling down the front window shades hours before a trusted Christian friend arrived to drop off the ham. Dinnertime, the family of four would eat the ham with pineapple and peas on paper plates—circumventing their usual kosher dishware.

Stewart had no clue to the origins of this meshugenah ritual, but he liked recreating it as a memory of his parents' idiosyncrasies. I always suspected one parent had secretly converted long ago. But I hadn't inquired, and after they had both died from lung cancer, four months apart, the year Stewart and I married, it no longer felt acceptable to ask him. Truth is, I intended to finally put a stop to this unsettling custom the following year when our Hallie would be a little person of her own. Enough was enough. Maybe we could start honoring them instead with a Christmas trip to their favorite vacation place, Miami Beach.

11

But I agreed to do it just once more, with the sole purpose of pleasing my husband.

~~~

That Christmas Eve, however, none of us ate the sacrificial ham. Never even heated it up. With the grocery bag safely on the back seat of my Outback, I pulled out of the supermarket and headed home. I shivered, partially from post-Ethel nerves, partially from the cold air. The sky showed no promise of white fluff falling to beautify the area. Just a chill in the air. With Hallie-the-Solid-Sleeper no doubt still napping, I hoped to squeeze in a few minutes on the exercise bike, followed by a shower, before starting dinner.

I turned on the car radio and flipped the knob past numerous stations until I landed on WBCN, one of the only Boston stations not playing Christmas tunes. The songs had sounded pretty in late November but were irritating by now. As I listened to Charles Laquidara spoofing holiday songs, I laughed the whole way home on the jammed highway, then off my exit onto Massachusetts Boulevard and around the rotary by Old Town Hall. I continued laughing as I travelled down the windy back roads approaching home. As I turned onto our street, I kept giggling at the radio personalities' jokes—then stopped short when I spotted a red Camaro parked in front of our garage.

Again? My husband thought he'd surprise me, this time, with a belated Chanukah gift? On Christmas Eve? It looked like the exact car he had selected for my thirtieth birthday two years before. I had refused it, annoyed he'd chosen something so flashy, particularly with a baby on the way. He sulked for days. This year, for Chanukah, the dog-patterned flannel pjs were precisely my style, along with the certificate for dinner at the Top of the Hub and, yum, that sexy black dress he selected. They were all good enough for me. So what that I had rejected the flashy purple ski bib; my old black one was good-enough, plus we never skied anymore, now that we were busy, devoted parents. Truly, what was Stewart thinking with this car purchase? And, wait, this one had a dented bumper; why would he try again with a used car when he knew I loved the Subaru?

I squeezed in beside the Camaro. My light mood vanished, replaced with an ache at the base of my neck. I rubbed it with one hand while pulling up the emergency brake with the other a bit too hard, causing my whole body to quiver. Stepping out of my door, I leaned onto the Camaro's passenger side window, cupped my hands around my eyes and squished my face up to the glass. Through my own annoying reflection of medium-length dark curly hair, a too-pointed nose, close-set brown eyes and fleshy lips, I could make out a red jacket adorned with a gold "TWA" pin. Beside it sat one of those little black suitcases stewardesses drag behind them at airports. I wrapped my wool coat around my shivering body and scanned my brain. Hmm, who might this car belong to? One of Stewart's co-workers dropping something off? On Christmas Eve?

I rubbed my neck and temple a few seconds, then opened my rear car door. As I leaned in, I caught sight of my reflection in the window again. This time my lips were puckered and multiple worry lines pirouetted between my brows, the combination contorting my features. I took a big breath before hoisting the grocery bag, and then balanced it awkwardly in one arm as I fished in my pocket for my house key. I climbed the few steps and unlocked the mudroom door.

Straight ahead, a little hint of light sneaked through the closed porch blinds, just enough to see a black purse resting on the round glass kitchen table, keys beside them—also sporting a TWA logo. Hmm, did he have an airline account?

"Hullo? Stewart?" Silence.

Without turning on any lights, I dumped the few groceries onto the counter, noticing, for the first time, how phallic the zucchini I'd chosen looked. I picked up the ham in its shiny red paper and black netting and dangled it from my fingers as I checked out the lower level. All dark and quiet in Stewart's office. So strange. Even Ringo didn't come running.

"Hullo?" I asked again, keeping my voice low so I wouldn't wake Hallie. No response.

Where was everyone? Downstairs in the basement exercise room? Nope, the light switch was off. This was crazy. Despite chills, I felt sweat form on my forehead. Oh, maybe Hallie woke up early and they were all out walking our cocker spaniel?

Checking to see if the house was, indeed, empty, I hugged the ham to my breast and stood before the stairs to the upper level. Until that moment I had never known the house we'd called home for three years contained so many carpeted stairs. But during this climb I counted each step as I crept up, wondering about all those Thursday west coast business trips Stewart had taken since well before Hallie was born. Those trips had extended into Sunday because flights back home were way cheaper, he'd explained.

I took another step and tried to remember the last time we'd made love. Was it the long Columbus Day weekend, or way back in summer? And what was the excuse he used the last time I leaned my head on his chest in bed, something about being too tired, worn out from all the extra hours on sales calls?

I scanned my memory for details about the new account someone from the bank recently called about, with my husband dismissing it later as a foolish error.

I tightened my hands firmer around the six-pound ham costing only $9.99, the unusual bargain I'd been curious about. My legs felt weak and my breath shallow. My head throbbed, the earlier discomfort now reaching migraine proportions. I hoped I wasn't coming down with a bug.

As I turned the corner of the stairway, I startled. I was looking right up at Ringo's wide-open brown eyes. He was wagging his little stump of a tail but stayed put, guarding Hallie's room. I climbed the final stairs and heard my daughter's naptime Bach playing from behind the closed door, but no other sounds. Still napping. So where was her babysitter? Her *Dad*?

I gazed down the long hall toward our bedroom and back at Ringo, who glanced away. Holding the ham in my right hand, I tiptoed closer and took a deep breath before opening the door one tiny turn at a time with my other hand.

The first thing my aghast eyes captured was Stewart and his red lingerie-clad bimbo lifting their heads from each other's private parts, her long blond hair falling about her ham-sized breasts, and a huge gold cross dangling into her vast cleavage. As I exhaled and heaved the ham at Stewart's prematurely bald head, I felt my breakfast rising from my stomach into my mouth, regurgitating over a sight no one should ever walk in on. Especially a loving spouse.

"What the hell! Jody—" Stewart shot out a protective arm and the ham dropped to the rug with authority.

"Hallie's right down the hall...you were in charge of her...how *could* you?" The words came out of my mouth in slow motion, like someone else's voice.

As my husband tugged to cover the two of them with our white floral quilt—embroidered with my Bubbe's precious handiwork—a pink plastic object resembling a giant pacifier exploded into the air like off a trampoline. It bounced a bit and landed near my feet.

I stepped backwards and hugged my arms around my body, trying to contain the shivers and suppress the putrid musky smell of that woman in my bed. Ahh, the odd scent I'd noticed on Stewart now and then for a long, long time.

Trapped under the quilt, the blond sounded like an adolescent girl trying to be all grown up: "You promised she'd be gone for a long time, Stewie!"

He sat up, ignoring her, and narrowed his eyes at me like I was the stranger in the bedroom. The bushy, black hairs on his chest, which I used to like to twirl my fingers through, now made him look like a petite, bald ape. I steadied myself on our bureau and tried to swallow down the rising oatmeal.

"Jody, it's not what you think."

"Oh, no? You mean she's your urologist doing a house visit, *Stewie*?" A strange sound emanated from deep inside me like the squeak of a deflating dog toy. I watched motionless as Ringo rushed in, jumped on the bed, and landed his front paws on Stewart's crotch, his rear paws on the woman's head. All my cocker spaniel needed was a Superman cape.

"Ouch!" The woman screamed as she shot up in bed, tented by the blanket like an erection gone wild.

"Shit!" Stewart howled. "You okay, Brooke?"

It was that—the name, *her* name, and his asking after *her*, not our child, or me—that released a scream from me that could have been heard all the way to Boston. Ringo jumped off the bed and raced back to his post, the pink, plastic sex toy dangling from his jowls.

With each breath I took to attempt to calm down and face the reality my marriage was now unequivocally over, the squeaky toy sound from inside of me became louder. My head ached so badly I wanted it to just roll off my shoulders. My lungs felt ready to collapse, and fragments of food rose into my throat. My eyes fell on the ham—the ham I had bought for him, his *stupid* ham—and suddenly I dove toward it and hurled it at Stewart and *Brooke*.

"Get out of my house *now*! And take the cheap piece of pig with you—both of them!"

I barely made it to the hall toilet before I retched.

16

~~~

After they left and I had checked on the blessedly still-napping Hallie for the millionth time—had he drugged our baby in addition to everything else?—I paced the whole house, then grabbed a huge garbage bag and paced again. I tossed shit of Stewart's in the trash from every room—his smelly athletic socks laying around in his office; his favorite worn hooded sweatshirts I despised in the hall closet; his coaster collection in the den from places he travelled to on business—with her?—and I dragged his old set of skis and poles up from the basement and shoved them out the front door. I'd been begging him to sell those for years.

Exhausted, I finally sat at the kitchen table and called my best friend. She insisted I go take a migraine pill. She'd flag a cab from Boston and head over.

"Be there in an hour, depending on the stupid Christmas traffic," Ruthie said. "And you're kicking him out for good, no option."

We hung up and I pictured my tiny friend, with her big brown eyes and jet black hair nearly down to her waist. Streaks of prematurely silver strands popped up, here and there, with a mind of their own. We'd helped each other through so much, and I really needed her now.

I waited for Ruthie's arrival with an ice pack on my head and an odd pain in my gut. Four years of marriage down the drain. It was far from a perfect union, but it was good enough, and I had never questioned whether he was loyal. And now poor Hallie's life was about to be forever changed. I wanted to wake her and hold her, but that would be selfish. Let her sleep a bit more. Thank God she had missed all of this.

I poured myself a small shot glass of Stewart's repulsive scotch, and then I took the phone into the living room and lay down on the couch. I must have imagined I'd just downed Fairy Dust, because I dialed, of all people, my

17

mother—forgetting that her most memorable comment after my high school prom date dumped me was: "I did not want you going out with a Catholic goy anyway."

Wrapped in my thick velour bathrobe, pacing my kitchen floor as far as the phone cord would allow, I ranted to Mother about Stewart. Despite her shrieking at first, like she'd seen a mouse, she stayed silent—an actual miracle. But eventually her lips parted, and the Fairy Dust wore off: "Oh Jody, sometimes that is all we get in life, imperfect men. They all have affairs—well, not your father, he knows he'd lose me in a flash. Try again with Stewart, dear. Maybe buy something silky—how about a garter belt? We can go shopping sometime and—"

I dropped the phone on the couch and raced to the bathroom to throw up again.

I did not answer when she called back.

For more than a year.

Chapter One
Early 1998

The house felt cozy and warm as Hallie and I took shelter from the brisk winds outside, although with the sky lowering its winter curtain so early, I needed to turn on the lights. It had been a busy afternoon of meetings for me, and day care for Hallie. Ringo grabbed his worn stuffed turtle and dropped it at Hallie's feet for a game of fetch. Thus began his fun part of the day. Mine too. Home with my loved ones.

We all snacked on Cheez-Its and chocolate milk, and I showed Hallie how to balance a cracker on Ringo's snout while the dog waited patiently for his treat. After clearing the table with her assistance, I settled the two of them into the den so she could color while I went to change out of my work clothes. Kicking off my black pumps, I flopped onto my bed, on my back, and leaned over to press the play button on the answering machine on my night table.

"You cannot avoid me forever, Jody. Call me. Mother."

Not again! I had refused to pick up when she called, or return her calls, ever since she rang my doorbell a month after Stewart left, and I stupidly let her in. But we didn't even get past "hello" because she stared at my toddler-toy-strewn living room and shouted, "Maybe if you cleaned up your house you could clean up your life!" I nearly pushed her out the door, bolting both the bottom and top locks. I went into my study and blasted music for an hour. Finally, I peeked outside. There was a God: her car was nowhere to be found.

After that, her calls came less frequently, yet I couldn't escape her periodic poison on my answering machine. I was shocked she was wise enough to not show up at my door again, although I'm not sure what I would have done if she had. Jail time might have been in my future.

On the other hand, whenever I heard my father leaving a message, I answered. He limited the conversation to topics like Hallie's newest vocabulary words, whether my car was up to date with oil changes and whatnot, or if the heat was warming up the house okay in the cold weather. This kind of dialogue made it clear he was concerned about me and Hallie, but I needed to fight my own battles with Mother, and work my way through my decisions about Stewart, on my own.

I paused the machine and tossed my suit jacket over the handlebars of Stewart's exercise bike. It served its daily purpose as a great temporary closet until the rare times I finally pedaled it. That's why I asked him to leave that one item behind, and take everything else, no matter how insignificant, including every last belt and tie and widget off his tool bench, and every piece of dirty underwear and other stuff still in the laundry basket, and even the tux my mother had bought him that he wore only to my family's posh black-tie events. And of course, I demanded he take the tainted bed.

A few days after the "incident," after he'd rented an apartment three towns over, with a bedroom for him and one for Hallie, I insisted he get our bed out of my house, along with our bureau and end tables. As well as his entire office contents, and anything else remotely belonging to him. I also insisted he confiscate the bedspread Bubbe had embroidered for us. Sadly, no amount of washing could erase the scum from my mind. He didn't argue about any of it, so long as he got to see his daughter. Besides, it was my house, purchased mostly with my family's money, so he couldn't fight me for that.

He arrived with the U-Haul as scheduled, with Hallie safely out of the house at day care. He also brought along a hired helper, as bulked up as a bodyguard, who carted in a stack of boxes and packing tape. Stewart and I did not meet eyes, although we were nearly the same height, and it was impossible to miss the thick bandage on his nose thanks to my marksmanship with the ham.

Halfway through moving things out, he sought me out, finding me in the laundry room, folding Hallie's clothes. I think he looked directly in my face, but I gazed at the wall above him. After a quick apology for his "mistake," he said that Brooke only visited now and then, because she lived in Florida—with her husband.

"We don't love each other. It's just for kicks, Jody."

Did he truly think that might make it all okay?

I turned my back on him and walked away, securing my bedroom door behind me.

The rest of the time he and his bodyguard were in and out of my house, I loaded the dishwasher, folded more laundry, threw in another load, and otherwise tried not to notice my life was continuing to unravel right around me.

After they pulled away from the curb, I tore myself away from the window and grabbed the vacuum and a huge container of Glade Air Freshener. I spent the next half hour vacuuming every inch of the bedroom rug and spraying the entire empty room, walls and all, until it smelled like a gardenia garden. When I was done, I slammed the door behind me, collapsed into a fetal position on the hallway rug and sobbed, swearing to never enter that room again.

Ruthie and I had moved everything of mine out of the bedroom that ugly Christmas Eve. As soon as she arrived, she tucked me into bed to sleep off my migraine, promised to read books to Hallie before feeding and bathing her. She eventually woke me to put my sweet girl to bed. The minute Hallie fell off to sleep, Ruthie ushered me to the kitchen. She pulled out some bourbon from her overnight bag. I grabbed the soda and two glasses. After we'd downed a few and made a list of everything cocky and obtuse and sexually deficient about every man we'd ever dated, Ruthie unveiled the clove-scented air freshener she'd brought over. I giggled uncontrollably, remembering the fabulous evil-spirit ritual we had carried out after the last of her noncommittal boyfriends had moved out a couple of years back. Perfect! My friend was a genius!

We tiptoed up to the bedroom and she cracked opened the door. I grabbed the spray from her hand and let a solid spritz blast just inside the door. She pushed the door open and as we entered, I blasted the stuff about the entire room as we both recited: "Out damned spot! Out I say!" in our best Shakespearean Lady MacBeth accents, eventually falling on the floor, hugging and crying and laughing and spraying more all at once.

When it stunk like a whorehouse, we carted out everything of mine, tipsy armfuls at a time. We reminded each other to hush while slinking past Hallie's bedroom door. Ringo sat there guarding her door and looking at us like we were strangers, his eyes narrowed and his tail stump pointed down.

We moved my clothes, shoes and books to the nearby guest room—why hadn't they screwed in there at least, so I didn't have to abandon my entire bedroom? And we stuffed anything sexy I wore just to please Stewart into a Hefty trash bag large enough to fit a dead body. A few times I would cry, remembering our lovely trip to Aruba, or a special dress I wore on an anniversary, but then I'd wonder what was ever real? And I'd dry my tears and soldier on.

As the night wore on, we sorted through my jewelry and knickknacks and packed up anything reminding me of him. Ruthie would save those at her place until I could decide what to donate or sell—including my engagement and wedding rings, which she slid off my finger to place in her safe deposit box at her bank.

By the time we were done, everything had found a place. Including one item we each took turns prancing around in— a pair of red patent leather hooker heels, never worn—which Ruthie decided to take home in case she "got lucky."

Then we split the entire quart of mint chip ice cream she'd purchased after she had made the taxi driver stop at a convenience store.

~~~

Soon after, I converted the lower level guestroom, directly below Hallie's room, into my bedroom. The first thing I did was plug in her baby monitor so I could hear her downstairs. I purchased an antique oak bedframe and dresser I found in a secondhand furniture store near Boston University, had a local furniture store deliver a spanking new double mattress, and hung up framed "Life" magazine covers of Princess Diana beaming her innocent smile. Every other spare wall or counter contained photos of Hallie in colorful frames I found at five-and-dime stores. Any pictures Stewart took of the two of them were placed in Hallie's bedroom only.

Although I allowed her father to see her every other weekend so long as that woman never entered the same air space, it became challenging to hate Stewart while Hallie loved him. I argued with him on phone calls while Hallie was at day care, but I faked it around him when we made her transfer to each home. We both tried hard to act normal, making her time alone with each of us special. And in between her visits, whenever I mentioned Daddy I used a singsong voice—while imagining him as Godzilla. But other than carrying through with my lawyer for a separation agreement, something had kept me from moving ahead with a divorce until recently.

Perhaps my mother's early phone messages had influenced me some? She'd say things like, "Give it a couple of years to let the dust settle, dear," and "I hear he's being a good father, maybe you should try again?" I didn't hear things like "I'm bringing over corned beef and knishes so you'll eat something," like some of the older Jewish mothers in my neighborhood did when they heard the bad news. We even got homemade chicken soup if anyone heard one of us wasn't well. Between them and my Christian neighbors, with their lasagnas and chicken dinners cooked wonderful new ways I never would have imagined, Hallie and I ate well without my needing to spend much time cooking.

I accepted the help the first year, but kept it mostly to quick exchanges outside my front door, as I preferred focusing my time on my daughter. Other than time with Hallie or going to a movie or dinner with friends occasionally, my closest night-time companions for twelve months were my Monet puzzles. Analyzing the pieces occupied me after Hallie fell off to sleep. I carefully studied each wistful, pastel-shaded piece to help locate its partner. I tried to match the darker pieces where haystacks created ominous shadows and where water lilies clung together as they floated into murky waters. Who knew so many variations of blue existed?

~~~

I returned to the answering machine and pressed the play button again.

"Hi, it's Rhonda…." Oy. Did my sister really think she needed to identify her grating voice? "I know you don't want to hear what Mom has to say, but come on, pick up the phone for *me*. Let's chat, call me."

What? Was she studying lingo on Geraldo Rivera reruns for a segment on "Sisters Who Don't Get Along And Never Talk But Suddenly Share Intimate Details"? When she gave birth to her daughter several months back and I visited her in the hospital—being sure to show up when only Dad was there, not Mother—she asked me, in front of her friends, if my husband was still screwing the stewardess.

No thank you, Rhonda, I will not return your call to "chat."

I peeled off my black, fitted skirt, flopped onto my lemony-smelling black and white striped comforter and sunk into the downy material. Ringo sprinted in and jumped on the bed. I kissed his warm furry head and motioned for him to go back to Hallie.

"I'll make your mac and cheese in a bit, honey," I called to her. "I'm getting into my jammies." I smiled at the thought of my sweet daughter engrossed in her latest masterpiece, the multi-colored crayons spilling off the coloring board by now and settling into the tan shag rug I planned to replace soon. She was so well-behaved and content while I transitioned from part-time working woman to single mother. After dinner, we'd do our new nighttime ritual we both treasured, singing along to her favorite Raffi songs, and holding hands as we danced about in a circle. We'd laugh whenever Ringo jumped up to join us. Afterwards, we'd calm things down with a quiet bath, book and, eventually, bedtime—but I often kept her up late to extend our time together.

"I'm making a picture of you and Daddy!" she shouted.

"I can't wait to see it," I lied. Well, I wanted to see her artwork, but the ones with Daddy in them stung.

I clicked on the tiny TV resting on its metal base in front of the bed. The Friday evening ABC news blared yet another report about President Clinton's assumed affair. I scanned for a glimpse of my father's brother in his characteristic navy blue pinstriped suit. Yup, there was his arm in the corner of the screen. Uncle Nathan had started representing President Clinton when he was accused of having sex with an intern. This was right up my uncle's alley, as he handled media damage control for the most intriguing clients. In the past he'd helped manage press leaks surrounding a French hotelier who'd been sued for having sex with an underage movie star, a Hollywood playwright caught plagiarizing, and a leading man on Broadway who turned out to be a woman. I never understood much about my uncle's job, and I wasn't sure I liked the sides he defended. Yet no one in the family said much about Uncle Nathan's work, except that through the years he had turned famous, mega wealthy—"a big macher," my father would say. He had moved the family into a posh Frank Lloyd Wright-style glass mansion in Westchester County, New York, when I was in junior high school. The three-level home was carved into a hill, with bedrooms partially underground. The grounds contained a swimming pool surrounded by an enormous patio, and a tennis court tucked into the woods far below. It was the perfect place to hold our family reunions on my father's side—the only side, since my mother, an only child, had long been orphaned.

The next reunion to honor my Bubbe's birthday was half a year away. We'd been doing this as long as I could remember. Of course, they were meant to be fun—with games and races in the pool, tennis competitions, poolside drinks with little umbrellas, and fancy restaurant dinners. Yet every year as we drove onto my aunt and uncle's long gravel driveway, and I knew the alarm was pinging in the house to announce our arrival, a knot formed in my belly. My family and I certainly lived in a nice home too, with a neighborhood pool and all. But this place made me uncomfortable, perhaps because I knew my mother expected me to be on perfect behavior. And I had to pack only clothes she approved of. When my sister and I were still living at home, she'd purchase new fancy fashions for all of us for the weekend, including hats that my sister and I "misplaced" the minute our mother turned her back. It was the only time Rhonda and I were ever in cahoots, but with her on my team, we got away with it.

These annual visits began in my aunt and uncle's former house as long ago as I could remember. Throughout the nearly four-hour drive to New York, my mother would remind Rhonda and me to be polite and not fight—which of course always led to our fighting even more. Mother would then send Rhonda off to play downstairs with our two little cousins while I had to stay back with the adults.

What I came to dread most every year was the part no one talked about: all the ongoing one-upmanships. Didn't anyone else notice and squirm? As kids, my sister and cousins continuously showed off new toys or gadgets and bragged about winning spelling contests or earning sports trophies; as adults, they, and now their spouses, spent hours bragging about everything from prestigious work goings-on to new cars to technology gizmos in their expensive homes. Okay, fine, so that was their style, not mine, but they also laughed about anyone who didn't live like them. When my Cousin Ellen's husband first entered the scene, he tried to fit in by boasting. But his beefed up brags only roused snickers by the others. I seemed to be the only one feeling uncomfortable for him. Stewart hadn't fit in either, but somehow they left him alone because he could talk sports with the guys—brownie points right there.

Even my mother participated in the one-upping. Every year I'd watch her compliment something of my aunt's—her newest prestigious paintings, new ultra-modern furnishings. Yet the tone of voice Mother used meant it was not to her liking, like the round metal-based seats that "look trendy—but aren't you disappointed they're not comfortable?"

The only ones who never tossed digs and quips were my father and Uncle Nathan. They always got along like, well, like relatives should, at least in my mind. With warmth and laughter, kindness and respect. And every year during the weekend, starting from when I was little, if I pointed out any of my reactions to my family, I'd be hushed and told not to be so serious and sensitive. For a while, I tried joining in on the bragging: "I made this outfit in home ec; look at my beaded bracelet my boyfriend gave me; I wrote the cover story for the college magazine, here, I'll show you; don't you love my new earrings I made in a silversmith class?" But as no one commented on anything that interested me, I just felt worse. Especially at the end of each weekend, when I'd watch with shock and distress as all the excess food went into the trash. Even then, I hated waste.

But I returned every year to honor my Bubbe—and try again to fit in and have fun.

This year, however, I dreaded the reunion more than ever, especially after skipping last year, when Mother concocted a story about me being off on "a business trip" with Stewart and Hallie so no one would learn about our "issue." Apparently, Rhonda was sworn to secrecy, too.

Still, I was finally ready to put to bed everyone's lies, and start living my life my own way. Trouble was, I had no clue what that meant yet, nor how to go about figuring it out without Mother's interference. I wasn't interested in all the perfection, competition and materialism. That kind of lifestyle, "Mother's Narcissistic Way," had never allowed me to feel like my own choices, or self, mattered. And Stewart's strong personality kept me transferring my obedience to my mother onto loyalty to him. Mothering Hallie, and training Ringo, were the first real experiences I had with feeling like I was truly happy being myself.

Now I felt ready to find out who the rest of my true self was.

~~~

The phone rang. Distracted by all of these thoughts, I grabbed it.

"So, you are alive? I thought I would see a story about you in the newspaper soon: Daughter kidnapped!"

I used every ounce of willpower, down to my pinky toe, to not hang up. "Look, Ma, what's to talk about? I'm never taking him back, and I gave it your ridiculous timeframe, well over a year now. Even Stewart was probably shocked I hadn't filed for divorce yet."

"I am just worried you will not find someone else who is Jewish and makes decent money."

She paused, and I exhaled loudly to keep from swearing. "He was screwing her for a long, long time, Mother! And I'm sure he still does when it's convenient for the two of them—despite her having a husband!"

"Jody Horowitz, I did not raise a trash mouth."

I leaned my head in my hand and jostled the contents. Why was I bothering with this woman, just because she gave birth to me long, long ago? I willed myself to keep quiet by wrapping a long curl around my finger. Hanging up was out of the question—I'd been doing that on and off for too long, and it just delayed the real truth—that I couldn't truly move on with my life so long as I succumbed to her emotional control over me. Since the "incident," I'd only let her see her grandchild when my father would take Hallie for visits to "Gammar Ida"—not that my daughter asked to see my mother. She had more fun visiting her great-grandmother, my Bubbe, where Hallie already sensed she could be herself and just play, instead of worrying about touching things at Gammar Ida's house. Or having to recite everything she had learned at "school" since her last visit.

After a long pause, Ida said, "Okay, sorry, we do need to try to talk though, do we not? You have missed all the holidays, and the only time Hallie has visited her new baby cousin you were not even there. This has to end, Jody."

I took a giant breath and exhaled so long I thought I'd pop a lung. It was the first time she'd ever used the five-letter word "sorry." I imagined those letters flashing in gold on my wall. Clearly they were meant to buy her something. I just didn't know what yet, but maybe it was time to learn what her real issue was. Eventually I had to face her. Had to find a way to forgive her so I could move on with my own life. I was not sure I could ever forgive her, but perhaps I could at least close the lifelong chapter on letting her control me like a puppet.

"How about we try to start over, Jody? Meet me at ten-thirty Monday morning at the Pillar House. We will have breakfast. But do not bring Hallie. And dress properly."

"I wouldn't dare bring her to watch her Gammar Ida chew me out for no good reason. Ma, it's my life, not yours, and I'm moving ahead with a divorce whether you agree or not. And by the way, I haven't worn ripped jeans since college—at least a decade ago. I kinda sorta know how to dress properly, even if you don't like my style."

"There you go again, taking my words too sensitively. Well, see you there. And please show up; do not embarrass me in front of the workers. You know this is where I meet with clients."

Hmm, "please" was a new word for her too. "Bye, Mother" was the best I could do.

Ida hung up without saying goodbye. I banged the phone into its cradle and felt the familiarity of doing that same thing whenever she called home from work to talk to me when I was a teenager. Without ever asking about my day, she'd launch into how busy she was at the office, and what chores I needed to complete for her, and how to prepare dinner—even though she'd left detailed notes on the kitchen table. Meanwhile, my sister and I followed her instructions every single day—yet she still didn't trust *me* to do it right?

~~~

After I'd put Hallie to bed for the night, I called Ruthie and told her the latest.

"Yeah, you need to go," she said, "but Ida gets only ten minutes to be sane, or you find some polite excuse to leave, like 'Oh dear, I think I left the oven on, gotta run.'"

I needed Ruthie's help deciding if I would be the compliant daughter or avoid the breakfast meeting altogether. It's not as though I'd actually agreed; I'd been ordered. Some things never changed, but I needed to change, because she clearly wouldn't. Only Ruthie truly understood it wasn't as easy as some might think to cut off completely from my mother's toxic parenting. All kinds of emotional and financial consequences would ensue. And shame. Always the shame. Like the time I broke a precious antique vase of hers by mistake while goofing off in the wrong place in the house; she scolded me for days despite my crying, and later begging, for forgiveness. Or when I cried to her as a preteen and said I needed more from her, and she replied, "What you need is a shrink." Or when I was away at college and she called to tell me my sister needed a biopsy for an abdominal cyst and I asked, "It's not cancerous is it?" and my mother wouldn't talk to me for weeks for saying "that word"—until it came back benign.

"If Ida's reasonable, which of course would be a fluke," Ruthie continued, "order breakfast and tell her your perfectly good rationale for the divorce—one year late, if you ask me, but you've already heard it from me a million times in English, Yiddish, and probably Pig Latin."

I wanted to join in her mockery but could hardly manage a smile, except when I imagined her long ponytail swinging as she spoke forcefully and bobbled her head all about.

"And be sure to remind her your attorney's well aware of the prenup," Ruthie added.

My mind raced to my mother's announcement a decade earlier when our parents presented Rhonda and me with large monetary gifts placed in new bank accounts. My mother insisted that when we married, we must create prenups "prophylactically" to protect our money and future inheritance from our husbands. As she spoke, I imagined sperm swimming around hundred dollar bills, so I asked if a prenup was like a money condom. "You will see, smart-mouth," is all she had said back then. Of course, I was now sorry she was right but glad I'd followed directions.

Ruthie continued. "If Ida makes a scene, stay composed, but buzz outta there. And don't look back. Heck, first get me one of those fancy crab things with asparagus and hollandaise sauce, and freeze it 'til I see ya."

"Thanks, as always," was all I could manage. Despite the best pep talk, I knew this meeting with my mother—no, with Ida, I'd start calling her by her name, too—might well dissolve into our usual roles, with her demeaning tirades whenever things didn't go her way, and my shifting into fight or flight mode instead of just calmly holding my ground.

~~~

"To be early is to be on time; to be on time is to be late; to be late is to be left behind." Ida's crazy motto whirled about my head as I pulled off the Route 128 ramp and into the driveway of the Pillar House. I deliberately arrived early for a change so I could be first. I circled around the huge parking lot of the white historic mansion-turned-restaurant. *Good, no black Mercedes with the vanity license plate "IHPRNT yet.* "I parked near the door and climbed out of my car. Rather than asking to be seated at a table, I stood in the portico in case Ida was obnoxious from the start. Then, per Ruthie's plan, I could bolt.

"Jody dear, I'm over here." Ida approached from the bathroom hallway, no doubt checking her weekly salon-washed-and-sprayed bouffant hairdo in the mirror. As though reading my mind about her car, she said, "The Mercedes is in the shop. I have a rental."

I giggled quietly as I observed my five-foot-one mother in her black mink coat with her hair dyed a little too black; she reminded me of the bear cub Hallie and I had recently seen at the Franklin Park Zoo. I leaned down low and placed a kiss on my mother's out-turned cheek, her usual greeting. I almost choked on the mix of Giorgio perfume and foul breath. It was as though something long ago had crawled into her body and died, bits seeping out with each exhale. *Maybe those are tiny pieces of me in there,* I thought.

I followed the hostess and Mother to her favorite table in the farthest corner of the restaurant, noticing how charming she acted to strangers. She asked after the hostess's children and nodded hello to the wait staff and few customers scattered here and there at this later-than-usual business breakfast hour. Hmm, had Ida planned it for ten-thirty in case I embarrassed her?

As soon as the waitress walked away, Ida whispered, "Oy, have you ever seen a backside that big?"

I wanted to tell Ida to shut her trap, that the woman was lovely, and I'd heard quite enough of her absurd comments through the years. But I couldn't start off by reacting to her crazy-making mishegas, so I pretended not to hear. Still, she recognized the look in my widened eyes and muttered, "You're so self-righteous, Jody. It is, indeed, the biggest backside ever!"

Instead of screaming at her, I dug my fore-finger nail into the fleshy skin of my thumb, hard—until my heartbeat normalized.

Mother planted herself in the seat facing out toward the restaurant's brass chandelier suspending from a gold-leafed coffered ceiling. She motioned for me to sit across from her. Aside from the blank wall, the only view I was afforded was of my mother, who looked a tad more wrinkled around the creases of her eyes than last time I'd seen her. But then again, I had bags under mine. I kept my black wool jacket on but unbuttoned, since I suspected this tête-à-tête would make me perspire.

"How've you been, Ma?"

"How could I possibly be with my daughter avoiding me?"

"Well that's getting us off to a good start once again." I tapped my fingers on the table. "What's good on the menu?"

"I always order the Western omelet, rye toast, marmalade." Ida removed her fur, placed it on the chair beside her. "My clients eat like pigs because I am paying. Lawyers are the worst. No wonder they all have big bellies."

I rolled my eyes toward the menu then lifted my head and thought about how to change the subject. She wore a wide, gold-braided chain necklace I'd never seen before. For a change, I actually liked it. "Nice necklace, is it new?"

"Daddy bought it for me when we were at dinner at the Ritz." She nodded toward my multicolored art glass hanging on a black cord. "I see you are still wearing jewelry with a 'small j.'" She fondled her necklace. "When are you going to start wearing jewelry with a Big J? Who is going to pay for nice things like this for you after you divorce Stewart?"

"Since when do I need things like 'this'? Not my style. Please, Mother, stop. Plus my work for the association pays a decent salary even though it's part-time. You know this! Besides, I love my job, and it allows for flexible time to be with Hallie." I gazed directly into her eyes. "It's the right thing, divorcing Stewart. It's not open for discussion. In case you're concerned, I'll receive child support for a long time, and some alimony. And I don't expect to be single forever, just for now."

"Well, I am upset you are making this decision. When Daddy told me the other day, I nearly fainted."

"The last year hasn't exactly been a piece of cake for me either. Stewart's remorseful, and a decent dad, but he still sees *Her*. Having *Her* anywhere near Hallie is a deal breaker for me. He knows I'll stop his partial custody. He's honoring it. I can tell. Hallie never mentions her."

I realized I'd been having a conversation with myself; Ida was looking at the menu and then her watch. I paused my soliloquy to see if she'd even notice.

"You cannot just start over, Jody. Especially with such a young child. Who will want to take that on? And look at you, you look so tired."

"You're kidding, right? I'm a good mom holding my life together, and this is what you point out? Yes, I'm tired! Of a lot of things. But I'm only thirty-three. Plenty young enough to start over. This wasn't my choice to dump our marriage upside down, but I need to be with someone loyal. And with better values! I deserve that and just wish you'd see it too."

"Give him another chance," Ida snapped. "Time has passed; maybe he has come to his senses."

I could barely contain myself in my seat as I watched her politely fold her hands across her beige silk blouse, her gold and blue scarf squished between her arms and her ample breasts. To help calm me down, I pictured her as a quirky Dickens character.

"Didn't Dad tell you it's no longer up for discussion? I'm filing for divorce, and that's that."

"You should have told me at the same time as Dad."

"Why? I knew you'd react this way. Isn't it time you tell me why you're so against this divorce? It's not like you loved Stewart or anything. It's not like you've liked anyone I dated, married or, for that matter, expressed the foggiest interest in."

I stopped myself from losing it. If I continued, I'd probably end up shouting my old argument that Yolanda, our family dog, nurtured me far better than she did. At least our German shepherd played and goofed around with me, kissed my tears when I cried, and cuddled me when I was lonely.

Ida looked up to study the chandelier. "Did I tell you we have been chosen to print all the materials for the Museum of Fine Arts?"

I nodded but shut off my ears. She was avoiding the confrontation and turning it into her incessant need for praise for expanding my father's printing business, and its panache, over the past twenty years. I was proud of her on days I could admit it, and I was proud of Dad and what he had built even before she joined him, but I wasn't going to feed her ego right now. I stayed silent.

"...so how will you go about finding another decent Jewish husband with a two-year-old?"

"*Decent* Jewish husband?" The waitress, heading our way, heard my elevated tone and turned back. "I'm divorcing a man who screwed up—literally and figuratively—and that's how you describe him? And, Ma, your granddaughter will be four at her next birthday."

"Two, three, whatever. A burden to a new husband. And, worst of all, you will be the only divorced Horowitz. You should be ashamed of yourself! Daddy and I are so embarrassed."

I banged on the table a bit too hard. "Ahhh...now we hit the crux of your issue! But damn it, don't you twist things around about Dad. I wish just once you'd let him speak for himself. He supports me on this—and has confidence I won't be alone with Hallie the rest of my life. It sure would help if you did, too."

"Look, you are getting fresh. Maybe I should just leave without buying you breakfast. Why can't you just be more like your sister? She is so much more like us."

"Holy shit, you're going to start that again? Perfect Rhonda? You do know she gave up her dream of owning a clothing boutique so she could earn her accounting degree and MBA just because you wanted her to be CFO of the company? And she married her first ever boyfriend just because he was a Jewish doctor, which so excited you! Yup, she sure is the perfect daughter, following your precise expectations—at what cost to herself, I might add, if she even has a self, with that husband of hers calling all the shots while he—" I caught myself and stopped talking before I let out incriminating information about Alan. Not that Ida would believe me. She, meanwhile, sat there flipping through her daybook, pretending she wasn't listening.

Why was I sticking up for Rhonda anyway? What had she ever done for me, her baby sister? Even when we were little, if I wanted to play dolls with her, she'd scowl at me and pick up a book. Yet when we were older and she'd be babysitting me, if I tried to study for a test in my bedroom, she'd call me an AP nerd and turn up the sound on the TV on the other side of my wall. If I invited a friend over, she'd make me cancel or lock the front door and not let me near it—even if our parents had said it was all right. It did me no good to tell on her—no one listened, always telling us to work it out ourselves. Now, as an adult, she claimed to have shaped her life exactly the way she wanted it, perfect husband, perfect house, new pearls for just about every occasion, hundred-dollar shoes, and invitations to whatever prestigious events she and Alan could worm their way into by making donations. Yet ever since she stopped working for my parents to raise Tiffany, she spent most of her time at the gym, leaving Tiff with the young nanny. Was that her idea of perfect?

I glanced at my watch. It was barely ten minutes into this stupid meeting. I needed to keep trying to let Ida implode, instead of me. Digging my fingers into the sides of my chair, I plunged in.

"Mom, please, stop comparing me to Rhonda. Sorry I've somehow let you down just by being me, and now my divorce is pushing you over the edge. But it makes no sense, really. You never thought Stewart would ever be successful enough as a sales consultant—though we were doing just fine for our needs." I started to take a sip of my water, but halfway to my lips I realized it was a bad idea as the glass jiggled in my hand.

"Oh, Stewart was good enough. Just try again with him. How was the sex dear?"

I slapped the glass down, water slopping onto the tablecloth. "Believe me, Mother, sex was not the issue. We were good-enough, so I thought, in many ways, including that one, until he couldn't keep his—"

"Enough! Look, the family reunion is less than six months away and frankly while everyone else is talking about business deals and whatnot, your divorce will be humiliating. Pity we cannot use the 'Stewart's on a business trip' excuse again. Just bring him, Jody. He is Hallie's dad. Pretend you are a happy family again and maybe, just maybe, it will actually happen."

"And should he also bring along Brooke, in a little red bikini? Maybe we can have a ménage a trois in front of Uncle Nathan, Aunt Bernice and the cousins while I wear the garter belt you'll select for the occasion from Saks? I'm sure Bubbe would just love this plan for her birthday weekend." I reached for my pocketbook, preparing to leave.

"Ever since Stewart left, something has happened to you. You were always sensitive, but now you are over the top." Ida stood and swung her scarf over her shoulder. She grabbed her mink coat and turned, but I tugged at her scarf, forcing her to turn back close enough for me to grasp her arm near the shoulder so she couldn't shake free.

"What's *happened*? I kicked out a man who screwed another woman and you're asking what's wrong with me instead of, maybe, helping cook some meals for us or offer to babysit once in a while, or even just show me some, God forbid, *emotional* support? And you expect me to bring him to our already messed up family reunion filled with forty-eight hours of determining who's most successful? Sorry, Uncle Nathan wins that one. And Aunt Bernice will always have more kindness, class and expensive designer *everything* than you. Give it up, Ma." I exhaled and let go of Ida's arm, motioning to the waitress.

For the first time I could remember, my mother stood motionless until the waitress approached. Ida maneuvered around her, moving her short legs so quickly she resembled a furry black Pomeranian dog trying to act fierce.

"I'll be dining alone this morning," I said. "Sorry for any inconvenience. Two Eggs Benedict, one to go, sauce on the side on both. And black coffee please."

I stood and switched seats, facing out. I couldn't wait to call Ruthie, tell her Ida had flunked, and I had won, sort of. And to come to the house to get her Eggs Benedict soon. And, oh yeah, please advise me on what the heck to do next.

Chapter Two

Hallie dashed ahead inside the lobby of the Jewish Housing for the Elderly. The click-clack of her new red shoes on the linoleum tiles made me smile despite my tense mood. She stood on tippy toes to press the elevator button. The door opened as I arrived, and we stepped inside.

"Going up?" Hallie asked in a deep voice. Each visit when she asked this, I made up a new destination to play the game. Today, other things preoccupied my mind, but I forced myself to reply in the customary way: "Eighth floor, please. Pet Department." She stood tall and business-like while playing doorman for me, oblivious to the brown pigtails jiggling about her angelic round face and big hazel eyes.

The elevator moved upward as sluggishly as most people in the building walked—except for my still-youthful Bubbe. I turned to face my little doorman. "Honey, listen, I need to explain some grown up stuff to Bubbe today. So you'll be playing by yourself for a tiny little bit." I held up a bag containing her travel coloring supplies.

"Yippee. I'll draw Bub-beeee."

We stepped out of the elevator, but when I spotted Bubbe way down the hall, I grasped Hallie's shoulder. "Shh,

40

let's let Bubbe finish talking to that man first." I crouched next to Hallie while we watched my grandmother outside her door, her groceries resting at her feet.

Bubbe handed the man what looked to be a small coin. As he approached the elevator with his empty cart, I dug into my purse. Hallie raced toward Bubbe.

"Hello! Here, this is for you, sir. I am Mrs. Horowitz's granddaughter. Thanks for helping her." I handed him a five.

"Why, thank you!"

His Aramis aftershave assaulted my nose, but it was preferable to the lobby's pungent scent of urine disguised as Mr. Clean, which remained nestled in my nostrils for hours after every visit.

The man entered the elevator and turned around. "By the way, I would do it for free for Mrs. Horowitz! Such a classy lady. I'm hoping she'll let me bring the groceries inside sometime. I keep offering."

He disappeared behind the elevator door just as I managed a smile. I wondered if this handsome, well-put-together, seventy-something-year-old man could possibly be trying to court my ninety-two-year-old grandmother? Then again, she looked eighty, was in great health, and no doubt lied about her age.

Down the hall, Hallie attempted to jump into Bubbe's arms despite the two grocery bags she was hoisting. Sadie Fine Horowitz lifted the packages and hugged her great granddaughter right between the bundles, Bubbe's humongous breasts flopping over the grocery bags. She planted a kiss on Hallie's head.

"My sweet Hallie girl! I vas hoping you'd come today!"

I raced toward the two of them. Bubbe wore a flowered apron over a striped polyester housedress, and her trademark Jean Nate perfumed the air.

"Let me carry those, please." I extended my arms and enunciated each word loudly and succinctly so my grandmother could hear.

"I've got it, don't hurt yourself," she said.

Although I was much taller and obviously way more fit, I knew my protective grandmother preferred to lift things herself.

"Come, Hallie darling, let me get you a snack. Come, Jody. I made rugelach and hamantaschen this morning. And bought some dog bones. No Ringo today?"

"Too many errands," I lied. I was too anxious about what I needed to tell Bubbe. I couldn't focus on walking the dog around to visit with eager residents, as usual.

As we entered the airy, three-room apartment, I breathed deeply. Yum, the smell of baked goods instantly relaxed my neck muscles. She was one of the only grandmas I knew who made delicious jam-filled hamantaschen all year round instead of only at the Purim holiday. Boy did I want those sweet treats right now. My mother and I hadn't spoken since the restaurant the week before, and while Ruthie and I agreed "the next one to talk loses," I nervously awaited Ida's next move on the chess board of our relationship. I wished the sweet smell of those freshly baked pastries, mixed with the familiar scents of my grandmother's home, could enter my pores, relax my spine, and envelop me in a blanket of worry-free peace.

Bubbe got busy separating bathroom and kitchen items from her grocery bags: I spotted two, thirty-two ounce containers of Listerine, two tubes of lipstick, deodorant, a large bottle of Jean Nate, and pink nail polish.

"Must've been a good sale," I teased, even though I knew her discount obsession went deeper. It stemmed from her roots as a Russian immigrant who came to America with her family at a young age. My grandmother could pass for a much younger woman if it weren't for her hearing aid, with its old-fashioned cord extending from behind her snow-white hair to an amplifier hidden in her "brassiere." Even when staying home baking and reading, which is how she spent most of her time, she always wore her favorite heart-shaped drop earrings and pink lipstick. And kept her nails manicured, visiting the manicurist downstairs every Thursday. Though she'd been alone for twenty years she still wore her wedding rings—one narrow gold band and another sporting a small solitaire diamond. Whenever she left the apartment, she pinned a locket to her chest, its enamel floral heart hanging from a gold-plated bow. "He's vit me all the time," she would say whenever anyone asked to peek inside. Bubbe's picture was on one side, Grandpa Bert's on the other.

My own hand still looked lonely without the diamond ring and wedding band I had removed on Pig Night, the name Ruthie and I had coined on New Year's Eve for that wretched night I had discovered Stewart with *Her*. Ruthie and I had clinked champagne glasses and toasted to "Sanity in '97." The toast was mostly for me, but also for her. She hadn't had a boyfriend, or a job for that matter, for quite a while. Now here it was 1998 and she'd found a great client she could work for from home most days, but she still lacked in the companion category. And her parents—though quite opposite from mine in most ways—were on her back about it. As for me, my work and parenting were deeply satisfying, yet despite grieving my shattered marriage and unclear future, pursuing a new man was nowhere on my radar screen. More consuming was the situation with Ida. I was hoping my grandmother could help in this area.

I stuffed a hamantaschen in my mouth, eating it in one bite, and then tied my long curls into a ponytail to help unpack Bubbe's groceries. Over-the-top cleanliness in her kitchen was my grandmother's main peccadillo—stubbornness her other.

Hallie had settled around the kitchen table, swinging her feet below her chair and munching on cookies. In her other hand, she held a fat crayon as she outlined Bubbe wearing what looked like an apron and carrying a round object emerging from multiple-sized fingers. Hallie was also adding something small next to her great-grandmother. I admired how intense she was while coloring, not wanting to be interrupted until she was through. A budding artist, or just a happy kid? Fortunately she had been young enough to adapt well to her parents living in separate homes.

As Bubbe and I finished unpacking, I gobbled down a few more cookies. When we were done, with my daughter still intent on drawing, I found my opportunity.

"Right back sweetie. Have to show Bubbe something in the bedroom. Here's a golden crayon if you feel like adding Ringo."

"Okeee, Mommeee," she said without lifting her head from her work.

I motioned Bubbe toward the bedroom. If Hallie heard the word "divorce" it would mean nothing to her, but the word "Stewart" might well draw attention.

"Vat? Vat?"

I shushed her with an index finger over my mouth and motioned again toward the bedroom.

The crowded room contained two single beds with dark mahogany head and footboards. I leaned against the closest one and pulled a note out of my jeans pocket. Bubbe knew about Stewart's affair but never said much about our separation, not even asking about a divorce unless I brought it up. With hands trembling, I unfolded the note and passed it to Bubbe like a kid in grade school. Lifting her glasses from their chain, she propped them up on her short round nose and sat on the closest mattress, covered with one of her matching worn bedspreads. It reminded me of the "tainted" one I'd tossed, so I glanced away. Ida had offered to upgrade these bedspreads a million times, even buying a set once from Lord and Taylor, but Bubbe insisted she return them. Bubbe and Bert had picked them out when first married, and when she learned how to needlepoint, she added their initials and a heart. These bedspreads were to stay. Forever.

I moved to stand beside the antique dresser and scrutinized Bubbe's face as I watched her eyes taking in my note: *"I wanted you to be among the first to know I'm moving ahead with a divorce. Hallie will be fine. I'm sorry to disappoint you, but it's the right thing to do. I'm still going to live in our house—it's mine legally. Mom and Dad know, but NO ONE ELSE is to know for now."*

Bubbe stood and let her glasses dangle again. Using both hands, she ripped up the note. She walked the few steps to the trash can and dropped in the tiny paper pieces. I watched her wipe at her hands carefully, as though each piece had been a shard of glass she wanted no part of. She walked toward me, her eyes filled with tears, then wrapped her arms about me.

"It's fine for me if it's fine for you. His loss. You'll find someone with better character." Warmth filled my heart as she unwrapped me from her arms. "And by the vay, you could never disappoint me. You and me, we're cut from the same cloth."

I motioned her back and handed her another note: *"Ida insists I try again and bring him to the family reunion, to your birthday celebration. She's embarrassed for the others to know I'm getting divorced. It's okay if I refuse, yes?"*

I repeated in my head, like a child: *Please agree, please agree.*

"Ida's meshugenah!" Bubbe slapped the side of her head and scrunched up the note on the way to the trash. She turned and walked back to the kitchen.

"Another masterpiece!" I heard Bubbe say to Hallie. I waltzed back into the kitchen with a lightness in my step I hadn't felt in a long time. Bubbe was taping the picture on the wall beside the others. The wall was as filled with artwork as a museum.

I examined Hallie's picture. The round object atop Bubbe's fingers now contained something resembling raisins but was probably meant to be a plate of cookies. Hallie had added me to the drawing, with long legs and a large pink body and head. And my daughter, wedged between us in the picture, was a tiny thing with long pigtails. Ringo was at the top, resembling a sun with legs. I wondered if it was healthy that Stewart wasn't in this picture? Maybe she understood the difference between her two families?

"Lovely, lovely family picture, honey." I kissed her on the top of her head and smiled at Bubbe.

The three of us sat in the living room trying to match llamas to llamas and emus to emus with Hallie's zoo animal match cards. Then we gobbled down tuna fish sandwiches on Jewish rye with sour pickles, Hallie's favorite. After the fifth round of yawns from each of us, I packed us up to leave.

In the small foyer, Bubbe handed me a big box which I knew came from my cousin. "Take zis linen dress Ellen sent me. She meant vell, but vhen will I ever wear it? Besides, it vill wrinkle the first time I wear it! Get it taken in to fit you. Maybe just once they could visit from that fancy penthouse apartment of theirs, instead of just sending things from Bloomingdales? Between her packages and what her brother's wife sends, I could open a NYC boutique right here for all the old folks."

"Great idea! Well, they mean well, I'm sure."

"Sure, sure, like your sister, but even though she's not working for Harry anymore, I haven't seen her in a month or more. She's too busy to drive one hour to show her new baby to her Bubbe now and then?"

"The nanny's the busier one, I suspect. Rhonda's probably busy going to the gym and whatnot."

I hardly needed to explain to Bubbe that I never saw Rhonda except with the family, not that I saw anyone all together for the past umpteen months. For as long as I could remember I was just an annoyance to Rhonda, and she was never the kind of fun, dependable sister my friends talked about. My grandmother understood Rhonda and I were sisters born from two different planets. As it was with me and my mother.

"I'll ask Harry about everyone tomorrow," she said.

In the old days, Hallie and I, and sometimes Stewart, had joined my father on his weekly Sunday night dinners out with Bubbe, and usually Ida came, too. But after Ida's brilliant show of empathy on Pig Night, I refused to go, sticking solely to these one-on-one visits, which Bubbe and I preferred anyway.

"You'll be back to see me again soon, maybe next Saturday, yes?" Bubbe asked.

"Can we Mom-mee?"

"Yes, of course, we'll be back soon, but you're with Daddy next weekend and gymnastics starts up again the weekend after. We'll work something out."

"Okeee. See you soooon though, Bubbeee."

Bubbe leaned low and made loud wet kisses on her great granddaughter's cheek until both stopped giggling long enough to catch their breath. "Say hello to your Daddy for me, dear."

"He says hi too." Bubbe and I glanced at each other with smirks on our faces, most likely with the same thought: Hallie learned nice manners from me, but also from her Daddy, so it seemed. Bubbe and Stewart had gotten along fine, but he had never gone out of his way to see her, despite no longer having parents or grandparents. Looking back, I guess "family" wasn't his thing.

Bubbe plopped a plastic sandwich bag of her home-baked cookies into my pocketbook. She knew my weakness. Whenever I announced "Backwards Meal" to Hallie, she shrieked with joy, because this meant she could eat dessert before a meal, as long as she ate her "real" food. This was routine at Bubbe's, with all the fresh hamantaschen and rugelach assaulting our senses. Clearly my daughter had inherited my sweet tooth.

"I hope to see you soon Jody dear, but if you're too busy, you know, dating, or something, just let me know."

"Maybe I should start dating so I can double date with you and Mr. Aramis who wants to bring your groceries inside?" I winked at Bubbe, who looked confused for a second, then blew a kiss goodbye and swatted my tuchus with her dishtowel.

Chapter Three

From behind the closed door, I heard the phone ringing in Bubbe's apartment and assumed it would be Uncle Nathan. He had begun his Saturday phoning system right after Grandpa Bert died. Nathan called his mother every Saturday to check on her and say hello whether he was home, in Europe on business, or even, sometimes, when he was meeting with the President or a world leader, just to impress his mother.

Somehow, Bubbe had no trouble hearing her two sons' voices on the phone, although she couldn't make out many words when anyone else called (go figure!), so she and I created a system. I would say my name loudly, she would acknowledge me. Then she would ask me questions. I'd reply with a booming yes or no, but other than that, we couldn't hold much of a conversation in between visits.

As Hallie and I skipped to the elevator, I found myself thinking about Grandpa Bert's funeral and the shiva afterwards. I was twelve, that awkward age between kid and teen. We had spent the day at my grandparents' Atlantic City apartment. Bubbe had removed the plastic cover usually protecting her couch. For the first time, I felt its plush upholstery after my grandmother invited me to sit beside her. I cherished my important post next to her on the soft couch, despite the itchy red, white and blue sailor dress my mother had made me wear.

My father and Uncle Nathan sat nearby submerged in Grandpa's deep, plaid-upholstered armchairs. The cushions were so well-used they retained permanent imprints where a lifetime of tuchuses had sat. I watched them as they received their visitors, reminiscing with everyone about their father and their happy boyhood. They told stories of playing stickball with the neighborhood kids, and catching a quarter out the window to fetch a bottle of milk for someone's mother—keeping the three-cent change if they were lucky. They sat in those seats like kings, drinking scotch in short squat glasses that clinked whenever the glass met their lips and jiggled the ice. They occasionally puffed on cigars, and while some people waved away the ensuing smoke, I liked to breathe in the familiar scent of my father's happiness, following it with my eyes as it drifted about the apartment.

My mother, who usually complained about Dad's smoking, didn't remark even once about the smell wafting about. Other than when she briefly greeted a visitor, she spent much of the day combing through Bubbe's big pile of photo and keepsake albums jammed with photos and other proud family documents. Sitting across the old walnut sofa table in a smaller version of Grandpa's comfy armchairs, Ida flipped through pages of each book, one at a time, providing running commentary. She muttered about this person's hideous shoulder pads; that person's necklace clashing with her blouse; the bright yellow silk dress she had fit into so well after that grapefruit diet for Grandpa's seventieth birthday party; and how Jackie-Kennedy-like her hair had looked.

"I never should have stopped going to the French hairdresser," she announced to no one in particular. Sometimes she'd comment on how big my father's belly looked, or how wide Rhonda's hips had grown, or how many letters from dignitaries Uncle Nathan had received. And why wasn't there more nachas about Harry? Occasionally she'd come over to show me a picture.

"You were adorable in that Cinderella outfit at Halloween," she said, showing me the photo of a blue taffeta dress and tin-foil tiara she'd purchased despite my begging her for a Flintstone's Bamm-Bamm costume. Or she'd point to eight-year-old me playing piano, unsmiling, a pixie haircut with bangs too short in the center where I'd cut them myself the day of my one-and-only recital. Or she'd share my elementary school report cards—with all A's but too many "shy in class" comments at the bottom.

I'd sometimes hear my sister and little cousins giggling from the bedroom down the hall. A part of me felt left out, yet I preferred holding Bubbe's hand while she talked with guests. Whenever I sensed in her voice she was about to cry, I waited for her to massage my fingers like they were pieces of rugelach dough. From my seat, I observed everyone stuffing their faces with bagels, whitefish, smoked salmon, and my aunt's sweet lokshen kugel, which I nibbled on now and then after she brought me some.

But by mid-afternoon, something felt twisted in my gut. I turned to my mother. "People are acting like it's a party! How can they do that?"

"What?" She looked around before tucking her face back into a photo album. "Oh, they're just trying to forget about death."

Forget about death at a *shiva*? To me, this was like forgetting about liver when it was on the place-setting right in front of you and there was no dog under the table to drop it to.

"Just stop trying to control everyone else, Jody. Go eat something, you'll feel better."

But I rarely felt better that day. Several times, I excused myself from Bubbe's side to grab a few chocolate rugelach.

51

I'd slip into the bathroom, cry a little, munch some rugelach, and then dry my tears and return to Bubbe's side.

~~~

While digging into my bag of cookies from Bubbe, I glanced in the rear view mirror. Hallie was asleep with her head leaning on her stuffed Dalmatian, Lucky. I felt filled with love for her and relief that my grandmother was on my side. I was about to bite into a cookie when I realized it was a dog bone! Bubbe was full of surprises. I plopped it on the car seat and dug back into the bag. I fished out a chocolate rugelach and chomped on it just as we drove by a favorite farm with grazing cows. I smiled.

At the earliest family reunion I could recall, Aunt Bernice's shiny pink-and-white cow-shaped cookie jar she kept on the kitchen counter soothed my broken heart after my sister had blocked the way for me to hold our new baby cousin. I had left the living room sobbing, and Bubbe came to my rescue. She dried my tears with her pink silk handkerchief, then glided my index finger over the stitches of her embroidered initials—SFH—until I stopped crying. She took my hand and led me into the kitchen, lifting the cow top with a "mooo," handing me a rugelach, and not only making me giggle, but making me feel as though she was the only person in the world who loved me.

And here I was now, nearly thirty years later, not talking to my mother, again, since the episode six days earlier, but feeling, finally, as though with Bubbe on my side, I could seek a life of my own and let the Pinocchio strings to Ida go.

Chapter Four

"Honey, Mommy's running late for her meeting, please let go."

The day care teacher hurried to my rescue. "Let's go play with Barbie in the dollhouse," Madison said, offering up Barbie in her pink ballerina outfit.

"No!" Hallie's frown remained, as did her sticky breakfast-in-the-car fingers clutching my skirt.

I kissed her cheek and tried again to gently unfasten her fingers. I could easily remove them and leave her for Madison to deal with, but I hated to do so, especially since this behavior was odd. "Please let go. I'll count to--"

"I want to come with you!"

"Look, I'll tell you what...I'll, I'll bring back something special."

"Ooh, fortune cookies?" Madison and I both smirked at Hallie's specific choice. I glanced at my watch. "Can't find those today, hon, but I'll bring back something else. Now go on with Madison."

"No! I want fortune cookies!" She stomped her Sesame Street-sneakered foot on the tile floor.

Why did she have to turn into Oscar the Grouch on the rare day I needed to get into Boston for an early meeting? And what was her issue this morning? Sure, we were a bit rushed, but this was unusual for her. Perhaps she was reacting to my stress.

"Fortune cookies, Mommy!"

I looked at my watch again. "Take your sticky fingers off my good wool skirt *now*!"

Unaccustomed to my raised voice, Hallie released my skirt and cried. I kissed her quickly on the head, and as soon as she hugged Barbie to her chest, she stopped crying. I flew out of there feeling rather shitty about the whole damn thing.

~~~

With Hallie moving slowly all morning, I'd only had time for coffee. Not far from Boston, I slid into the only super mini-mart with a parking lot I recalled. It was packed, but I managed to catch someone pulling out. Once inside, my choices were a greasy breakfast bomb or a sweet-cheese Danish that would bounce my sugar way up and crash me down in the middle of my meeting. What was I expecting to find, an omelet? Starving, I grabbed a bag of peanuts then scoured the cookie aisle and grabbed some sandwich creams for Hallie. Hurrying to check out, I almost knocked over a display of fortune cookies. Was it Chinese New Year recently, or just my daughter's lucky day? I placed the sandwich creams down off to the side, took a container of fortune cookies and slid into line, giggling out loud.

"Excuse me, where'd you get those fortune cookies?"

I turned and gazed into deep-set Bermuda-blue eyes. Framed by thick dark eyebrows, his long, oval-shaped head narrowed into a square jaw-line, with the hint of a dimple at the chin. A head or more taller than I, he was long and lean, fitting just right into a blue blazer and tan khakis.

"Uh, down the aisle over there."

"Thanks. I'll have to come back later, actually."

"Go grab 'em. I'll save your place."

"Hey thanks." He disappeared and I stilled my racing thoughts. I knew it was just some guy in a mini mart—I mean, he could be a creeper or an axe murderer—but he was the first man to catch my eye since I was separated. Maybe it was the prominent nose and slightly heavy beard stubble— like so many Jewish guys I'd known back in high school, including my biggest crush—but taller. Whatever, he felt familiar. And appealing.

He returned and held up the plastic package. "I could use some good fortune." He smiled, and his white teeth lit up against his dark skin. "You needing some good fortune too?"

I placed my items on the counter and turned back to him. "Yeah, I lost highly complex negotiations with a three-year-old this morning. How 'bout you?"

"That will be seven ninety-nine," the cashier interrupted. I placed eight dollars down and collected my things. "Good luck with your fortunes," I said, tossing him a smile. His eyes looked far away. I turned to leave.

"Child who eat cookies in car seat create *crumby* car." He shrugged and grinned. "It's the best I could come up with under pressure."

I chuckled, and my heart flip-flopped over this warm, corny guy. But what else could I say to stall, especially with scads of sleepy, impatient people all around us rushing to pay? I scooted away, glancing behind me once more. Was he checking out my tuchus in my fitted red wool coat, or was it my imagination? He shyly turned back to the cashier. I smiled.

Back in the car, I considered waiting for him to come out, but I not only had a meeting to get to, I felt awkward. Flirting was never my thing. As I backed out and drove off, I wondered how another woman might have converted such a sweet meeting into getting to know someone. I was certainly out of practice.

~~~

I rode the elevator from the parking garage to the top floor of the downtown Boston building. The door opened directly across from double glass doors leading into the Graphic Design Society offices. I was grateful a colleague had set up this meeting with the director. My goal as the Public Relations Association's executive director was to convince him to design our fiftieth anniversary commemorative booklet for free. I pushed open the doors and was immediately captivated by oversized photographs lining the reception area walls. Two in particular captured my attention: one of an old woman with a lined face and sweet smile, another of a young woman standing in the rain. She had curly straw-colored hair and sparkling eyes that looked mischievous.

"You must be Jody Horowitz." The receptionist startled me.

"Oh, excuse my manners, yes; I was lost in these lovely photos." I set my briefcase down.

"Thank you. Mr. Puricelli took them. He's an amazing photographer. Please, have a seat." She motioned to a coatrack and a sofa. "He will be here shortly."

I removed my coat and hung it up. I had no problem killing time on that cozy couch. I would daydream about the friendly, funny, handsome man I'd just met. He was probably even Jewish, and maybe even available? Yet I ran off for a meeting with an old guy who's late?

"Ah, here you are," the receptionist said. I turned with outstretched arm, ready for a handshake.

"*You're* Jody?" Sam Puricelli's mouth dropped open and his eyes bugged out like a cartoon character. He grasped my dangling hand and placed his other one over it for a few seconds. "Wow, I guess all those fortune cookies I just inhaled really worked!" His face beamed. Mine felt paralyzed, like the rest of me. I willed myself to talk.

"Uh, this is really rather, well, awkward, to be honest. Should I look for the Candid Camera hidden somewhere?" I glanced around.

"Yeah, we do this to all first-time visitors."

The receptionist looked askance at her boss and busied herself at her desk.

"Actually, I'm speechless," Sam said. "And believe me, that's rare. Come." He half motioned, half led me into his private office.

"Er, one sec. My briefcase." I felt relieved to have a few seconds to grab my bag and pull myself together. Meantime, I also scanned my brain for any Italian Jews I'd known, hoping this instant crush of mine was Jewish, though unlikely with a name like Puricelli. One guy from high school came to mind. Italian and Jewish. I hoped this would make two.

I entered the conference-room sized office and sat where he motioned. My two competing personalities wrestled— business woman or about-to-be-single-again, wannabe flirt? How could I possibly maintain a professional mindset with that room-brightening smile and those alluring eyes—and no ring on the fourth finger left hand? As he eased his agile body into his chair behind a handsome mahogany desk, I looked around the room, stalling. An L-shaped tan leather couch was at the far end near a large conference table, and behind it was a massive window showcasing Boston Harbor. As my eyes swept back toward him, I realized that more photos of the woman from the hall dotted the cream-colored walls. Definitely a wife; my Dad never wore his wedding ring either. What a scumbag this guy was, flirting with me in the store, and giving me this grand flirty greeting.

"…between here and there?" The end of Sam's question snapped me back.

"What did you ask?" I realized my voice sounded edgy, and I needed to calm down and do this deal no matter the odd circumstances. I softened my tone. "Sorry, I was lost in the photo of the pretty woman behind you."

His skin paled and he closed his eyes for a second. "Oh, uh...I was asking if you know a short cut? You must have beaten me here by at least six minutes."

"No, no shortcut. Just heavy on the pedal to be on time to meet with what I expected was the senior bigwig from the GSA—not a peer, to be honest."

"I see, and I'll assume you meant in age, not status? Perhaps you mixed up my name up with our founder, my late, great father, Sam Puricelli, Senior? Long deceased."

"Yup. Sorry." I sat up taller in my seat, trying to switch to professional mode after noting Jews do not have juniors or seniors after their names, and besides, this guy was taken.

"It's all right. He's been gone a long, long time. I miss him just about every day and it's an honor to be confused with him!"

"So much for doing my research. Don't hold it against me." I snickered a little too loud. "Well, whichever 'Sam' you are, let's talk. We have some big ideas we really could use your help with."

"Great, I'd love to help, and it seems, from what I've heard from Tim at your place, you're creative, considerate and easy to work with." He leaned back in his chair and smiled.

"Hmm, those exact words? I think I need a raise." This time I laughed naturally, as I relaxed some. I was trying hard to let go of the confusion and my disappointment, and to just focus on my sales pitch to get the work done free.

Sam smiled and tapped his pen on his mahogany desk as though he were trying to will himself to focus, too.

"So, Ms. All-around talented, what say we get on with this project?" His pen appeared to tap for an entire minute before I could finally move my lips to reply. While a part of me wondered if he were like this with women all the time, the mutual attraction was overwhelming, married or not.

"Yes, let's get on with this project," I mimicked. I shifted in my seat, crossing my legs with their sheer black stockings and black pump heels. I hadn't done it intentionally, I was just settling in, but I noticed his eyes followed my moves. We looked at each other in silence for a few seconds as I adjusted the collar of my white cotton shirt and smoothed my black suit jacket. Then I opened my leather folder and pulled out a pen.

He cleared his throat more than once. "Look, I don't mean to be discourteous or break any sexual harassment laws, so please tell me to stop if you want, but I can't concentrate on work until I know if you might have dinner with me sometime soon, well, if I'm not being presumptuous, of course, and if you're also, um, how do I say this, *free* to have dinner? I notice you don't wear a ring, apologies if I'm being disrespectful, which I probably am, I'm sorry." He paused his babbling and raised his eyebrows comically like a boy asking for another cookie. Despite his wife smiling down behind him, I found his sudden awkwardness endearing. This was all too surreal. My eyes bounced around and took in a framed certificate from the Rhode Island School of Design...a signed baseball in a plexi holder...a framed photo of a middle-aged man and a boy...a plaque having something to do with the words "karate." That last one meant he definitely was not Jewish, hardly knew a Jew who did karate. So what? He was married, for God's sake. What the hell was wrong with me?

He was waiting for my answer. The smile had vanished.

"Well, before I can answer," I hesitated, clearing my throat. "I must be equally presumptuous and say your photos are magnificent, yet I'm wondering if your lady-friend would mind us meeting for dinner?" I motioned to the woman on the wall behind him, and then grimaced as I realized I sounded snooty, like Ida.

Sam's face turned ashen. He straightened in his chair and stiffened. He stared right through me while taking a breath that seemed to take ten minutes to travel from his abdomen all the way to the tip of his head. Finally, he exhaled for what felt like at least ten days. I could not believe I was dealing with another cheating asshole.

"Um...my wife...she's, er, deceased." He took a few quick breaths as though trying to keep his emotions intact.

"Oh my God, I'm so sorry for being so rude." I leaned forward and placed my hand over his. "So, so sorry."

Sam set his hand over mine and rested it there in silence. It felt so comfortable, more like comforting a friend than sitting with a stranger who had just revealed such personal information. When he eventually spoke, it was in slow motion, as if he were keeping time with a sluggish metronome rhythm "Don't be sorry. You needed to learn I wasn't some two-timer, I get it, and—"

"No, I shouldn't have questioned your intentions. And, you are correct about no wedding ring. I'm free to have dinner with you sometime." I avoided the missing parts of that story.

We released our hands back to our laps, although I sensed neither wanted to let go. I wanted to tell him I had been hurt and made a fool of, so trust was an issue. But this wasn't the time or place.

"Jody, when I saw you at the store, something just called out to me." The spark was back in his eyes and voice. "I realized afterwards it was the first time I hadn't thought of Shelley for ten straight minutes in the nearly fourteen months she's been gone. In fact, I was kicking myself for not getting your name and number. So even though my head's in pieces right now—this is all rather difficult and I won't lie, I'm struggling here—I'd very much like to have dinner with you sometime."

"I've gotta admit, something grabbed me when I saw you in the store, too. You actually reminded me of my fourteen-year-old crush."

"Hope I've matured."

I loved his frankness and admired how forthright he was. I struggled with sharing intimate emotions. And so had Stewart, who was a classic sports, beer and closely-held-feelings kind of guy. I felt so comfortable with Sam; I wanted to curl up in his leather chair—on his lap—and doze off to sleep, keeping this dream going for hours.

"So, what do you say, Friday night possible? Can you find a sitter?"

"This…Friday…night," I said slowly, thinking. "Well, I might be taking my daughter to, er, Shabbat services, um, the Tot Shabbats are Friday nights, we sometimes go." What a liar, we'd been three times. I couldn't wait to tell Ruthie about my cleverness as I tried to discern if he knew anything about Jews. I couldn't date someone who thought we had horns.

"Ah, Tot Shabbat." He smiled.

His answer confused me. Could it be he was Jewish after all? Maybe he has a Jewish mother? And he must have children; he knew about cookie crumbs in cars! His response made it feel like we had started playing "Jewish geography," the "game" Jews play when we suspect someone's Jewish. We dance around the direct question by asking, instead, if you know Mark Rubin from XYZ company, or what you thought of Adam Sandler's Chanukah song, or if you've ever been to the Catskills. I was hopeful again. I did want Hallie to have a Jewish stepfather one day, although, this was just one dinner, I reminded myself. "You've been to a Tot Shabbat with your children, too?"

He hesitated. Swallowed hard. "Uh, no. No children." He looked down at his desk, obviously trying to compose himself.

Oh God, did his wife *and* children die? That would be too much to bear for anyone. This rollercoaster ride of emotions was exhausting. Plus we had work to do. This was business, not joint therapy.

"Well, actually, I guess I can take Hallie next week instead. And I can find a sitter Friday night, yes. I can probably get my ex-husband to take her, actually," I lied, not quite knowing what to call Stewart, who, according to the law at least, was still my husband. "Oh, wait, I'm wrong," I blurted, remembering Stewart already was with Hallie Friday night, but I had blocked out Friday's plans. Not only was I attending a family neighbor's pre-Bat Mitzvah Shabbat, but that meant I needed to be in the same air-space as Ida. Including the next morning at the actual Bat Mitzvah service. I dreaded it and planned to avoid her by sitting with my childhood friends.

"Oops, I totally forgot, Sam. I have to go to a neighbor's Bat Mitzvah that evening, you know, the Shabbat service the night before."

"Funny, I went to a family Bar Mitzvah last weekend! How's Saturday night, or do you have the celebration bash that night?"

"No, it's a morning service followed by a luncheon, but I'm just going to the service. So Saturday night's perfect." I practically floated around the room, knowing his family Bar Mitzvah meant he was Jewish, or part-Jewish, after all! I cleared my throat. The timing seemed right. "But one question. No matter what's ahead for us personally, I hope you'll still design the booklet for the P.R.A.?"

"Are you kidding me? If it's a way to interact with you a few times a month, at the very least, for the duration of this project, you betcha."

"And, er, gratis?" I uncurled my crossed legs and placed them firmly on the floor.

"I think I might even offer to pay *you*." He winked.

While some women may have found this offensive, after what I'd been through, I craved it. Somehow, we shifted gears and got down to business.

Chapter Five

"Nice legs, baby," a jerk in a yellow truck yelled out his window. I ignored him and was glad to see he kept driving down the road. These annoying catcalls happened now and then when I jogged in my favorite purple Lycra outfits. I bought them when I first started running, not realizing real runners just wear t-shirts with cool sayings from races they've run. But these were my most comfortable jogging clothes, so I wore them anyway. I ran only for the exercise or to clear my head, and only when Hallie was off with her Dad, like this not-too-cold day.

While I had never done a single race, Ruthie had raced for years. She introduced me to it because she was so sick of hearing me complain about having an entire person to lose after Hallie was born. Now, thankfully, my temporary pillow-like belly and padded hips were back to normal. But these days I hardly ran, while Ruthie was training for the Boston Marathon with the Dana Farber runners—something I'd never even consider. I was always a slow runner, my long, lean legs better designed for stockings than sports, or at least that's what Ida would tell me when I was younger, but now I knew I could do both!

Stewart had loved my shapely body—until I became pregnant and he stopped touching me like he used to; that's possibly when his affair started, but I tried not to think about it. Besides, now I had Sam to daydream about while I jogged. He was off on a brief business trip out west.

So far, Sam had been different from any man I'd ever been with. Even after several dates, and sweet, late-night phone conversations telling me he couldn't wait to see me again, he didn't convey the same sexual overtones he had that first day. Was he only ready for a friendship?

On our first date, he didn't seem to want to just be friends. He had placed his arm around me sweetly as we headed to a dimly lit corner table at Charley's at the Mall at Chestnut Hill. We comfortably shared steak tips and sweet potato fries, and with each glass of chardonnay consumed, we leaned closer across the table toward each other. But when Sam wasn't talking with a glass or fork in his hand, he placed his hands on his lap, while I rested mine on the table, hoping he might caress one. No such luck, so I concentrated on the easy, open conversation, with not one lapse.

We learned we were each skinny kids with acne, better looking and more popular by high school, when we both recalled kissing way too many frogs. I thought about saying "*Ribbit,*" and puckering my lips, seeing what response I'd get, but I didn't. We found out we were passionate about our jobs, watched *Friends* religiously, and avoided movies with blood and gore. He preferred plain 'ole vanilla ice cream for dessert (*horrors, how dull,* I thought, as I was a chocolate chip cheesecake lover, or better yet, chocolate mousse!). His favorite childhood memory with a parent was of skating each winter on a town pond with his Dad, while mine was deep sea fishing with my father. Sam told me he was an only child, and I revealed I wished I were one, too, although I avoided details about Rhonda's and my non-relationship.

By the time the waiter had cleared our mutually-agreed upon raspberry sorbet with one spoon—romantically feeding each other alternate bites while smiling at our corniness, we had sobered up on cappuccinos and decided to continue the evening briefly in his Camry. He led me to the parking lot, taking my hand. As soon as I lowered myself into the front passenger seat, the smell of his natural, pine-like scent, mixed with the spearmint deodorizer hanging from the mirror, gave me an odd sense of familiarity and comfort.

"I have something disappointing to tell you," he revealed as soon as he settled in and closed the door.

"Nothing could possibly disappoint me. We've had such a fabulous evening." I wrung my hands in my lap, wondering if the specialness was about to be ruined. Maybe he wasn't feeling ready to date yet?

"I didn't tell you the whole truth," he said, turning slightly in the dim light to look at me. "That family Bar Mitzvah I mentioned? I know I made it sound like it was my family, but, you see, I'm not Jewish. My parents raised me Catholic."

I swallowed hard, my head sober, yet my thoughts spinning from confusion. I hadn't even thought of this issue all night. I had assumed his mother was Jewish. How else could there be a *family* Bat Mitzvah? And hadn't we just been sharing our life stories? Apparently, in my inebriated state in the restaurant, I'd missed that I was the only one who mentioned anything about a Bat Mitzvah. I'd shared with him my uncertainty about whether I might be more religious these days if I had had one. He had listened empathetically, nodding with what felt like understanding. Yet he had changed the subject—hadn't he?—without saying whether he had a Bar Mitzvah, or revealing anything about the Jewish family he'd referenced that first meeting. Then what family was he talking about? A cousin's interfaith kid?

To be fair, although I had talked a bit about Hallie, I had dodged all conversation about my so-called "ex." And he hadn't mentioned his wife, so I still had no idea why he'd acted so emotionally when I asked about children in the office. There were, of course, worlds more to learn about Sam, and now I was learning something uncomfortable and disappointing.

Suddenly, I wondered, maybe Shelley was Jewish? I turned toward him, mouth pursed. I could only see a shadowy version of his face; my eyes hadn't adjusted to the darkness yet.

He continued. "I suspected you thought I was Jewish, but I was so happy to learn you were, so I kept quiet about myself. I know lots of Jews prefer dating people from their own faith, and I didn't want to lose the chance for us to get to know each other. But I'm hoping two things. One, that you're not limiting yourself to dating only Jewish men, and, more so, you can forgive me for leading you on." He paused. I stayed silent, taking it all in. "I admit it, I was wrong. I let you believe something probably important to you. But please, give me a chance; my wife was Jewish and her family and I are still close, and I've grown to love and respect the Jewish culture and values, maybe even more than my own." He paused again, and this time I sighed a silent relief. It was starting to make sense. "I know this might become a deal breaker for you," he said, then quieted his tone and added, "I really, really hope not, Jody."

I wanted to comfort him, but I was a bit confused about all of this myself. I stayed silent in the near-dark as I pictured myself lying to Ida that morning when we talked briefly at the Bat Mitzvah service. She and my father had skipped the Shabbat service the night before and I had hoped they'd skip the Bat Mitzvah, but no such luck. I had hugged my father, said a few words to him, and he walked away, leaving the two rivals together. In Ida's and my two-minute, cool greeting, I kept the peace by lying to her, telling her I'd try to stay open to a relationship with Stewart, while at the same time admitting I was, nonetheless, continuing the divorce process. She scowled but remained stoic, avoiding a scene, and then we separated. But throughout the event, just knowing I had an upcoming date with a wonderful man, whose family was Jewish, kept me resilient enough to feel confident around Ida.

I had traveled so deeply into my own thoughts that I still hadn't spoken to Sam.

"Talk to me, Jody, please. Yell at me if you want to. It can be our first fight!" He laughed, then immediately turned serious again, bumbling his way through my silence, as I struggled to find my voice. "In the past, Jewish women didn't want to date me, even though I grew up in Marblehead, surrounded by Jewish neighbors, and my first girlfriend was Jewish. She came with me to all the cotillions. So funny, stepping on each other's toes as we learned all those dances. But then one day her parents made us end it just like that. Afraid we were getting too serious. Broke our hearts. Snuck out to see each other until they caught us and moved out of Massachusetts.

"By the way, my first name is actually Samuele like my dad, but I never use it. And I only go to church twice a year to accompany my mom on Easter and Christmas—it's just not my thing. And somehow I never related to Catholic girls, maybe something about their tendency to be closely held with their emotions? I was never sure what was missing, until I met Shelley, so full of feeling, and we just clicked." He paused. "Like you and I have. Anyway, I don't know anything about your family, yet, or you, on this issue, but she and her family never minded our different religions, and look what she and I built: a house of love. And now here I am, an 'honorary Jew' looking for that again." He laughed. "Uh...I think I'd better shut up and let you tell me how you're doing here, you're way too quiet. I'm getting worried, and I sound like I'm ready to ask your Dad for your hand or something. I'm really failing at this dating stuff, huh?"

"Give me a sec," I managed to croak out, finding his awkward boyishness ridiculous, yet endearing. I smiled in the dark, despite feeling jealous of his obvious love for Shelley and her family. The chill I'd been feeling diminished as he had babbled on, and then retreated after the remark, "an honorary Jew." In middle school, I had called a close Irish friend an "honorary Jew" when he suggested my family name our new German Shepherd pup "Yiddish." The breeder had required a name starting with the letter "Y" for the kennel's twenty-fifth litter. We chose Yolanda, instead, but my friend and I laughed about that memory for years.

"Please, don't let this be a deal breaker," Sam continued. "Truly, I'm sorry I waited all night to bring this up. Guess I hoped to charm you into not turning me away."

I thought about the wonderful evening and my hopes for possibly starting a new happy relationship. I considered Ida's wrath when she would eventually hear. And Dad's disappointment. If we kept dating, I'd have to survive Rhonda's mean comments, disguised by her usual sarcasm. Hmm, and Bubbe. What would Bubbe think? *"You could never disappoint me, Jody,"* ran through my thoughts.

I turned toward this sweet, honest man sitting beside me. He had shared emotions more openly than ten men put together. You had to love this guy.

And Ruthie would never talk to me if I put my family before my heart.

"Tell me about those *cotillions*, Samuele."

He leaned across the seat and we awkwardly hugged, silently holding onto each other until a policeman drove close and waved when he saw we were fine. We giggled like teenagers and gave him the thumbs up signal. Soon, Sam asked me to point out my car in the near-empty lot, then drove beside it, took my keys and hopped out to start it and put the heat on to warm it up for me. When he returned to the car, we hugged again. I contained myself from stealing a kiss. I didn't want to be first to express my desires, yet I felt dejected after settling for a final hug as we said goodnight.

Fortunately, the lingering sensation of his arms around me, and the fresh memory of his head resting on my shoulder, lasted the whole drive home.

Before climbing into bed, I woke up Ruthie to tell her the whole sordid story. In a hoarse, sleepy tone she admonished me lovingly, as only she could.

"Who cares he's not Jewish for God's sake? His wife was Jewish. Get over it! Besides, he'll know how to daven next to Harry and Ida at High Holiday services like the best of 'em." Then she said she loved me, asked how the Eggs Benedict I'd never delivered from the Pillar House was coming along in my freezer, and we hung up.

~~~

The following date, Sam had suggested a weeknight movie, again meeting halfway, this time at the Chestnut Hill Cinemas. He embarrassed me in an endearing way, coming back from the snack counter balancing two sodas and one of those huge buckets of popcorn to share. It was like he bought something that screamed "I'm Part of a Couple Again." Afterwards, we went for coffee and pastries next door, but the date ended early because I had a babysitter instead of an ex-husband that night, and Sam had work the next morning. Again, no kiss, yet his hand-holding in the theatre, and his warm and funny personality, made me feel safe with his affection.

By the next date, however, this no kiss thing was starting to test my patience.

During a Boston Celtics game, we shared pizza and Edy's gourmet ice cream while watching them beat the Knicks. We'd met at the Boston Garden, not too far from his condo in South Boston. He came by MBTA train, and since I had left my car at the closest "T" station to my suburban home, we both hopped on the "T" together after the game. But my transfer stop came up quickly, so off I went into a surge of people. The train wasn't exactly conducive to that first kiss I was longing for. But what about him...wasn't he longing for one?

The next date was on such a frigid night and, again, we met by T, this time for a concert at Passims in Harvard Square. So, our goodbye in zero degree weather was swift, but he had rubbed my shoulders earlier while waiting in the line to get into the club, so I felt encouraged.

Finally, by date four, Sam invited me to a special dinner at the romantic Bay Tower restaurant, overlooking Boston. He insisted on driving the thirty minutes from his place to pick me up at home, though the traffic he'd encountered left no time to even show him my house; we needed to return to Boston to make our reservation. Because he also planned to drive me home at the end of the night, I had made arrangements for Hallie and Ringo to sleep at my sister-in-law's in case he invited me back to his place instead. Or wished to stay at mine. I was more than ready.

At the restaurant, we sat in one of those rounded chairs that always looked so romantic—which Stewart had refused to sit in. With Sam, it felt as cozy and natural as I had imagined. We shared a bottle of champagne and oysters, laughing about their aphrodisiac reputation. Dinner started with Belgium endive salads and followed with such fresh grilled swordfish it tasted like it had been prepared right off the boat—and probably was. We also shared grilled asparagus, and I was momentarily tempted to lift up a piece with my fingers and suck it gingerly, but it was too risky. I settled for accepting his hand in mine in between courses, as we took in the view of the sparkling city lights around us and swayed to the jazz pianist's romantic sounds. The chemistry in the air between us could not only be enthralling me.

Just after ordering dessert, as I left for the ladies' room, I felt the warmth of mutual love blooming, and it wasn't just the champagne doing its job. I nearly floated down the hallway.

"Please, open it," was all Sam had said when I returned. There, resting beside my chocolate mousse sat a small red box wrapped with gold ribbon. He sat up stiffly in his seat, focusing more on the package than on me.

"Oh my, what's this?" I fumbled with the ribbon, unsure how I felt about receiving what appeared to be jewelry from a man I'd started falling in love with but who had never even kissed me. I pictured Ruthie hovering above us, asking if we were in fifth grade and about to go steady. I lifted the top as cautiously as if I were unfolding a report card, afraid to see something I didn't expect inside. The box contained a two-ounce spray bottle of Red Door, a perfume I'd never heard of. I was allergic to most perfumes, but even in my confused state, I knew this wasn't the time to tell him so.

"Oh my, thank you." I took the cap off and took a quick sniff. "Lovely. Thank you." I placed one hand on the side of the bottle and the other hand still held the cap. I had no clue what to do or say next. I was relieved it wasn't jewelry, yet either gift seemed too soon for a fourth date. Then again, a kiss, or more, hadn't felt too soon for a fourth date—maybe I had my priorities skewed? Still, I didn't sense that kiss was even about to happen now.

"Put it on. Uh, would you mind?"

"Of course not. Sure." I wondered for a second if he meant on my wrist or my neck. Either way, one spray of perfume wouldn't bother me, so I pushed aside my dangling silver and gold earrings to spray a bit near my ear. I had barely set down the bottle when Sam leaned close and tucked his face into my neck, lingering for a few long seconds. I held still, thinking maybe this was his tactic for a first kiss. Nope. He sat back up, returning to the awkward stiffness—yet I noticed tears in his eyes. I sat quietly, perplexed yet wondering if...

"Perfect on you, exactly as I hoped." He leaned in for another quick inhale near my neck, then instantly pulled back and fussed with his drink.

I quietly exhaled and placed the cap back on the perfume. I felt my mood shift away from my heart and into my thoughts. Had Sam not been so awkward, maybe I would have simply accepted the gift with joy. But I couldn't help thinking about Shelley and if this had been her scent. The rest of the evening, Sam was sweet and polite, leading me through the doors he always held open for me, but not even kissing me goodnight when, to my disappointment, he drove me back to my house and although I invited him in, he declined. He walked me to the door but said he needed to visit his mother early the next day.

"Please, invite me another time," he said. "And I hope to meet Hallie soon."

I nodded.

"And I look forward to introducing you to my mother sometime soon." He leaned in for a long hug, tucking his nose into my scented neck again. Then he released me, squeezed my hand for a few seconds and said goodnight. He blew me a kiss as I stepped inside and closed the door behind him.

I immediately washed off the perfume best I could, and then dialed Ruthie, waking her once again. She listened to the whole story. I longed for her interpretation.

"You keeping the perfume? Get any hives yet?"

I laughed at my friend. I was in emotional pain and she was focused on the perfume. "Yes to the perfume, no to the hives, thank God. It takes more than one spray. I'll break the news to him soon. But, ya, I'll keep it. I may try it again."

"Shucks. I figured I could have the perfume and go after him if you get impatient." She went on to advise me to just be happy and have fun. Stop analyzing him. Maybe he just couldn't handle being with a new woman while he had such amazing memories of his wife.

She was right; I hadn't wanted to think of another woman in the restaurant with us, but she had indeed materialized with my chocolate mousse—which I managed to consume in its entirety despite the jumping beans in my stomach.

Sam and I had a few daytime dates since. We were never at a loss for words, and we shared lots of the same interests. Except for the one I was waiting for?

Even during meetings in his office for brief check-ins on the project, my fantasies ran wild the few times his secretary announced she was off to lunch. But Sam would just continue talking about the logo, the typeface, the layout, until I wanted to point to his couch and scream STOP. But didn't. And after each meeting, we'd share a lingering hug before opening his door, but that was it, not even one kiss! I was dying for that first kiss, or for him to touch me in a sexual way, but it was as though he'd locked up those earlier powerful emotions. Yet his warm words kept me confused.

~~~

As I continued to jog in my purple Lycra outfit, another trucker honked. I ignored him, but I couldn't stop wondering if a stranger found me appealing, what was wrong with Sam? Was he just scared to get sexually involved again? He certainly appeared to be willing to be close in every other way. I knew I should ask, yet I wasn't sure I wanted to hear his reason.

Sometimes I even wondered if he was gay, but I dismissed the thought: Shelley was the obvious proof, though it was nearly impossible to let myself think about him with his wife. The woman was dead; why was I so jealous? I had tried encouraging him to tell me about her, but he refused, albeit gently.

I rounded the corner toward home, glad my run was almost over. But all it had really helped me sort out about Sam was that I felt emotionally spent despite this new relationship awakening pleasures long faded. It wasn't easy living alone with a three-year-old, while taking care of a dog and house. And keeping up with the work project Sam and I were moving along. Still, I was strong and soldiered on. Yet always lurking in the back of my mind was my deception to Mother about staying open toward Stewart. In reality, reuniting with Stewart was unequivocally not an option, despite Sam's perplexing attention. Most days I thought he was just what I needed to help keep my life moving forward more happily. Except on days I feared he was too Mommy-attached or never going to give up Shelley enough to truly love me.

Or maybe it was just too early for a new man in my life? Didn't I have to figure things out with my family, and myself, first?

Chapter Six

Ringo licked at my sweaty feet the moment I removed my running shoes. I couldn't bring him on long runs when I went too many miles, even with his athletic body. I stripped off my soggy outfit and let my hair out of its restrictive ponytail, the curls falling onto my sweaty neck. I checked the mirror to make sure the pale brown spots on my face hadn't darkened too much from the sun. Not too bad. Whenever I ran, I applied a strong sunscreen to the spots my dermatologist had explained came from something called "pregnancy mask," a skin reaction to pregnancy hormones after giving birth to Hallie. Well, she was worth it.

I stepped into the shower, pleased with my run. It felt good to push my body. I had four months until the annual weekend to celebrate Bubbe's birthday with the New York cousins, and I wanted to feel fit. But I had two more important curveballs to deal with. Which would I be ridiculed for more? Revealing my divorce and Stewart's cheating, or bringing a Catholic into our midst if I chose to defy Ida and bring my boyfriend? I could barely imagine driving into the compound with Sam. His jaw would drop while taking in the expansive, plush estate. Maybe I shouldn't bring him, or just not go! But shouldn't I let Hallie get to know her extended family better?

~~~

Just out of the shower, still wrapped in only a towel, I went to my desk to check my email before Hallie returned from Stewart's in a few hours. He had finally taken my request for the divorce more seriously, but was still stalling on filing his financial papers. I needed to make it clearer that this was not an option.

I opened up my email to try to draft something to Sam, who had written the day before from his post in California where he was photographing animals for the Wildlife Society's annual calendars. He had asked me to join him on his next trip there, and while a part of me was thrilled, another part wasn't sure I could just pick up and get away like that.

I started by checking my AOL daily news report, and catching up on no-good news. Then I answered one quick work message and scanned the newsletter from the soup kitchen I volunteered at now and then. After deleting fifteen junk messages, I noticed an email I'd missed from Ruthie, and a new one from Sam. I pounced on the one from Sam. I'd seen him for lunch after a work meeting just before he left, and he was sweetly romantic, bringing me flowers and chocolates. He didn't ask why I hadn't been wearing the perfume, and I wondered if he even noticed. He was warm and huggy, as usual, but I still felt a physical reserve from him.

Email to Jody from Sam:

Taking a break from this photo gig and writing you from a plugged-in Starbucks across the country. What a high tech society! Drizzly out. Much too raw for this time of the year in San Diego. Nicer back home? Well I'm off to scout out my photo assignment. I'm happy to be here, but awaiting my return home knowing I'll see you soon and we'll have time together. Love, Me. P.S. You will come with me during my next trip in a few weeks, yes?

I released a deep sigh. Sure, I wanted to go. What fool wouldn't accept a basically free trip to San Diego, other than my airfare, with a wonderful man? Yet didn't we need to define the relationship first? I closed the screen and clicked to open Ruthie's message next.

Email to Jody from Ruthie:

Flowers and chocolates?! And so handsome? This guy for real? I got it: Next time Stewart comes to pick up Hallie, get Sam to walk around nude. That'd put his Royal Heiny in his place. Better yet, can he walk around nude at my place the next time my folks come? They're starting to hint that if I can't find a nice guy, maybe a nice woman who wants children would be acceptable! Oy vey! Ta-ta. Love ya, RuRu.

I laughed at Ruthie's sign off. "RuRu" was what I called her way back in junior high school when we met. Back then, all the girls were playing around with nicknames. I became Jo, which stuck, but fortunately Ruthie's RuRu didn't last long. Still, she used RuRu with me now and then to lighten me up. Our connection went so far back that she was one of my few friends who understood my sensitive psyche from my family's long-standing criticisms. Her family was different from mine, more down-to-earth in many ways, but just as invalidating of her special qualities, like her intelligence, humor, and empathic side. Still, she wasn't as sensitive as I; she'd grown up with a tough brother and developed a harder shell, for good and for bad. When we were younger, we teased about running away and living in a box in Harvard Square. After my parents presented me with the well-funded bank account, RuRu suggested our tiny box could be elevated to a giant condo if I would only let myself dip into that money.

Email to Ruthie from Jody:

Love the RuRu! Made me smile as always, thanks! I should just call you, but I have so much to do before Hallie comes home in a couple of hours. You are too funny re: Sam at your place! Tell your parents I said to chill. The right guy will show up eventually, Ru. He will! As for Sam, yes, he's sweet but still nothing going on, not even that first kiss. The newest is he invited me to come out to California during his next photo gig in San Diego. On the one hand I'd love to go, but I'm just not sure I can handle it, even if I can get Hallie and Ringo all set. It's about two weeks away; wouldn't I have to tell my parents where I'm going, and then that opens up the usual can of worms?! And he brought up his salary situation again, the stuff I told you about on the phone. He's still so relieved that I said it doesn't matter. How could I share my ambivalence—that while I don't think I care in my gut, the reality is, in my family, "real men" aren't artists and photographers—and they make good money. Oh, God, I feel like a snob. Like my family! And how are you, my dear friend? Xoxo Jo

My buddy list announced Ruthie was back online and was typing. In a minute, I saw her response.

Email to Jody from Ruthie:

Hey there! Only have a minute. Working on the Pine Street Inn grant today then have to go for a long Marathon training run. But hey, any kind of romance sounds good to me; I'm in mourning over how long it's been since I've had sex with someone other than myself! Not that you are in any better shape in that arena, I now learn! He's still Mr. Asexual? What's up with this dude? And what's up with YOU? Offering to send you to California and you're unsure? You're meshugenah! He can bring ME! I'll play YOU for the week! And I still don't believe he doesn't have much moula? Then where'd he get the fancy office? Hey, what's money to you, anyway? Use that family savings account, my foolish friend. So what if a few strings are attached? Just chill. Besides, you and lover boy don't both need to have money any more than you both need to cook. Oy—now you're gonna tell me Mr. Italian Mama's boy's gonna whip you up a veal marsala next date? Love & kisses, Ruthie

Email from Jody to Ruthie:

Don't worry about replying again, do your work. I'm just answering now while I have time. R: the office, he gets his space free—barters for it, I think. And, well, yes, he does cook, or so I've heard! All he's mentioned are his Mama's recipes: spaghetti sauce, lasagna, stuffed peppers. And lokshen kugel—guess who he learned that one from? But Ruthie, honestly, cool it with the bank stuff, please, I still have no sense of humor about it; haven't touched it. Call me stupid, but I call it smart—no worse ties to Ida than already exist! And re: the Mama's boy stuff, I think (I hope!) he's just a dutiful, loving son. That's a good sign, isn't it? Xoxo Jo P.S. If Harry and Ida knew any of this I'd be minced meat, don't you think?

Email to Jody from Ruthie:

You expect me to work while this good shit is coming straight into my computer? Seriously, lighten up, girl, they're only your parents. Ha! Really, Jo, it's your life—why do they still freak you out so much? I'm gonna have to coach you on the "Fuck You Factor," my friend. Truth is, Jo, no one can really make you feel insecure but yourself. Go girl! Kissy, kissy.

She's one-of-a-kind, I thought. Sure, I used the F-bomb now and then when pushed, but I'd never say Fuck You to anyone unless enraged. But her point was well taken; I'd let too many people run over me for too long. Also, Ruthie was so openly affectionate, where I often was reserved. Maybe it was because of so many situations when my affection was rebuffed, particularly by my sister at the annual family reunions. My stomach felt queasy as I recalled the time I tried to break the tension with Rhonda. Tried to be more affectionate.

~~~

I was fifteen and it was Rhonda's first year away at college. She had stayed in Manhattan to take summer classes at NYU. We all met at the New York Horowitz's house that summer. Rain had followed us earlier on the drive from Massachusetts, and as we arrived, the mid-summer sky was graying.

"Go ahead, kiss your sister," our father had said to Rhonda on Uncle Nathan's driveway at their old house, before they built the contemporary.

Rhonda was climbing out of a taxi just as Dad, Mom, Bubbe and I pulled in. I stepped out of the car and approached my sister. I'd read a story in "People" magazine about an actress who referenced her sister as her "soulmate." It had inspired me to try to become closer to Rhonda now that we were older and had been apart for most of the year. I made an obvious attempt to lean in and try to kiss her cheek to change the pattern she and I had been in for years. But Rhonda, toting a new Louis Vitton suitcase, wheeled the heavy bag just inches from my toes, and in one motion covered her cheek with her hand and turned her head. "Let's not break with tradition," she said.

"Speaking of tradition, I hope Bubbe made her chocolate rugelach," Cousin Ellen piped in, walking toward us in stylish bellbottoms. She'd let her hair go natural, hippy-like, no more putting it up in frozen orange juice containers at night to straighten it. It was long and frizzy and stopped just above the large breasts she'd obviously developed that year.

Staring at her, I couldn't help thinking of Janis Joplin. Imagining eleven-year-old Ellen on stage screaming "Me and Bobby McGee" helped me focus on something other than the embarrassment of my cousin seeing Rhonda rebuff my kiss.

"Yes, yes, I have my rugelach," I heard Bubbe saying as she climbed out of Harry's Mercedes.

Fortunately, she had missed the Jody-Rhonda exchange, or so I hoped. I didn't like Bubbe seeing the worst side of her family. After any squabbles, she'd tap at her hearing aid in frustration, perhaps to let everyone think she hadn't heard the negative stuff.

"And who is zis?" Bubbe asked after we had all gathered near Rhonda's new fancy suitcase Ida was admiring. Cousin Barry had approached this warm, fuzzy little driveway reunion. A tall blonde girl towered over him and hung possessively onto his not-quite thirteen-year-old arm. She waddled as she walked in her skimpy, tight mini-skirt.

"Bubbe, meet Nancy, Nancy Rodder, er, um, Nancy Rodder*man*," Barry stuttered. Nancy pulled slightly away from Barry. She scrunched up her tiny nose and forehead, cocked her head and squinted at Barry. I noticed him stepping gently on her foot and winking at her. She stared at him with a puzzled expression. He looked at Bubbe and smiled, then repeated his girlfriend's full name—Nancy Rodder*man*—and tapped at her shoe again.

"Oh, er, yes, I'm Nancy, er, Rodder*man*, nice to meet you, Mrs. Horowitz. I've heard so much about you."

Cousin Ellen turned away to stifle her laughter as the entire "mishpucha" watched Barry's attempt at turning Nancy the gentile into a Jew.

"Nice to meet you, dear." She handed Barry her suitcase and walked toward the house. Everyone assumed Bubbe had believed the stunt, except me, because I noticed her looking slightly skyward while rubbing her locket with Grandpa Bert's picture between her fingers.

Thunder suddenly crackled from a distance and everyone rushed inside. Rain meant we would be forced to spend the day stuck inside, no tennis, no swimming. No diversions from the intensity of some of the conversations, and from the tension that, without fail, ensued between two people every visit. But rarely the same two. Who would it be this year?

Harry and Ida? Me and Ida? Ellen and Bernice? Every year, the main antagonists-of-the-moment rotated. Never Bubbe, never Barry, never Rhonda with anyone other than me; never, never the loving brothers, Harry and Nathan. I didn't want it to be me and Rhonda anymore, so when I happened to open the bathroom door just as she arrived to use it, I took the opportunity to ask her about rejecting my kiss.

"God, get over it," she said. "It's called sarcasm. Sarcasm is funny. Stop overanalyzing everything." Then she walked into the bathroom and closed the door.

Approaching the kitchen, I overheard my mother and Aunt Bernice talking. I peeked through the opening of the swinging door.

"I presume you're pressuring Barry to drop the shiksa?" My mother was asking Bernice. Ida twirled her bangle bracelets as she spoke. She wore a navy blue pants suit with white anchors adorning the sleeves. Today she was the Admiral, I noted wryly, as she often wore an armed forces-of-some-sort style of dressing.

"I'll worry about his choices when he's old enough for marriage," Aunt Bernice said. "And, well, Ida, that's not a very nice word." Her back to Ida, my aunt scratched her eyebrow in that nervous habit of hers, then pounded the chicken breasts with a mallet—despite already appearing flattened. Bernice always dressed simply but tastefully, and that day she looked elegant in a brown fitted knit dress that hugged her shapely body. Simple gold earrings accented her look.

"I never allow my girls to date goyim," Ida said.

I knew she was lying. I'd dated a few non-Jewish boys in high school already, and Rhonda had, too. Ida just made it so difficult for us that we couldn't sustain the relationships.

"You don't have a problem with goyim when it comes to a prestigious client." Harry's voice sounded playful as he entered the kitchen from the other side. None of them noticed me behind the other door.

"That's not family, that's business, Harold!"

"Oh 'Harold,' is it, I'm in the doghouse again? Remember, dear, I coulda married a goy, but I chose you." My father liked to brag now and then about the blond shiksas he dated in the old days. And a particular strawberry blond. Rhonda and I had heard all about Maria, the woman he wanted at eighteen, but his parents disapproved. "Love ya, darling," he added, looking at her voluptuous breasts. He popped a stuffed mushroom in his mouth.

Ida darted across the kitchen to the other side of the room, shoving open the door before I could move away, nearly knocking me over. She glared at me a second and then scurried away.

~~~

So many negative reunion memories diluted the fun times. What would surface this year? Especially if I invited Sam to be thrown into the Lion's Den. Turning away from the computer, I wanted to unscrew my head and shake out the memories. It was enough to fill a novel!

I spent a few minutes putting away a basket of clean laundry, then turned back to my computer, checked the weather in San Diego and scrolled through images of the hotel Sam planned to take me to. Was he going to reserve two rooms, I wondered, only partially sarcastic? I was tired of dreaming about his lips on mine, his body pressing against me. I wanted it to happen already. It had been about two years since I'd had sex. The longing was becoming unbearable.

Thank God Hallie would be home in a couple of hours, and I could focus on what really mattered, being with my precious gift, the one thing Stewart had given me that shone.

Chapter Seven

I knew I needed to reply to Sam, as he deserved a response, but I needed a snack first. Hopefully he assumed I was too busy to check email and, besides, he wasn't able to check his often either, except at a Starbucks where they were set up for computers.

I headed toward the kitchen. I'd have a quick cup of tea and a brownie, and then I'd unwrap myself from this soggy towel. I'd dress and settle in with the Sunday paper until Hallie came back. I turned the corner from the hall to the kitchen and—

"Hi, Mommy!"

I shrieked and lifted my hands to my face as though she were an intruder. My towel fell into a heap on the linoleum floor. As I dove to pick it up, Ringo raced into the kitchen and slid on the plush terry, pushing it toward Stewart, who had just walked in. A smirk across his face, he bent and seized it, but instead of handing it to me, he draped it around my naked body like a polite prince protecting his princess from the cold. I grabbed it and wrapped it tighter.

"Hi, pumpkin," I said with as confident a voice as I could muster while Hallie snuggled into me. I hugged her with one arm, keeping the other affixed to the towel. I glared at Stewart. He had abused the key I'd given him for emergencies, but I didn't want to fight in front of our daughter. "What're you guys doing home so early?" I asked Hallie, but I mostly addressed Stewart.

"Daddy took me to the carnival. Look what I made!" She raised her wrist to show off the friendship bracelet that some sweet, patient teenager had probably helped her create.

"Nice, dear." I glared at Stewart again.

"We went to the Needham carnival, and I didn't want to drive all the way back to my place and then back here, so here we are! Didn't think you'd be home yet…oops." Stewart grinned as he leaned against the doorway.

"Haven't you ever heard of this little thing called a doorbell?!"

"Glad I didn't, cause you're looking good, Jo, real good." He looked me up and down with that slight crooked smile I'd always fallen for. I looked away.

How dare you, I wanted to say. But my little girl was there, so I let it go. Besides, obviously he'd seen me naked for years. But we'd been apart for over a year now, and when he'd last seen me naked my body was still stretched and flabby. It was nothing like the taut, youthful-like skin I had regained, except for those stretch marks around my belly button to remind me my girl did, magically, emerge from this very body.

"Maybe we three can have an early dinner together tonight?" Stewart asked. Hallie jumped up from the floor, where she sat petting Ringo. "Yeah, Mama, yeah, let's!"

I shook my head. Unbelievable. Stewart knew better than to say that out loud in front of Hallie. "Uh, where's you-know-who tonight?"

"I see absolutely no one here but us three," he replied, again tossing me the smile.

I knew I shouldn't drop the question, but the answer would have created a high probability of us hollering at each other, so instead of walking into the bomb that would have ended with our daughter crying, I let it drop. I didn't like to make an issue about his girlfriend in front of Hallie, plus I suspected he honored the rule to be female-less when with Hallie, or I'd swiftly file for full custody, he knew that. Most women were horrified I let him stay in Hallie's life after what he'd done, but I believed Hallie was better off with him than without. Despite his foibles, he was a good dad.

"Legal Sea Foods at the mall?"

"I don't think so Stewart." I lowered my gaze. My mind firmly said "no," but my growling stomach and love for Hallie confused my emotions.

"Please, Mommy, just this once. We can all go to dinner and then you and I can come home and play, just us two...and Ringo of course." Hallie leaned over and nuzzled her head into the dog's soft fur. My little girl was showing interesting negotiation skills. As I watched her pet the animal that had once belonged to Stewart, too, the words "just us two" tugged at my heart. For so long now it had been "just us two." For once Hallie could have all three of us together, if only for a short while. Didn't she deserve this more often than just at her birthday party, her gymnastic recitals, and Hanukkah? Hmm, maybe we could have a glass of wine together, and I could persuade him to send those financial papers to his attorney.

"Okay. But just for a quick dinner, not Legal's."

Hallie whooped and I escaped to my bedroom to dress.

Dinner passed uneventfully, with all conversation aimed at or about Hallie. Our daughter grinned like a freshly carved jack-o-lantern throughout the meal. She took turns sitting next to me on one side of the table and then next to her Dad on the other side, and then back to me. We pushed her plate of mac 'n cheese across the table and switched her booster seat so many times, the waitress eventually brought over a second booster.

Throughout the evening, Stewart showered me with his usual dose of charm I had forgotten about; I'd long locked away memories of ever being smitten for each other. He held doors and put his arm gently around my back as we walked in and out of the restaurant, and instead of bristling, I found myself liking it. More than a few times, I caught him gazing at me a little too long, as though he were studying my face with a hint of regret.

Most of all, I felt grateful Stewart had driven us to a Ninety-Nine restaurant two towns away, where none of our friends or neighbors would be dining, something I hadn't thought of when I suggested "a quick dinner." A quick dinner, of course, would have meant eating somewhere in our small town where we three didn't need to become the topic of gossip, again.

But the longer drive meant we didn't return home until it was way past Hallie's bedtime, and the sky had blackened with thick clouds and hardly any moonlight. No surprise, Hallie fell asleep on the drive home. Stewart offered to carry her into bed, and since my body felt sore from the long run earlier, and my mind was nice and relaxed from the glass of wine with dinner, I accepted. Opening the side door, I let Ringo out to do his business and to avoid his rousing Hallie. Then I held the door open for Stewart, who cradled Hallie in his arms and headed upstairs to her room. The villain he'd become suddenly rematerialized as the doting father and husband I had once believed he'd been.

I followed them upstairs, gently removed her shoes, and lifted the bedcover. Stewart lowered her onto her Kermit the Frog sheets. He placed her stuffed Dalmatian, Lucky, by her side. I knew Hallie would be curious in the morning about sleeping in her clothes, but I didn't want to wake her. As we tucked the covers about her small warm body, I noticed the moon shining through the multi-colored window shade, casting a pale rainbow on the wall. I leaned over to kiss her at the same second Stewart did, and as we each planted a soft kiss on opposite cheeks, the scene felt choreographed by Disney.

We whispered goodnight and left her room, gently closing the door behind us. Ringo, who'd come back in the house through his doggy door, settled himself in his bed outside his best friend's closed door.

"And goodnight to you, too, Stewart." I ushered my estranged husband downstairs and toward the mudroom door. I was annoyed at myself for forgetting to bring up the issue of the financial forms during dinner, and now didn't seem the time.

"Whoa, your mood just changed. What's up? Come, let's sit and talk a bit."

"No, you should go."

"I promise, no funny business. I know it sounds like a pick-up line at a bar or something, but I'm your ex-husband, not some stranger."

"Oh, and therefore I should *trust* you?"

"Ouch. Yeah, I get it. Okay, I'll go. But honestly, Jo, wasn't tonight kinda special?"

The gentleness to his voice reached me somewhere deep inside. He was right. It had been a special night. No ghosts or baggage alongside our table, no worries about the future. Just a moment in time with a sort-of family.

"Yeah, it was nice. Though I had no clue I could be civil with you for longer than the usual five-minute Hallie exchanges. Not sure you deserve my civility."

"So I'm forever in the doghouse? Hmm. I guess if that's the only way to stay involved with you, I can take it. Ruff ruff." He made his eyes and mouth droop like a sad puppy.

Despite myself, I smiled. I pictured him in Ringo's crate, chewing a dog bone, which is where I once found our cocker spaniel after Stewart and I had a fight about who-knows-what. Back then, we didn't fight much, but when we did, he was always the one to end it, and with humor, which deflected the issue away from the topic. I always welcomed his ability to do that, as I tended to hold a grudge. But at that moment, despite the humor, my smile evaporated. A whoosh of issues passed by my eyes in disturbing images like in a bad dream: How lonely I sometimes felt while caring for Hallie alone. And other than an occasional house cleaner or babysitter, and a dog walker here and there, I handled all of it myself, only seeing friends, or even cracking open a good book, on nights Stewart had Hallie and I felt less sapped of energy. Then there was how lonely for physical intimacy I felt despite sweet Sam's attention.

By the time I had looked up and rejoined the world, Stewart was in his stocking feet, his shoes kicked off to the side of the kitchen, where he had just finished pouring some wine. He wore his blue and tan argyle socks, and even though they were old-fashioned, they were always my favorite. Despite my irritation at him, I couldn't help noticing I was feeling physically attracted to him for the first time since that awful day. I hated myself for those thoughts, but they hung in the air like the tempting smell of cotton candy when you want it because you liked it once upon a time, yet your wiser self knows it's sickening stuff.

"Gee, make yourself at home, why don't you? And with my wine and corkscrew. You appear to know your way around here, buster, don't you?"

"Just lucky guesses." He smiled, walked toward me and handed me a glass.

"To Hallie," he toasted.

"To Hallie. But really, Stewart, you must go after this." We clinked glasses and he waved our favorite video, Casablanca, at me, and before I knew it I was following him around the bend into what had once been our living room, the gray-blue faux-suede couch and glass and brass coffee table unchanged. I never used that room anymore; not since Ida had criticized the mess of toddler toys in there.

We started the movie and sat near each other on the couch, which felt both weird and familiar. I quickly became lost in the movie, yearning for the scenes with Bogie and Bergman. During the long mournful flashback scene set in Paris, Stewart left to use the bathroom. I was too focused on Bogie's distress, after Ilsa doesn't show up the next day at the station, that I hardly noticed when Stewart returned with the bottle of wine and poured more in each of our glasses.

A while later, I yawned a few times. He nudged me to go put on pjs to "get ready for bed, Jo, I don't bite," but I refused. Instead I took a pee break, and when I returned, I drank some more wine he'd poured.

Not long before the twist ending of the movie when Rick, Ilsa and Victor Laszlo arrive at the airplane in the thick fog, I went to pee again, and noticed my gait a bit unsteady from the wine. He suggested, again, that I put on pjs, and this time it sounded like such a comfy idea that I went into my bedroom, dug into the back of my closet for the one thing I'd saved: heart-patterned pjs he'd bought me the Valentines' Day he proposed. I pulled them on. I shuffled back to the living room in my gray fluffy slippers and cuddled under the couch blanket, drinking some more wine. I hardly flinched when he removed one of my slippers and then the next and began to massage my feet in his lap while we watched the end of the film. With the fog filling the TV screen, and the fog in my head taking over my brain with Stewart's familiar caresses, I felt his hands slide up my legs and touch me through the silk. And as his hands glided higher up on the silk—oh, my—his touch felt like magic pills carrying me away to some heavenly place of whiteness and calm. My body craved release and, even more so, the feel of a man's skin, and Sam just wanted to be friends, didn't he? And Stewart's natural scent was so comforting, that warm earthy fragrance I always loved. Ummm, it felt so good as he slowly stripped off my pants, and then his, and as my mind started to pay attention—*this is wrong, don't let this happen!*—I swatted all thoughts away; we weren't divorced, after all, just separated, and oh my, I had to catch my breath to not release a loud sigh, which might wake our daughter, as my body responded to his touch. A scene passed through my eyes as I envisioned Stewart finally ending things with Brooke. We were husband and wife still. Raised a daughter together. Were a family. My thoughts blurred together as he leaned back on the couch and in one swift movement pulled me on top of him. I felt him inside me and I sighed deeply with pleasure, and then somehow, disgustedly, my mind flashed to Ida, and though I tried to block her out, I thought maybe she was right; I should give him another try, and he'd attend the family reunion and all would be easier moving forward. Stewart's quiet sighs brought me back to the moment, and soon I felt his jerky movements and rode his rhythm as he tried to quiet the blissful sounds of his release. I lost myself totally, joyfully, into all of the sensual sensations, eventually collapsing onto his chest, feeling our naked, sweaty bodies sinking into the couch beneath us.

We stayed there together for a few minutes, but by eleven twenty-five on the digital clock across from me, it was over as quickly as it began. With my pajamas still discarded on the living room rug, all I wore was my shame after Stewart stood to dress, and revealed it was best if he head home.

"Brooke's due in on a stewardess gig in the early morning."

I threw a couch pillow at him and wrapped the throw blanket around me, twisting it closed. I stood and pushed him toward the door, pounding on his back with my fists.

"Sorry, Jo, you were really looking good, you know, and I sensed you wanted it, too, and, damn, it was good, wasn't it?"

I shoved him out the door and bolted it tight, then crouched on the mudroom floor and sobbed. He was right. I had wanted it. But I couldn't believe I'd fallen for the charms of Stewart Wolfman once again. Didn't I know by now that man would never grow up? So what if he could hold down a decent job and be a good father to Hallie? He could not carry out a normal, mature, loyal relationship so long as he was driven by what was in his pants, not his head.

I was so thankful I'd never taken that man's last name. It was awful that Hallie would carry that name throughout her early life, and maybe forever. And I would just have to accept it, including those many times teachers and nurses and doctors and even the postman still erroneously addressed me as "Mrs. Wolfman" no matter how many times I'd corrected them. Why did I confuse this rotten-souled man's interest in sex with devotion, commitment, love of our family? *What was wrong with me that I was tricked so easily?*

~~~

Poor Sam, I don't deserve him, I thought as I lay awake all night after I'd buried the pajamas in the bottom of our trash and took a long, hot, soapy shower, scrubbing myself like I was removing filth. Thank God I'd just finished my period so there was no chance of....oh God, I couldn't even think of it. Another baby by Stewart when I was falling in love with Sam?

Sam! Oh God, I no longer deserved him. I'd let him down in a way he could never know. I'd be sure he would never learn about this night. Damn Stewart for leading me on tonight, and damn him for ruining our marriage for a woman who flew in and out of his life. Literally.

What was it about men that they regress to their youthful, carefree days just when they're needed to be grownups? In our early years together, Stewart had revealed an inner image of himself as an acne-pocked, skinny nerd. Great: I helped him feel so good about himself during our marriage that, at the worst possible time, he took his newfound self-esteem to another woman's body. Couldn't possibly have been a coincidence, the two of them in our bed when I was due home that day…he was being self-destructive. What a fool! And with a shiksa nonetheless, to use my father's derogatory word. Attention from shiksas meant a lot to Jewish boys, especially those who'd been nerds in high school. It was like they were getting some prize, or screwing parents who pressured them to only date Jewish girls.

Stewart had married a Christian woman, briefly, the first time around, but by the time I met him, he had divorced her, and all Stewart would say about why it ended was "Eh, we got married too young." Then he added, "But I'd never leave you; you're my best friend and lover." Bullshit.

And now I'd been the fool to let him back in.

I thought I had analyzed all of this ad infinitum by now, although it had been quite a while since I had focused on his betrayal. This time, I suspected Stewart must have cheated on his first wife, Regina, too. Or maybe even more times during our marriage? Poor Regina; she must have felt these same sickening feelings when she learned he had married me. Maybe she even wanted to warn me, but didn't. And now I'd let heartless Stewart open up the tightly sealed lid to the whole mess once again…while I had someone sweet like Sam waiting for me in the wings.

I practically crawled into the bathroom, slumped over the toilet and threw up.

~~~

THE NARCISSIST'S DAUGHTER

Two a.m. I'd be a mess for Hallie tomorrow; I *must* force myself to sleep. Tomorrow I'd advance the divorce, have my lawyer subpoena the asshole. At that moment, Ringo jumped on the bed, perhaps hearing my muffled sobs. I hugged him to me and laughed out loud, remembering a cartoon saying, "The more I learn about men, the more I love my dog." And the one saying, "Husband and dog kidnapped: reward for return of dog." Maybe there was hope: I could laugh, and as my mind raced through all the earlier men who had hurt me, abandoned me, I saw each of their faces dissolving into the head of a dog, one a pit bull, another a big fat bulldog, I even saw my father as a drooling St Bernard head. Then there was Sam, the sweet loyal golden retriever. He had been a perfect gentleman so far. Loving fully, even without sex. And now I would lose him if he found out. I wasn't a liar, but this set a new precedent. Stroking Ringo's fur some more, I finally felt myself falling into a much-needed deep sleep.

Chapter Eight

"Don't shoot, don't shoot!" I screamed at the gunman as I grabbed Hallie into my arms and crouched underneath a nurse's station, hiding my baby under my body. We waited, trapped, hiding from another round of attacks. Gunshots rang out, hitting the walls, the medical equipment, everywhere but where Hallie and I hid. I held my breath, rocking my little girl to my bare breast. Where had my clothes gone? I was naked and—

Suddenly—all was quiet. I peeked through a crack to see if my attackers were finally gone.

The nurse at the far side of the room seemed unfazed. "My God," it's Regina, I realized, although I had only seen Stewart's first wife in photos, but the perfectly round face and red hair distinguished her. Regina was making notes in a patient chart. For a second she caught my eye, smiled, and then floated out of the way, leaving her shift.

Stewart appeared across the room, and Sam passed by him in a physician's white coat, disappearing into a hallway. I tried calling out for Sam but couldn't form the words. Without warning, the gunfire began again, this time near Stewart. As though hearing nothing, he reached into his pocket, pulled out a mirror and looked into it, smiling.

The entire time, Hallie remained folded inside my body, singing quietly to herself. I reached my arm out from under our hiding spot toward Stewart, hoping he could help us. He caught a glimpse of me, grinned, then looked down at his watch and walked in the other direction. He brushed past one of the gunmen, no, it was a woman, two women—Ida and Rhonda! I watched as Stewart took Ida's arm and the two of them glanced my way then motioned toward the hallway. "Let's dance," I heard Stewart say to my mother. "No, no, let's eat," she answered. "Feed me." And they disappeared into an elevator, Rhonda following.

All was now quiet again. Feeling shaky and abandoned, I crawled out from under the nurse's station, still naked, and reached for Hallie's hand. Hallie smiled at me and I hid my distress as best as I could. "Let's go Mama, it'll be okay," she said. She reached for my hand and tugged me toward a brightly lit corridor leading out of the infirmary. In the distance, I heard Ringo barking and knew everything would be okay.

~~~

"Mama, mama, wake up, wake up." Hallie was pulling on my pajama sleeve, waking me from this terrifying dream. "Someone's at the door."

Chapter Nine

God, I've got to get out of here, I thought, now that Hallie was off to brunch and then to the science center with Stewart's sister. Suzy worked nearby and was a Godsend to me and Hallie. Ten years older than me and single with no children, she silently made it clear she was in our camp. She even offered to help out with Ringo sometimes. She had apologized for ringing the bell so early that morning, but she had slept at a friend's house near here after work, had the day off, and thought she'd check in with us. It was as though she sensed when I needed a break or some support. There was no way Stewart had told her about last night, as the two barely spoke. Nor did I tell my sister-in-law anything more than what Hallie would tell—that we all had dinner together, although I hoped Suzy hadn't noticed Hallie was dressed, while Mommy was just waking up in pjs. No matter, Suzy was a saint and her coincidental timing gave me the day to sort through my nightmare...the real one and the dream.

I had to get some air. I threw cold water on my face and then ran my fingers through my hair in an attempt to fluff it up a tad. I slipped into khaki pants and a baggy sweatshirt, laced up my sneakers, and stuffed a few dollar bills into my pocket.

"Come on boy, let's go for a walk." Ringo carried his leash to the kitchen. His tail wagged so hard it looked like he would lift off the ground.

But first I checked the flashing red light on my answering machine. Probably from last night while we were out to dinner. It was Ida. I wanted to hit the delete button, but stupidly didn't.

"Hello, Mother here. I know we haven't spoken much but I've been meaning to tell you the date for the Jewish Philanthropists' Benefactor event. It will be held here two weeks from next Thursday, and I expect you to come. Do wear something chic, including someone attached to your arm—Stewart perhaps, to save face for now? And I have made the event for seven p.m. to accommodate Alan's schedule. You will not have any trouble finding a sitter I presume. You must not bring Hallie. Call me soon, please. I must firm up my guest list. And where are you on a Sunday night, by the way?"

Ida was speaking to me like everything was normal between us. Had she not noticed I was no longer her puppet? She didn't even trust me to know better than to bring a child to an adult event? And I should bring *Stewart*? And wear something chic? Did it never end? Would she try to dress me in itchy taffeta and those uncomfortable Mary Janes she favored for me as a child? Well, maybe she would, but I was no longer going to stay stuck in my life under her control. And, Alan, accommodating Alan Yadlowsky in choosing the time for Ida's big annual event? *Alan*? Alan, the bastard who dated Rhonda for so many years and only proposed marriage after he'd learned there was money in this family! Alan, who often ignored me because he didn't like what he referred to as my "touchy-feely" personality, but the week before he provided his sperm for Rhonda's first artificial insemination, he whispered to me that if I'd come with him into the little bathroom with the sterilized jar and red light, he could complete the "task" in no time. Then he laughed a hearty laugh as though to say it was all a big joke. I wanted to tell my sister, but I knew she'd just say I was jealous, or couldn't take a joke. Ida was adjusting the time of her event for Alan-the-Doctor—her show-off name for him when introducing him to strangers? Hmm, Ida's party was being held when I could be in California, secluded from all of this, relaxing with Sam. He could be my ticket away from it all.

I hit the delete button on my answering machine, grabbed Ringo's leash and locked up the house. As soon as we stepped outside, the cool air felt invigorating, just what I needed to attempt to retrieve my strength and sanity from last night, and forget about all this bullshit.

We walked a mile on the peaceful wooded road. Not long after reaching the edge of the downtown area, with its handful of restaurants, stores and coffee shops, I turned back.

"Jody? Is that you?" I heard the painfully familiar voice of Brad by the town parking lot we'd just passed. Damn, not now. I pulled Ringo's leash in close and picked up my pace.

"Jody?"

I turned to see Brad tugging at his suit jacket, trying to hide a paunchy midsection. His face was puffy, he had a double chin and barely a strand of hair covered his bald pate, once covered in thick black hair. And was he always quite this short? He looked so awful it hardly mattered that I looked like I'd spent the night sleeping in the street. I wanted to bolt. "What brings you out this way?" I asked, barely audibly.

"You, my lovely." He plopped his briefcase on the ground and leaned back against a telephone pole, resting his hands between his parted legs. I wasn't sure if this was supposed to be a come-on or another way to hide his stomach. Either way, it—he—disgusted me.

"Come on Ringo, let's let Elvis play with himself." I tugged on the dog's leash and started off the curb. My usual tolerance was shot, flushed down the toilet with Stewart's betrayal, Ida's obnoxiousness, Sam's blind unknowing loyalty, and now this crap.

"Stop, I'm sorry. What's wrong?" Brad hurried after me, grabbing my arm. "Can I help in some way?"

I glared at him, his face solemn and his jacket now askew, revealing the full-on beer belly. I'd heard this heartfelt speech many times before when he had acted sincere one day, withdrawn the next, cocky and flirtatious the day after, finally leaving for the other woman he had denied. It was nearly ten years ago, yet the roller coaster ride of emotions rushed back.

"Tell me, what's wrong?"

I raised my spine as tall as possible and pulled my shoulders back in a stance I'd learned in dog training class to command control. "Brad, you're the last person I will ever share anything with." I turned to go, but he grabbed my arm again.

"Jo, all I ever meant to do was love you. I fucked up. I still think of you, you're the woman I let get away. Two divorces and I still think of you. You married?"

I yanked away from his grip. "You and your damn lies; you're at it now, telling me you're here in town to see me. Damn it, I deserve better than lies and bullshit!"

"Okay, okay, calm down. I meant what I said about you, really. You were always sweet and kind, and sexy I might add, but I didn't think I deserved you. I was a prick. I know that now. I'm here for a meeting with a client. He asked me to come to his office this morning to discuss his retirement plans." He pointed across the street at the dental office sign.

"But I was early, and I saw you. Hoped you'd still find me *sexxx-y.*" He winked.

"No! I unequivocally do not!" I kicked at the curb. "Sling your shit at someone else. And, fuck you, Brad, just fuck you!" I tugged at Ringo's collar and ran off. I imagined Brad standing there with his jaw ajar, used to getting whatever he wanted.

"Thanks, Ruthie," I said in my head. *"I guess I took the intensive 'Fuck You Factor' course myself!"* Although my body was trembling, I felt carefree. Around the bend, I tied Ringo to a pole at a Shell station. I desperately needed water...and maybe a soothing brownie. As I walked into the convenience section, the headlines of *The Boston Globe* caught my eye, showing the President at yet another press conference about the mess heating up again with "that White House intern." I knew Uncle Nathan was probably standing two paces away, just off camera. I wished he could fix my love mess right now, too. I should have stayed away from Stewart's temptations just as Monica should have stayed away from Clinton. Poor Hillary.

Poor Sam.

"Two twenty-five please." I paid and turned to leave when something peculiar caught my eye. A sign next to a display of laundry detergent must have once had a sign "biodegradable," but the "bio" had faded. I walked away, sucking down the water. Then I opened the brownie wrapper and repeated the word I had seen on the sign. Degradable. *Damn it, I've felt degraded long enough from those who supposedly love me.* At that moment I had an epiphany: I had been stuck between the proverbial rock and hard place for way too long; unless I could let go of the past, try to accept, or at least tolerate, all the narcissists who had hurt me, and choose my own path without needing their approval, I would remain stuck forever!

I guzzled more water and tossed the brownie, still in its wrapper, into the trash. *The hell with all of them. No more walking over Jody!* I entered the phone booth at the far side of the gas station, popped in a quarter, then punched in my mother's business number. Ida wouldn't be in the office until later. She'd hear the message then.

"Hello, this is Jody," I said in a professional tone. *"I got your message, Mother. I will make a donation to your cause, but I will not be attending. I will be on vacation in California with a new and wonderful boyfriend whom you probably won't approve of because—horrors!—he isn't Jewish, nor a doctor or lawyer. I've actually been seeing him for a while and kept it from you so I didn't have to hear your insults. And you're probably shaking your head right now, and once again disappointed in me, but you'll excuse me while I get on with my life instead of the one you've continually planned out for me. Oh, and Hallie is all set while I'm away,"* I lied. *"Please do not think I'll need you to babysit, not that you have ever offered. And, do not call to discuss this. I can assure you I will not answer."*

I hung up without saying goodbye and prayed my sister-in-law could watch Hallie and Ringo while I traveled. I was relieved not to attend yet another annual benefactor dinner in the massive Great Room my mother had built the year after Uncle Harry and Aunt Bernice had moved into their Westchester County mansion. This year, I could breathe in fresh La Jolla air and love of a kind man, instead of rivalry and self-importance.

Next I called my divorce attorney's office. She took Mondays and Fridays off to be with her kids, but she'd check her messages.

"Beatrice, it's me. You said I'd know when I was ready to push harder, and you were right. I'm ready. Go ahead and subpoena him for those documents he's sitting on, and

let's focus mostly on the custody stuff. I'll call you soon and explain what's going on."

Another phone call, to Stewart's answering machine. I knew he'd have either left for work meetings or still be asleep, curled up with Brooke and not answering the phone. After I heard the familiar short message, I unleashed my fury. *"If I wasn't totally clear before that you are continuing to fuck with me, now I know for certain. Get the fucking documents filed NOW or you'll be hearing from my attorney really soon!"* I slammed down the receiver just as I heard someone pick up.

One final phone call. No quarters left, so I punched in my credit card number.

"Hi, sweetheart. I hope you check your home messages soon. I'm so sorry I haven't answered your recent romantic emails. I wasn't feeling well, sort of sick to my stomach; didn't want to worry you about it. The good news is I'm fine now, truly fine. It was just something yucky I guess I hadn't fully digested. Call me. By the way, I want you to meet Hallie as soon as possible, and then my grandmother, too, and, when, exactly, do we leave for California?"

Then to myself I said, "The sex will come; love this man his way—now."

PART TWO

MINDY POLLACK-FUSI

Chapter Ten

Hallie held Sam's hand as we entered Bubbe's building. Ringo and I lagged behind so the cocker spaniel could sniff the familiar scents. He figured it was his visiting day, when elderly people with hundreds of smells all over their fingers, clothes, walkers, and wheelchairs would pet him and feed him biscuits. I had trained him well; all he had to do was sit, shake hands on command and look cute, which came naturally to him with his long floppy ears and sleek haircut. Kissing the customer was a bonus, only upon request.

But the dog had a different job that day: he was there as my pet therapist, to calm my nerves as I introduced Sam to Bubbe. I had mailed Bubbe a note to tell her about Sam, and to plan the meeting. I hoped she would receive my news well. And not mind that he wasn't Jewish.

"What's not to love about him?" Ruthie had reminded me when I spoke with her on the phone that morning, calling her to receive a last-minute boost of confidence. "If Bubbe doesn't like him, you've been withholding something about him, girl."

Hallie was now busy teaching Sam the routine of running to the elevator and pressing the "up" arrow, which I had already clued him into. I caught up to them and Sam winked at me and said, "Eighth floor, lingerie, please."

"But Sam, that's the floor for *girls*." Hallie crossed her arms over her chest as though he'd said something naughty. Sam and I looked at each other with curiosity, wondering where she'd learned that word.

"But it's also for men who want to buy things for their best girls, and maybe I just want to buy something for you and Mommy?"

"Ernie underwear for me!" Hallie announced before returning to her formal stance as elevator operator.

"And might Mommy like something silky?" Sam winked at me.

"It depends how this little get-together goes. Hope it goes as well as your first visit with Hallie! Look at you two now, inseparable." Sam had arrived at our house a few days back to meet Hallie. He carried in a huge blank canvas and finger paints. While I had prepared dinner, they bonded over gooey fingers and a joint painting of rainbows and roses. My two artists had stolen my heart all over again.

"Hallie dear! Ringo! My loved ones, so vonderful you are all here," Bubbe's voice boomed from up the hall as we approached her apartment. "And, Sam! My, my, Jody told me you vere handsome, but look at you!"

"I see where Jo gets her shyness." Sam leaned down to kiss Bubbe on her cheek. Bubbe beamed.

"No rugelach today, sorry. Instead, I made blintzes and chicken soup with matzo balls and chopped liver and gefilte fish. And a sponge cake with fresh strawberries. Oy, my manners, bragging about my cooking and keeping my family in the hallway." She ushered us in.

"And *my* manners," Sam said, pulling his arm from behind his back and presenting Bubbe with a tiny bouquet of flowers. "For you, Madam." He dipped into a bow. "You brag all you want about your cooking, and I'll brag about my homegrown flowers. I grow them year-round in a special greenhouse window in my condo."

"He's handsome and talented," Bubbe gushed. "If you don't vant him, I'll take him."

"Sold," Sam said, walking into the adjacent kitchen and lifting the cover off the pot of chicken soup. "Um, um." Ringo was right behind him, sniffing to see if Bubbe had dropped anything on the floor while preparing the meal.

"Okay, you two, knock it off," I said to Bubbe and Sam. "We all know how much you each want to love each other for my sake."

"Yeah, I'm usually mean, silent, and abusive. How about you Bubbe, you just putting on an act, too?" Sam winked at Bubbe.

"Well, yes. I bought the gefilte fish and lied to impress you. But I made everyzing else!"

"Good, 'cause I love the stuff in the jar." Sam pulled out a chair and plopped down. He lifted a fork and knife and pretended to await his food in good-humored anticipation.

I sat, too, and Hallie busied herself with the puzzle Bubbe had set out for her on the living room table. Bubbe fussed over all of us like a mama bird feeding her newborn babies. As she served up one dish after another—noting happily that Sam finished every morsel—she talked about everything from Boston politics to teenagers' manners these days to working women to President Clinton's troubles with "that Monica woman," which keeps Uncle Nathan so busy. I suspected it wasn't all idle chatter; my wise grandmother most likely was testing Sam's values. And his politics. I knew he'd pass. In fact, I had once asked him if he were truly this compatible with my preferences and my values, or just faking it to get along? Didn't he have any faults? He had stopped mid-bite in the restaurant, spinach deliberately sticking out from between his teeth like a comical dog revealing what he stole from the table. He removed it, and then spoke in an evil voice like Jack Nicholson playing the Joker, "I don't like cleaning pots and pans, I've been known to forget to put the toilet seat down, and I am sometimes so early to parties the hosts are still vacuuming their rugs. Other than that, yes, I'm per-fect." Then in his own voice he added, "Did I add I'm a recovering perfectionist?" I chuckled along with him, and I knew if these were true they sure were minor faults. He had never expected perfection from me, like all the others in my life had. Myself included.

After a nice, long visit, Ringo scratched at the door to go outside. Sam offered to take him. "Especially since I know Bubbe won't let me help her with the dishes, am I right?"

"Next time maybe, but not today."

"Aah, there'll be a next time! I passed the test, Jo."

"Go now, go. Take Ringo, and bring Hallie vith you. Zat'll give me and Jody time alone to talk about you. Then I'll send her down. But first, give me a big kiss goodbye."

"There's that shy streak again, and I hope this isn't the kiss-off." He planted a noisy kiss on her cheek.

"Go, you, get out of here. Come see me again when you two come back from this exotic trip to California." Bubbe patted him on his behind and kissed Hallie goodbye.

The door closed and Bubbe turned to me. "He likes my cooking, and he eats seconds!" We both grinned. "But truthfully Jody dear, he displays good values and character."

"He's been a good son to his mother his whole life and a good husband to his first wife, and he treats me with kindness and respect."

"Then I like him for you, enough said. Has he asked you to marry him?"

I averted her eyes. "No, no, we hardly know each other. But it already feels right. And he knows I'm still married to Stewart, technically."

"Ah, the legal stuff. But in your heart you are divorced, yes?"

I nodded, thinking shamefully of Stewart slipping out the door the other night.

"I see that you like this boy. If he vants you, you be vith him. Go on the trip vith him, get rid of Stewart for good. Go have the life you deserve, the one I've been vishing for you."

"It's tough making a commitment to someone who isn't Jewish." There, I'd put one toe into the subject.

"But he likes gefilte fish." Bubbe walked toward the sink full of dishes. She was making her point clear; his religion was a non-issue to her. Then she stopped and turned back around. "Anyvay, ven you were in the bathroom, he told me he was prepared to raise his children Jewish when he was married to Shelley, and he even considered converting to make them all a more united family."

I stared at my grandmother. This was new information to me, and while I was happy, I was shocked he had shared this with her. Maybe that's one reason I adored them both; they were emotionally open and forced me to unlock the latch on my closely held heart. "He's a good man. He's good to me," I said to my grandmother's back.

"Vat? Vat did you say? His food is for you? You like spaghetti and lasagna, huh?"

"No, Bubbe," I laughed, knowing she was playing games with me. "Well, yes, I like those foods, but I said 'he's good to me.'"

"Huh? Louder, dear." Bubbe shut the running water and looked me square in the eyes. "Say it again, dear? I'm not sure I heard you correctly."

"He's good to me!" I practically yelled, grinning.

"Oh, yes, I heard loud and clear. I hope you did, too."

Chapter Eleven

Sam and I had one "check" on my side of the family, so a week later, ready to take another risk, we scheduled the next special get-together.

"They'll love you, Jo, just relax." We had just begun the hour-long drive toward the north shore of Massachusetts to meet not only his mother, but Shelley's parents too. The sun edged out from behind a cloud, promising to be a good day. I had pleaded with him to meet his "parents" separately, but Sam insisted an "interfaith" gathering would help me feel more at ease.

"Trust me, babe," he said, putting his hand on my knee. "Isaac and Debra are still like parents to me, always will be. They want nothing more than for me to be happy again, and they'll see, in a flash, how happy I am around you. Plus my mother loves having them over."

I was eager to meet them all and to see Sam's childhood home, perched high above the Atlantic Ocean.

"I guarantee you'll like them...and they'll love you."

"But I'll never be Shelley," I whispered, as though to myself. I was setting him up to ease my insecurity, yet I knew I might fail the test. Shelley was still his, forever locked in his heart, perhaps taking up even more space than I did, for now.

"That's true," Sam replied rather matter-of-factly. I felt the knot that sometimes twisted in my stomach when her name came up. I folded my hands tightly in my lap, smoothed my skirt, and clamped my jaw shut.

"Look, I see how uptight this makes you, but I can't always keep boosting you. You have to do it for yourself more." He cleared his throat, and then softened his tone. "The facts are, well, you won't ever be Shelley. We both need to accept it, and we both need to help each other with this over time. But I love you for being you, for your instant acceptance of me and my past, your compassion toward people you care about, your creativity in so many categories, your intelligence, your amazing parenting skills. See, not just for your sexy curly hair like she had, but that kinda helped us meet that day in the store, so what the heck!"

He stopped at a traffic light. Leaning over, he kissed the side of my head and took my hand in his for a moment. I felt a twinge of guilt for revealing my insecurities when he was so loving and self-content, and much less complex than I when it came to love, trust, and just about everything.

After our conversation, Sam became quiet. I wondered about his thoughts but decided not to ask. I detected pain on his face, his brow slightly contorted, his mouth tight. I unfastened my seatbelt so I could lean way over to silently kiss his cheek and gently rub the back of his neck. He choked up. With just my eyes and the tilt of my head, I let him know I wanted to know what was wrong.

"Hard to talk about."

"I'm here if you feel like telling me. Something about Shelley I presume?"

"Ya." He focused on the road, his jaw slightly twitching.

"It's okay, talk or don't. I understand this stuff's tough, even though I can't really understand, of course. But you spend so much time tending to me. I'm here for you too, you know, you silly boy!"

We drove silently for a few minutes, which felt like hours. Finally, he spoke in a tone I'd never heard before. Weak, lacking confidence, like a school boy asking a girl to a dance. "It's just sometimes I feel I'm betraying Shelley, loving you as I already do, so soon. My heart just can't give her up, it's just too tough, Jo." He glanced sideways at me and then paused. I returned his gaze but remained silent, wondering what was coming up next.

Sam choked up a few seconds and wiped his eyes with the back of his hand. "Yet I have to give her up! God knows she's...gone. Forever. And in an odd way, you're a reminder of that. Love, loss and guilt are all part of the pendulum I guess."

I stroked his cheek. "So, how about you tell me about her, finally? Particularly before I meet her parents?" I had waited so patiently for this moment. Difficult as it might be, I needed to learn more about the other woman.

Slowly, gently, I coaxed out of him that she was not only beautiful, with her golden curly hair, dark blue eyes and pale freckles—as I'd of course seen from the photos, but also the most patient and kind woman he had known. She was a fabulous cook, artist, and kindergarten teacher who adored children.

I wanted to crawl into a hole and cry, sadness rising in my heart, but also my confidence waning into the gutter again. Still, I persevered so he would feel safe mentioning her when he needed to. While a spouse's death was something I couldn't grasp, I sure knew it was an entirely different scenario than being cheated on! I wondered, again, about the horrified look on his face the first day we met, when I asked if he had children.

"Tell me more, Sam?" was all I said. I could do this; we needed to do this.

Sam kept his eyes on the road, and told me they had started trying to get pregnant a few months before she passed out at dinner at his mother's house. They had all hoped her fainting was a sign she was pregnant; instead, they discovered a malignant brain tumor, and within five months, despite aggressive treatment, she was gone. Just like that.

"She was so strong, Jo. She fought to the end and, throughout, she was mostly worried about me, how I would be...after." He paused to compose himself and turned to look at me sweetly. "You two would have loved each other, actually. Though she would have hated your family." He managed a smirk despite the tears filling his eyes.

My head ached for my boyfriend's pain. I stayed quiet, composing my thoughts. It was easy to be envious of her time with the man I now loved, but mostly I felt devastated for Sam. I tried to imagine what it might be like to lose a wife, a friend since college, the woman who should have been the mother of his child. I placed my hand over his on the steering wheel. He moved our hands to his lap. I spoke slowly.

"It's all right. I can handle hearing this now. I'm glad you feel comfortable talking to me about Shelley. Not sure I could have handled it before, but you've made me feel safe. We don't need to remove Shelley from our lives. I know you couldn't, wouldn't want to. Just so long as I'm feeling safe with you and strong enough to handle it, we'll keep her in our lives." He moved his hand to wipe a tear, then he took mine back.

"But hey," I said, "maybe on my weaker days you can give me some wiggle room?" I laughed and mussed his hair. He managed a smile and mussed mine back.

"One more thing about Shelley." He smirked this time. "My last confession, I promise."

"Do I need to sit behind the curtain?"

"Ha, ha, funny girl. Well, maybe, actually. Depends how you handle it." With his eyes, he asked if I was ready. I nodded. "The Red Door perfume?" he said. I nodded again, hoping an explanation might finally emerge about that intimate early gift, and the uncomfortable way he had tucked his nose into my neck to sniff the perfume several times. And when I eventually revealed I couldn't wear the perfume, he appeared relieved.

"Drumroll please," I said. "I knew something was up with this one. I'm all ears." I tugged at my ear lobe, tilted my head, and grinned in anticipation.

"It was a litmus test Shelley designed for me. Well, for 'you.' It was her scent, as you probably guessed. Yet it didn't smell the same on her friends, not as appealing. On them, she told me, it smelled like talcum powder." He lowered his voice. "So while she was, um, preparing things in the end, she sent me to buy her a bottle, which I thought was odd since she had plenty, but of course I indulged her wish. I had it wrapped and everything. Well...you can probably guess...she insisted I would find the right woman when the 'shoe fit.'" He glanced at me to make sure I was taking it okay.

I beamed. "Ah, I'm Cinderella! My love found me with a glass slipper!"

"Yeah, Cinder, I was falling for you harder than I thought I should. I hardly knew you, yet something told me you were the one. So I used the Shelley-designed litmus test. You passed."

"Obviously. I'm still here." I threw back my head and laughed. Then I put my hands together as if in prayer and looked at the heavens: "Thank you Shelley. Thank you thank you thank you. I promise I will always take good care of your man, er, our man." My stomach tightened. I felt like I could cry, as though I loved her just because of our mutual connection, and because she could design something as original and soulful as a perfume litmus test.

"Yeah, but that night, I was worried. For two reasons. That the perfume wouldn't smell great on you, but I also

116

feared Shelley had pulled a prank, rewrapping the gift with something else, like a box of condoms or something."

We laughed for a long time, probably as a release to all the sadness and loss we'd been revisiting, as well as any tension ahead at the luncheon meeting. We both needed to laugh. It was like hitting a "reset" button to free us for playfulness after so many serious topics had emerged on the drive.

The rest of the trip, we blasted the radio and sang along to oldies. We kept the windows of his Camry totally down, our hair blowing in the spring breeze. Occasionally Sam took my hand and kissed it. I sensed his joy at finding happiness again, and having shared some secrets—although I held mine deeply buried inside my shamed chest. As we reached the north shore and drove by the ocean's edge before turning up a few side roads and climbing the hills nearer to the house, he glanced at me and raised his eyebrows in question. Was I feeling more relaxed, safe and ready to meet everyone, he asked with his eyes? I nodded and smiled, giving him the signal I'd be okay, though butterflies danced in my gut.

~~~

"Interfaith time," he teased when he pulled into the driveway. "Corned beef and prosciutto on rye!" We both snickered. *If only interfaith issues were this easy.*

But the truth was, Stella, Isaac and Debra made me feel so welcome from the moment I saw them, despite no doubt struggling with painful emotions as they met the woman taking their dead daughter's place. As they approached the car, any remaining fears of mine evaporated. Stella reached us first, hugging me tightly into her soft body with its slightly thick waist and hips and ample bosom that felt so safe. She wore a flowered cotton dress and had tucked her long, snow-white hair into a loose bun.

"Welcome my dear."

Before I could even say 'thank you' she had moved away to hug her son. Isaac approached me next. I quickly warmed to his shiny bald head, broad smile, and green eyes, and he offered up a handshake that dissolved into a tug toward him and a noisy kiss on my cheek.

Debra approached next, hesitantly. She took my extended hand and buried it into both of hers. She silently took in my face. Her lips quivered for what felt like quite a few seconds. I waited, then helped her out, tried to break the ice.

"It's wonderful to meet you," I said, "and I'm so, so sorry for your loss." My eyes awkwardly darted about because I foolishly hadn't asked Sam to help me prepare for what to say about her daughter's death.

Debra remained silent, studying my face. Her lower lip trembled, and she still held onto my outstretched hand— probably way longer than she intended to. I focused on her eyes, a neutral stillness to my mouth. I took in the sweet, youthful way her shoulder-length, salt-and-pepper hair fell loosely about her tired-looking face. As her gray eyes moistened, she kept her gaze on me. I suspected that despite being physically here in the driveway, she was really far, far away.

Soon, Sam came over and hugged his mother-in-law, who dropped my hands and collapsed into his arms. Quietly, Isaac joined in the hug, his wide arm span reminiscent of a massive bird protecting its brood. Stella stepped closer and leaned into Isaac's side. I stood motionless, just a foot away, and watched, soaking in a family full of overflowing affection and feeling.

The complete opposite of mine.

Within minutes, Debra awkwardly patted my back and Stella motioned us all inside. I nearly gasped when I noticed the side and rear of the house overlooked the ocean. I wondered if someday Sam and I might live in this peaceful location in this quaint coastal town. The 1940s Colonial-style house perfectly fit Stella's "Early American" décor, which would have made Ida roll her eyes. But Stella, unlike my mother, cared more about people than items, I could already tell. The house appeared to be preserved the way it was when all three lived there. Or maybe she just couldn't afford to renovate?

The delicious smell of lunch hung in the air in every room as we all followed one another on Sam's quick tour of his family home. The aroma of spaghetti sauce followed us to the room Sam called the Captain's Room because it curved out over the ocean like the bow of a boat, where smooth water was lapping at the rocks below. The scent of garlic wafted upstairs into Stella's bedroom, with its faded blue, green, and yellow flowered wallpaper and mahogany bed set. The man's bureau was probably in the same spot as when Sam Senior was still alive. My Sam's childhood bedroom was now a sparsely decorated guestroom—with the exception of yellowing karate and art certificates cluttering one wall, which I took a minute to savor. The familiar smell of chicken soup lured us back to the kitchen, where dozens of well-used pots and pans of all sizes dangled from the ceiling in the one renovated space of the house.

Bubbe would fit right in with these people, I already could tell. And so did I.

"She's sitting next to *me*," Isaac announced as we all found our places around the mahogany dining room table. It was covered in a white lace tablecloth slightly yellowed with age. I could make out the initials, SSP. Perhaps a wedding present to the newly married Stella and Samuele, way before there ever was a Samuele Junior, who was a late-in-life surprise baby for Stella and her husband.

"How can I go wrong with two handsome men around me?" I flashed a version of my high school award for Nicest Smile to Isaac, then to Sam. And I meant it. My stomach had completely unknotted and my limbs were loose, relaxed. I felt happy. I could be myself with these people.

The conversation moved quickly and lightly, with lots of laughter throughout a meal that included Debra's homemade knishes and, for dessert, Stella's homemade pizzale wafers. Stella and Sam were duly impressed I knew, and loved, pizzales, which I hadn't encountered since my college roommate brought them back from school vacations.

"I'm skipping dinner tonight, that's for sure," I said as I helped Stella clear the dishes. The others had gone outside to sit on the deck. "This was two meals in one. Everything was fabulous, but you and Debra must have been cooking for days. Thank you for going to so much trouble on my account."

"Nonsense. We Italians like to celebrate with big meals for every happy occasion, just like the Jews do! The only difference is Jews celebrate with food even for the not-so-happy events, but we don't," she said, referencing the Jewish shiva, with its loud socializing and tables full of food, in contrast to the Christian wake, with its abundant flowers, but no food. "Shelley used to tease, 'All those long lines Christians wait on to comfort the bereaved, and no food when you're done?'" Stella paused for a few seconds, then continued as she washed dishes and handed me a well-worn blue-striped dish towel. "You know, Jody, I want you to know I, for one, have no problem with the religious difference between you and my Sam. When he first brought Shelley home, it was a surprise to me that Sam had chosen a Jewish girl, but it shouldn't have been a surprise. He'd grown up here near so many Jewish families, our dear, close neighbors. His very first girlfriend was Jewish. When he and Shelley became serious, I went to the priest, my good friend Father Claude, and I asked him how the church treats such marriages because Jews don't believe in Jesus."

As Stella talked, I took each piece of glassware, sterling silver cutlery, and blue floral Wedgwood china plate from her hands. I wiped each one and gently placed it on the granite counter. I was glad to be occupied during such a personal discussion.

"After he heard the whole situation, Father Claude set me straight. He said, 'Stel, Jesus loves all people; do you think He would really condemn the Jews to Hell for living a good life but not believing in Him? If Jesus were that unloving, why would we believe in Him?' And I told Father Claude, 'All my life I've believed in Jesus, I've put my faith in God, but still He took my Samuele from me so painfully so many years ago, I don't know what to believe anymore.' And Father Claude placed his arm around me and said, 'Stella, what do you think, God's really only going to come down and save the Catholics?' So that night from my bed, I asked Samuele a question," Stella continued. "And of course it was a rhetorical question, because he couldn't answer from Heaven, but I swear I heard his voice, so I repeated my question, 'Samuele, do you mind if our boy marries a kind Jewish girl?' And he answered, 'Stella, *kind* is all I care about for that good boy of ours.' I swear he said that to me, right there in my bedroom. I put on the light and looked for him, and of course I was all alone, but I know I heard his voice. So now all I care about is 'kind,' and I can already see you are kind. So don't worry about your differences. Just make a good life together, have many babies—more than I could ever have. It's good they be Jewish, they'll be smart and wise and kind like you and Sam. It's okay."

I don't think I can stand this moment, it's too beautiful, I thought as I bit my lip hard and choked back a lifetime of tears I feared were about to come flooding out. I placed the glass I was drying on the counter, still wet. Stella sensed my vulnerability, wiped her hands on my towel, then took it from me and hugged me tighter than I'd ever been held.

"What's this, a love fest without me?" Isaac marched in just at the right moment, helping me pull myself together.

"Look, we're bonded in soap suds," Stella said, holding me at arm's length and laughing at the two of us, wet from a combination of soapy water and tears. Isaac walked toward me with a dry dishtowel.

Sam walked in and took the dishtowel from Isaac. "I'll wipe that off my girl, Isaac—you stay away, thank you very much." He patted at my tears first, and then at my damp chest. He hugged me close for a moment. I felt overwhelmed by all the beautiful warmth and humor around me. No tension. No bickering. No competing. No sarcasm. This was all new. Even Debra, the quietest one, no doubt wishing I would go away and Shelley would return, walked over to me and Sam, and with tears filling her eyes, and everyone listening, said, "I give you two my blessing...from my Shelley, too."

There in Stella's kitchen, with its new butcher block island and old but shiny pots, no one knew whether the tears we all shed—a few of us with noisy sobs, others quieter— were happy or sad tears or, most likely, both. But we all knew we felt like family. And for the very first time, with a man I hardly knew but felt so good about, I felt what family should feel like.

Chapter Twelve

Dear Dad: *I am sending this note to your office so Mom won't be able to intervene as she has most of my life. And that you will hear me out. If you wish to share this letter with Mom, or even Rhonda, that's fine. I leave it up to you.*

As Mom may have told you, I am leaving in a few days— gone by the time you receive this—for La Jolla, California, with Sam Puricelli, my new boyfriend, of whom I am quite fond. I will be back the following Saturday night. Sam has treated me with more respect and kindness than any other person, besides Bubbe, since perhaps my kindergarten teacher. He is thoughtful, kind and sweet. He loves children and he and Hallie adore one another. And he is a third-degree black belt in karate—he'll keep us safe!

Dad, Sam is just a bit older than I am and previously was married for several years—to a Jewish woman I might add—who died of a brain tumor a little over a year ago. Yes, Sam is Italian, Catholic, but he is as familiar with the importance of Jewish tradition as I need him to be. He is a non-practicing Catholic, opposed to many of the church's old-fashioned teachings and beliefs, but he firmly believes in God and in living the Ten Commandments and a religious, ethical, dutiful life to God and family.

I know in your heart you are a good and loving man and a father who feels he gave his best to his family because you provided so much for us. I also know you love Mom very much despite her often-difficult side, and perhaps you, and only you, have a unique insight into her soul, one that has helped you sustain a nearly forty-year marriage. I respect you for that.

Yet I want you to also know that because of Mom's "power" over all of us, I, in particular, have not been able to make my own choices about my life. Rather, I have opted for the way I thought things should be rather than learning what I really wanted for myself. Had Stewart not had his affair and left, I would have made a life with him and stuck to my wedding vows, but, frankly, I would have been cheated out of a truer love, and the loyalty I deserve. I know this now, because of Sam.

With Sam, Dad, things feel right. I even met his family and his former in-laws and they are wonderful, warm people. Sam and I feel like the silly saying, two halves of one whole. In fact, I met him on a project for my work—he is a talented graphic designer and photographer. Please don't freak that he's not a doctor, lawyer or CPA! He's very well regarded in his field. His father, long deceased, was a prestigious designer in Boston, too. I know you're wondering what "the artist" makes for a living, but let me make it clear he makes enough to make me happy.

What also helps a lot is your mother gave me the thumbs up on Sam. I assume by now she's tried to kick you in the pants to accept him and me. I hope she has succeeded and this letter reinforces that I'm happy, and he is a good man. I'm moving ahead with my divorce to Stewart as you know, and my attorney assures me my assets—er, yours—are secure. Thanks, Dad, for planning so wisely.

I love you, Dad. Those three important words are not easy for any of us to say to each other in this family, but I

124

need you to know I finally understand you've really been the one who's kept us together by plugging away at life, succeeding, and never complaining. You taught me to be an optimist. You're a stronger man than I have been a woman, at least up until now.
Love, Jody

Chapter Thirteen

Tuesday

Email to Ruthie from Jody:

No wonder Sam comes to La Jolla several times a year! This place is my new drug of choice. He went off to his photo shoot and I'm a lady of leisure all day. I promised myself I'd get some work done, but the heck with that. Just jogging around the Coast Walk Trail in the sun, smelling the ocean air, and being alone here with Sam is enough to clear up my past months of fog. And you should see this hotel he splurged for. Good thing he gets to write off some of it! It's like a piece of Italy in La Jolla. Hey, how's your frame of mind before I go on and on? I'm bursting to tell you all this, but let me know if you're up for hearing it. Jo

Email to Jody from Ruthie:

Shut up about me. If I can't have a life, at least one of us can. Seriously, I'm okay. Picked up a couple of new clients this week, so I'm gonna be glued to this computer for a while, but at least it's bringing in the bucks. Send more good gossip, I could use the diversion, and it's good to hear you so happy. Hey, has he jumped your bones yet?!
Love ya, Ruthie.

Email to Ruthie from Jody:

As FAB as my time alone has been today, I can't wait 'til Sam returns for another night in the magical La Valencia Hotel. I know you want the dirt, but there still isn't much, except he has the body to match those karate belts he earned a long time ago. He's so modest, he hardly mentions it. But, I don't yet have in-depth knowledge about that body...kinda weird, but he finally went from no kiss to lots, umm, and it's wonderful just to feel his body holding mine in the middle of the night. Ru...we still haven't made love, and I'm too scared to ask why, it's probably about Shelley.Meanwhile, you'd hate this, and I'm wild about it: he sleeps in silk boxer shorts. I've wanted to rip them off a million times, but I'm really trying to let him have the controls. But I'm only human. We'll see if I can contain myself tonight. Or, maybe he finally won't. GTG. He'll be back soon. I'll try to write tomorrow. Jo

Wednesday Late Afternoon
Email to Ruthie from Jody:

"Mrs. Puricelli, your massage is confirmed for two-thirty in your room." That's the phone call I woke up to this morning! No we didn't get married, silly. Sam insisted I pamper myself while he's off for another day of shooting, so he arranged for me to have a massage. I'm loving every second of being a "kept woman." Okay, I'll admit it—I love feeling like Mrs. Puricelli. But it's an unusual time, no kid, no dishes, no distractions, no parents! Just us. And...well, the kissing and cuddling has continued...and it's lovely! But that's still it so far! I feel like a teenager waiting for the next base, ha, but I just have to wait it out. It's worth it for such a loving, attentive companion, and I've discovered he's very take charge—not only the massage he ordered, but he also surprised me last night by coming back to the room with a scrumptious dinner and wine...and candles. And this

morning before he left, he tucked the covers in all around me. That's when he told me he'd ordered the massage (which was delightful but weird to be semi-naked in a room with a man when my own guy hasn't seen me like that!). And tonight he wants to take me shopping at Prospect Place. I told him he doesn't need to keep doing this kind of stuff, especially when he doesn't have that kind of money, but he said I should trust him, it's fine, and it makes him happy to see me happy.

Hmm...should I start worrying he's a spendthrift or worse, a voyeur—was there a hidden camera in my room during the massage? Until I find out what's wrong with him, this just keeps getting better! And how are you my dear friend? Too busy with all that work to write? ☺ *Jo*

Thursday Late Afternoon
Email to Jody from Ruthie:
Does this guy think he's Richard Gere and you're Julia Roberts? When you return, I've got to meet him finally. Hey, we'll rent Meryl Streep in Heartburn to give this guy a dose of the reality you lived before him! That's real life, man. Or go buy him one of those funky California sayings, like 'My love for you grows stronger every day—now take out the trash, honey.' Seriously, Jody, you'd better grab this man. He may be the last old-fashioned romantic on the planet, if he's not gay or crazy. Have fun, you two. Maybe tonight's the night...GTG... Late for a date with my cat. Actually, hafta finish some work, these deadlines are nuts. Gd luck. Ta-ta. Love, me

Friday Morning
My head spinning, I dialed Ruthie and hoped she'd be home. No patience for email.
"Hello?"

"Ruthie, it's me. Sorry if I'm interrupting your work, can you talk? I've got to talk to you," I blathered into the phone.

"Yo, girl, this the story about the Big One?"

"No. Well, yes. Bigger than that. Sit down. Oh my God. No joke. Sit."

"Calm down, I'm here for you girl. Talk! I'll shut my trap and listen, but slow down."

"He, oh my God, proposed to me last night. Told me he can't imagine his life without me and wants me to be his— God, I can't even say it! He wants to spend the rest of his life with me even though he's never made love to me? This does not compute."

"No, this does not compute, agree. But go on...it's good. And start at the beginning please...I have no need to do my work with something this good to distract me!"

"What an incredibly romantic night we had. First he helped me pick out a sexy black dress at this unbelievable store. I swear it's where the stars probably shop when they're here on vacation! And then...oh, Ru, I'm sorry, I just can't focus. You know I've never been happier, but after he said, "So will you marry me?" or something perfect like that, all I could think of was Ida and Harry, and who'd have the heart attack first?!"

"Oy, you've gotta bring them into this wonderful story? Grow up, will you? You need your head examined, but you've had it examined, and a lot of good that did! Sorry. Now, get to the point! What'd you tell Lover Boy? Are you telling me you turned this once-in-a-lifetime deal down? Did you at least tell him you love him?"

"Yes, I said 'I love you' back, it wasn't our first time, but not without thinking I don't fully know—how is he as a lover? I mean we've done a few little things, but not the real deal. I started to talk about it and he looked confused or something, so I didn't say anything more. You think it's a Catholic thing? I was too uncomfortable to bring it up again,

and he didn't offer an explanation. If we can't talk about sex—or have it!—how can I agree to marry him? It's not the sixteenth century for God's sake. I don't understand any of this. He's really rushing things, don't you think?"

"Maybe, but who cares? I don't know what his reason is, but as long as his dick works, stop worrying about it. Stay calm, girl, and go for the ride. Hey, tell me, did he say his famous line, 'I'll always be here for you?'"

"Yes, you creep! When I said I needed time, he held me and said, 'I understand. I'm rushing things, I know. Whenever you're ready, you let me know. Until then, I'll be here for you. You've been there for me so many times.' When have I been there for him? All I've been is a neurotic mess that somehow he can see past! Ru, I better go. He's at a meeting now, then we're heading to the historic Hotel Coronado tonight. In the morning, he's taking me to the airport and heading up the coast to finish his work. I'd better jump in the shower."

"Well, I hate to not hear the more, shall I say, nitty gritty details, but I guess it'll hafta wait. Call me when you get home. Hang in there, sport. This is amazing stuff. Luv ya."

"You're the best, thanks Ruru. Love you, too!"

~~~

I hung up the phone and leaned back on the bed, feeling a bit dizzy with love and confusion. No one had ever paid this kind of attention to me. I was sure I didn't deserve it. He clearly didn't see all those terrible sides of me my family knew about. Even the side that had been lying to Ruthie lately. I was keeping too many secrets from my best friend these days, not telling her about my pathetic night with Stewart or about my fear Sam might be gay.

I made myself a cup of coffee and settled in at the sweet little writing desk. Before showering, I flipped open my computer to check my work email…and when I spotted a message from Ida, I spit out a mouthful of hot coffee onto my nightgown. When did she learn to use technology— nonetheless score an email address like that, YourMother@aol.com? Didn't Mother Teresa have rights to that? Or every Jewish mother out there? Why mine?! There she was in black and white, haunting me from the other coast. I stood and walked toward the bathroom—*I'm not going to read this.* But the tug was too strong. I succumbed.

Email to Jody from Your Mother:
  "Well, Jody, I must say your telephone message sent me to bed with a migraine for days. I would still be sick in bed if it weren't for my important event. It was beyond rude of you to leave such a foul message. I just do not understand your temperament these days, or your choices. And now you tell me you are off with a Catholic man. You do not understand why this is just not right for our family. Aside from the fact we owe it to our tradition, and those who died in the Holocaust, to keep our heritage going, you are embarrassing us dating this man. No one has brought any goyim into our family. Nor, as you know, ever been divorced. Ever. Period. Why don't you just come home and fix your life?"

~~~

My throat felt on fire, closing up on me, the feeling of bile coming up too. It was like I had consumed something I was deathly allergic to. I needed air. I flipped open the balcony door and walked out, grasping the handrail. I looked down at the cliffs beneath me, then farther down to the ocean. As all became a blur, I worried that I might topple over, making the news: Lady Found Dead at Fancy Hotel after Receiving Rude Note from Mother. I needed to get out of there. I ran into the bathroom and tossed my toothbrush and make-up into my toiletry case. Then I opened the bureau and pulled out everything of mine, not even folding my pants and shirts before throwing them into my suitcase. Feeling confused and frantic, I went to the closet and grabbed my things from their hangers. I stared at the black dress still in its sheer plastic covering as though I were Cinderella vaguely remembering a dream. I left it hanging in the closet on its lonely velvet hanger. I shoved the rest in my suitcase and zipped it close. Then I took out a sheet of hotel stationery and a pen. In shaky handwriting, I wrote:

Dear Sam:
I hope deep in your heart you can find a way to forgive me. You are so sweet to me, so good for me, so generous, too, but this is all much more than I feel I deserve right now! I have secrets you don't know about and they're killing me. Please stay and finish your work! I'm so proud of you and I want you to complete this wonderful assignment. I can't wait to see the calendars when they're done. I just need to return home to ground myself and settle some things. And please, I adore the dress, but it's too much money for you to spend on me. Please, please return it. Be patient with me. We need to talk. But I must go. Now. Forgive me.
With love, Jo

~~~

I managed to get a standby seat just minutes before the next plane to Boston lifted off. I settled in, and as I placed my purse by my feet, I noticed an envelope from the La Valencia sticking out of a side pocket. I unfolded it, lifted out the sheet of paper and read it:

To my beloved Jody—
Last night we shared a mixed message or two; we'll sort them out, those few.
Life is about being together, being whole, and even though there will be an occasional hole, we'll step over it with love.
Our inner thoughts and feelings are strong, and to share them with each other is not wrong.

I love you, Jody dear, and cherish all of the times you are near.
Sam (the bad poet)
P.S. What I just can't understand is why any man would ever leave you.

I covered my mouth with Sam's message and cried, just as the pilot announced the flight time would be five hours and twenty-five minutes and the current weather in Boston was forty-eight degrees and raining. When I could speak, I ordered a double gin gimlet, gulped it down, and fell into a sound sleep, so deep yet aware of a dream.

Dozens of couples were holding hands and entering a small but beautiful glass enclosure leading to a garden filled with rows and rows of multi-colored tulips. Some couples watched butterflies flitting about, trying to entice them to land on their hands; some smelled the flowers; some kissed and hugged on corner benches; some were engrossed in conversation. I was all alone and trapped outside the glass enclosure. Every time I tried to enter, couples squeezed past and closed the door on me. I tried once more to reach for the door, but this time it clicked and locked. I pulled hard and the handle came off in my hand. Frantic, I looked around for a key. Where was the damn key? I lifted up rocks, scanned the dirt floor. No key. I took one from my purse and tried it, but it crumbled in my hand. More couples maneuvered around me, as though I were invisible, and they easily entered the beautiful chamber. I threw down my purse in disgust and walked away, sad and ashamed.

Chapter Fourteen

"**E**xcuse me, miss, we've landed. Everyone is leaving the plane." The flight attendant shook my shoulder. "You okay, Miss?"

"No, can't you see that?!" I snapped at the blond, blue-eyed woman who uncannily resembled Stewart's Brooke. I glanced at the name tag: "Donna." Phew. "Oh, sorry, I'm not okay, but yes, I'll leave the plane. Excuse me for snapping at you. I'm just under a lot of stress." I noticed I was still clutching Sam's note in my left hand, despite five-hours of dead sleep.

"No biggie. I noticed you fast asleep during the flight and I was kinda checking up on you now and then, making sure you didn't plunk your head on the shoulder of that guy next to you, as he didn't look too friendly." She smiled and popped an after-hours stick of gum in her mouth and offered one to me. I shook my head.

"Honey, you look like a very normal lady, if any of us are 'normal,'" She snorted. "But I can sense you're going through something rough right now. 'Been there, done that' myself. Frankly, what woman hasn't?" She paused and I began to stuff my things into my carry-on tote.

"In fact," she continued, "remember me forever for this cute little ditty I'm gonna pass on to you. I heard it somewhere on one of those talk shows: 'The bend in the road isn't the end of the road unless you fail to take the turn.' Good stuff, whatever your problem is, honey, don't you think? You feeling any better yet?"

Still in a fog, I nodded and pulled on my jacket, eager to get off the empty plane.

I was no stranger to Logan Airport. After stopping in the bathroom and throwing water on my mascara-smudged, raccoon-like eyes, I stepped outside to catch a cab. But the line was so long, probably because of the drizzly weather which always backed things up. I wanted to keep moving. I'd try to catch a cab at the next terminal. Maybe it wouldn't be as busy.

Dragging my one small suitcase behind me, I kept walking, lost in my thoughts, until I found myself in total blackness on the ramp toward the Sumner tunnel.

"Asshole!" The driver of a swerving, honking cab leaned on his horn and yelled out his window. Seconds later, he jerked to the side and slammed on his brakes, causing a symphony of horns. I hugged the side of the road, frozen like a deer in headlights.

"Jody?" the driver shouted out his window. "Jody Horowitz of Oliver Road? Is that really you?"

I lifted my head and read the sign on the cab, "Thomas's Taxi." Tom was walking toward me. He was scheduled to pick me up when my original flight landed tomorrow. He must have done a Logan run for another customer.

"Jump in," he said, half demanding, half leading me as he might an elderly or blind person. "What the Hell's wrong?!"

I couldn't answer, couldn't believe I had been walking the ramp to the tunnel in a daze. Nothing like this had ever remotely happened to me before. The best I could do was mutter, "Breakdown. Maybe? Tom, please don't tell anyone how you found me."

"Hey, it's me I'm worried about, I coulda killed you—bad enough I almost killed a stranger, but a fav customer? Where to now, home? I'm off-duty, I'll take you there."

"No, no. I can't be alone right now." I paused. Ruthie would know what to do next. "Take me to 22 Winchester Street, off Beacon, just past Coolidge Corner."

It felt like I'd known Tom forever. He had driven me and Stewart to the airport whenever we took vacations. We were all so close in age, with Tom just a bit older, now pushing forty. We had grown friendly, though only during cab rides, and mostly limiting talk to sports. Still, his familiarity—and that he knew about me and Stewart being separated—made me feel safe while driving to Ruthie's.

We arrived in a flash. Tom opened my door and helped me into the apartment building. He waited with me in the small vestibule until buzzer number six answered its intercom seconds later.

"That you, Jo?" Ruthie shrieked.

"You were *expecting* her?" Tom asked. I just stood there, stone-like, dumbfounded that my best friend had guessed it would be me.

"Shit, who are you?" Ruthie asked through the intercom.

"Ms. Horowitz's cabby, and I hope you're her shrink."

"I'll be right down!" Ruthie didn't buzz us in, nor did she say anything to the cab driver when she burst upon us, wearing only a Patriots tee shirt, her black lace underwear peeking out. She instantly engulfed me in her arms. The three of us barely fit in the tiny foyer that reeked of a combination of pizza and cigarettes.

"Oh, honey, look at you, you're a mess," she said, patting my snarled hair, and pushing it back from my eyes. I shivered in my wet jeans and tank top.

"I was hoping you'd show up here. Sam's called a dozen times wondering if I'd heard from you. He feels responsible for your running away. Imagine that?! That boy is not only nuts about you, but nuts! Come up, come up."

Tom, in his worn jeans and blue and red Patriots sweatshirt that pushed against his protruding belly, dug his hands in his pockets and kicked at the dirt in the foyer.

"Oh, you wanna get paid, huh?" Ruthie said. "Come on up."

"Inviting me up in that tee-shirt is tempting, but, nah, this one's on me—you should be paid for taking her in, lady. See ya Jody, and, man-oh-man, good luck. Call me when ya need a ride back. That one's on me, too."

"Where'd ya find the cute cabby, Jo?" Ruthie asked after Tom had clicked closed the door and tipped his Red Sox hat at Ruthie through the glass.

Even in my state of distress, I noticed those two would make an interesting couple, their wits equally matched, even if their physiques, backgrounds and social class couldn't be more opposite. Maybe there was hope; I was finally thinking of something other than what a total immature jerk I'd been, and how I had sabotaged the one miracle that ever fell into my lap.

~~~

Ruthie managed to settle me into a hot bubble bath. She brought me some tea with Bailey's Irish Creme, a drink the two of us had enjoyed together in the old days when we were young and carefree, but I didn't want it. I placed it on the edge of the tub. Ruthie sat on the toilet seat, leaning forward and cupping her face in her hands.

I told her about running away from the hotel, my terrifying dream of always being alone, and of nearly getting killed. "I'm so scared, Ru."

"Sure you're scared. A nervous breakdown doesn't come with balloons, cake, and ice cream, you shithead. But you do get to have Valium or Prozac soon if you don't snap out of it on your own. Or, with help—mine and someone else's: Jo, I called Sam, told him you were here." Ruthie studied me as I placed my bubble-coated hands over my eyes and released a barely inaudible squeak.

"He wants you to call him as soon as you're able. The man wants to *apologize*. Jeez. You caught The Pope this time!"

I tried to speak but couldn't contain a flood of tears. Finally, I spoke, but each word blurted out in odd tones, different decibels, the way a pre-pubescent boy caught in a series of vocal hormone blips might sound.

"He wants to apologize to *me*? I, I, I don't deserve him," I stammered, lowering my body into the tub until I had buried my entire face in the bubbles. Ruthie grabbed me by the hair and jerked me upright.

"Shut up, just fucking shut up and listen to me. You've come a long way these past few weeks. Did you really expect to be 'cured' of Ida and the rest of them so quickly? Anyone growing up with that kind of criticism and judgement doubts themselves, assumes no one will ever really love 'em and protects their heart, and then the shit with Stewart feels like confirmation of that, hey I've lived it, too, you know that, so I understand it, sure....but Jo, you get the fucking Pope and still sabotage yourself? You were doing so well it was inevitable you'd fall off the wagon at some point, you total nutcase, but recognize it for what it is and pick yourself up. Are you forgetting that you have a child who adores and depends on you and who is the love of your life? Not to mention your Bubbe and that perfectly trained human-like cocker spaniel, and, well, me, and your other friends who are so important to you?!"

I glanced up at Ruthie but kept quiet, and she followed my cue, sitting silently on her perch on the toilet seat. Leaning toward my tea, I took a sip, allowing the sweet hot liquid to roll around in the back of my mouth. If I could taste, then maybe I could feel again too. Lying back in the tub and letting the bubbles bury me up to my neck, I breathed in the smells of lavender and of home, Ruthie's home, where I felt so safe and comfortable. But this wasn't enough to return to sanity. What did I need to feel sane again? Calling Sam? Apologizing? Calling Hallie at Suzy's, where the two expected me late tomorrow? Voluntarily committing myself to a psych ward? I cried again.

"Oh, tears, now there's something new and different! You haven't heard a word I've said, have you?" Ruthie turned and walked out.

A moment later she returned, the phone in her hand. "Either you pull yourself together and call the man, or I dry you off and drive you to Mass. General. Only the best shrink ward for Ida and Harry's girl," Ruthie added snottily, knowing that the senior Horowitz's penchant for only choosing doctors at "the best" hospitals would tick me off. "Or maybe I should just drive you home to Mommy?"

"Fuck you!" I bolted upright. "Give me the goddamn phone."

"Atta girl!" Ruthie screamed as though her horse had just won the Derby. She leaned halfway into the tub and splashed a wave of bubble bath up in the air, high fiving me in the same swift motion.

~~~

After an exhausted night's sleep in my friend's bed, with Ruthie sleeping nearby on the couch, I awoke as though from a three-hour film, the kind that drags the viewer through so many emotional roller coasters that they carry their heads out in their hands. Like "Schindler's List." Or "Sophie's Choice."

Well, Jody has a far simpler choice, I thought. I suddenly felt clear-headed and sane, and going to see my Hallie would be the final medicine I required.

The night before, Sam had grabbed the phone in half a ring and apologized for being so overbearing. In a nice way, he had explained, but in a way not unlike Ida had always been to me all those years. Calling the shots for me. Planning my life step-by-step. Removing me from my own decision-making abilities. Making me feel as though I were a character playing out my own life by somebody else's script. I thanked Sam for his enormous insight and for being a better psychology student than I had been; I hadn't even made those parallels, nor had Ruthie. And he was correct.

"But Sam, I'm a big girl, or at least I'd like to be. I should have known better than to have panicked the way I did. Nothing you did was in and of itself wrong, *nothing*, do you hear me? I just didn't cope well with all of your wonderful attention—I'm not used to it, I don't feel I deserve it, and I don't feel I can be good enough to give you what you deserve." I twirled my hair around my thumb, then dove in. "Honey, when you return, there's something important I must tell you about me and Stewart."

"Jody, nothing, *nothing* about you and Stewart matters to me! Frankly, all I want is to hold you tight and let you know everything's going to be all right. Hey, that can be a song," he said, half-snorting and half-chuckling like a kid telling his first joke. "Jo, we're going to be okay. Just trust me that I can see the real Jody inside of that damaged shell. The fun, supportive friend, the loving mother, the compassionate soul who hasn't had enough compassion aimed toward her, and believe me you deserve it. Just trust me on all of this until I can look you in the eyes and you in mine. I fly back on Monday—three more long days away from you, but that's the best I can do. And call your answering machine. I left you some messages you might want to hear."

Among the messages on my machine were several from Sam expressing his fear for my safety and his understanding, and another vowing to always be there for me, no matter what. I felt strong enough to hear it this time, strong enough even to listen to Ida's message when her voice came on next.

"Jody, hello, hello? I know you'll be home one of these days—tomorrow is it? Daddy just told me about your note to him and he said to give you a chance. I guess I can try. I missed you at the dinner the other night, actually, and by the way, it was well-attended, of course. We raised a lot of money. Best year ever. Listen, we know you'll be back by Sunday, and we're taking Bubbe out to dinner, then she's sleeping over. Daddy insists I come to dinner, so I want you to come. Hallie, too, of course."

What "of course" really meant was Ida was either on a new course to control me since the last one didn't work, or attempting to be the Good Mother and Grandmother as a means of dismissing her recent behavior. Her foul email had pushed me over the top, but I would never, ever let her know about the episode, because, somehow, she'd find a way to label me weak.

"No need to call back unless you can't come. I know it's a bit of a drive, but meet us at Legals at the Burlington Mall at six. Just go straight there. Daddy will pick up Bubbe." Ida hung up in her typical fashion—without saying goodbye.

Hmm. Two days away. Sam coming in on the red eye Tuesday morning. I felt strong enough to go to this dinner. Okay, yes, I could do this. And I would find a way to talk to Bubbe alone, maybe take her to the restroom, tell her the wonderful stories from our trip. And of course, I'd share the news of his proposal, although I still wasn't ready to accept. It was way too soon.

Chapter Fifteen

"**M**ommy, Mommy, Mommy!" Hallie shouted seconds after I entered Suzy's house. Hallie raced toward me, and I pushed past the wiggling Ringo to scoop Hallie up into my arms. "Hallie, Hallie, Hallie!" I echoed as I spun my beautiful daughter around and around until our giggles and dizziness blurred together like a noisy top. We landed on Aunt Suzy's rug in a heap of kisses, with Ringo forcing his body between us to try to lick at my face.

"Ooh, I missed my love-girl so." I planted a wet noisy kiss on Hallie's cheek and patted the dog with my free hand. "Show me what you made at day care this week, and tell me everything you did with Aunty Suzy even if you already told me on the phone, because Mommy wants to hear it all again and again, because I missed you sooo much on my trip!"

Hallie took my hand and led me to Aunty Suzy's dining room, where they had stacked all of Hallie's creations from day care. I picked up one at a time. "Ooh, look at all your masterpieces!" As I commented about each one, the vivid colors she had used brought me back to when I was small and my mother would set me up to paint. She would cover the kitchen table with newspaper and draw the outline of a rainbow, and I would color it in with the paints. I'd try hard to stay within the lines, as instructed. Once, I spilled the red paint on the white linoleum while my mother took a phone call. Ida swiftly hung up and made me scrub the kitchen floor with a brush that felt rough in my hands. Afterward, the painting stopped.

"This is you over here, I'll show you," Hallie said, dragging me back to the present, where I needed and wanted to be! No more trips to the past!

Suzy had taped up a few pictures. Hallie put her little fingers on the one of me—the tallest figure she had drawn. It had an oval face framed with brown curly hair, two eyes and a big smile. Arms came out from the head, and feet came off of the middle of the stem that formed the long body. "And this is Daddy." Right next to me was a shorter, stouter person with no hair but with a line for the cap Stewart often wore. And down near the legs was a little extra squiggle I interpreted as Stewart's penis. His being naked around her was still okay for us, but soon she would be old enough for it to stop. I made a mental note to remind Stewart about this.

Hallie wore a wide smile as she pointed to herself. Her most noticeable feature was a bright red, large curved line indicating her always-wide smile. In the corner of the picture was a dog, and beside it a smear of brown ink. "This is where I spilled some paint, but it's okay," Hallie said. "I can pretend it's a squirrel for Ringo to chase!"

"I love it all, honey. It's very special," I said, hugging her tightly. "It's more special than you can even know, including the squirrel! I can hardly wait until we can frame it and hang it up at home!"

I turned to my sister-in-law. "I can never ever thank you enough. You just can't know how amazing you are to help like this!"

Suzy, in her quiet manner, replied, "We'll always be one family."

That day and the next, Hallie and I were inseparable. We went roller-skating, made chocolate chip cookies, and played for hours with the new dolls I had brought back from California. Saturday night, we watched "101 Dalmatians" and shared a bag of popcorn, and afterwards, with Hallie in pajamas ready for bed, we made her favorite: "Lion's food," a blend of a little bit of everything from the cupboard, all stirred together in a huge mixing bowl. Flour, sugar, cinnamon, soybeans, basil, soy sauce.... We topped it off with a cracked egg, and Hallie mixed it all together before we fed it to the hungry lion that lives in the garbage disposal. I wiped down the messy counters while Ringo licked the floor clean of everything but a piece of fresh basil he rejected.

"Guess he doesn't like rabbit's food." I laughed as I picked up the stray herb and gave the floor a quick spray of 409.

Hallie curled her nose at the 409, and the two of us giggled as a drop of flour from her hair sprinkled down her face.

It felt so wonderful to laugh and just be a devoted mother once again. Hallie had helped me shelve everything on my mind: The upcoming dinner with Bubbe and my parents; my reunion with Sam in a few days; completing the project for the PR Association; and, toughest of all, facing Stewart soon at his attorney's office—the first time I'd be seeing him since that awful night. Being with Hallie was a joy. Life, thank God, was good again. Even better than before.

Sunday evening we cleaned up and drove off to meet Gammar Ida, Zayde and Bubbe at the seafood place, where Hallie looked forward to her usual mac and cheese despite the icky smell of fish.

Chapter Sixteen

"**E**xcuse me, are you Jody Horowitz?" the host at Legal Sea Foods asked me. I nodded. "There's a message for you to call your mother at home. It's an emergency."

I bolted upright from my seat at the table where Hallie sat coloring the big lobster on the children's menu. Emergency? Did Harry get in an accident on the way to pick up Bubbe? Or even worse, on the way back this way, with Bubbe in the car?

"What's wrong, Mommy?" Hallie asked. I was gathering Hallie's crayons, stuffing them into my purse. I slapped twenty dollars on the table to well cover Hallie's chocolate milk and my glass of Riesling I'd barely touched. "Aren't Gammar Ida and Zayde coming?"

"Honey, I'm not sure. Mommy needs to make an important phone call and I can't leave you here alone at the table. You can play by the phones." I tried to compose myself for Hallie's sake. I took her hand and we exited the restaurant into the mall to use the pay phone. Ida might have tried to reach me on my new cellular phone. Harry had bought it for me recently, insisting I have one of the early models just out, mostly for emergencies, yet I wasn't in the habit of taking it with me yet. Now I wished I'd brought it..

I recalled another difficult phone call when I was twenty-two. I had just arrived home to my small apartment in Cambridge after a ten-day vacation in Colorado with my college roommate, and I called my parents to say I was back. I had been on the phone with Ida for ten minutes, talking about my trip and Ida's projects and news about Rhonda and Harry, when suddenly Ida's voice changed dramatically.

"Jody, I have something very, very upsetting to tell you." She sounded so solemn. I sat on the edge of my bed and gripped the phone table.

"Well, dear, you know that what I'm about to say will be difficult to take."

"Ma, just tell me! What? What's happened?!"

"Well, you need to prepare yourself."

"Did someone die or something?"

"Now, dear…"

"Shit! Is it Bubbe, is she dead?"

"Calm down. You see…"

"What?! Just tell me!" By now I had imagined someone was in the hospital, or worse. But my mother had let me talk for ten minutes before telling me, so how bad could it really be? Sweat beaded up on my forehead. The summer air coming in through the one window in my stale apartment felt stifling. I could barely breathe.

"What is it? I can't stand this any longer—just tell me," I screamed into the phone.

"Well, um, last Monday, your beloved Yolanda died in her sleep."

"Oh, thank God it's just the dog! I thought you were talking about a person," I responded, my fingers relaxing around the receiver until a nanosecond later when I felt a shiver up my spine and I cried out, "My Yoyo? My sweet Yolanda?!" I pictured our German shepherd, nearly twelve, struggling with arthritis and now gone forever. Yoyo, the dog I was so attached to in my teen years when no one

146

understood or adored me as much as she did. My chest heaved, felt heavy, and I ended the phone call so my quiet crying could release into the deep sobs I felt welling up inside of me.

Back then, I wondered whether Ida had done me a favor with the big build up about Yolanda, or if she had just made the whole thing worse in her typical dramatic fashion. Was she doing this again now? An emergency, in Ida's mind, could be a way of getting me to call because they were running late. Or was the "emergency" something like a flat tire? I bit at a cuticle on the thumb of my free hand while punching in my parents' phone number. Despite rationalizing that it was probably nothing, my stomach ached.

"Jody, is that you?" Ida's new "caller identification system" probably read "Burlington Mall." "Rhonda's on her way over. Why don't you come, too, and I'll explain?"

"Ma, don't pull another 'Yoyo' on me. Tell me now what's up. I have Hallie with me and I have an obligation to keep her safe, to not be driving to your house with this big mystery on my mind." I pulled off a cuticle and it began to bleed.

"Yoyo? Oh, Yolanda. Jody, it's best if I tell you here."

I started shaking and turned my back from Hallie. "No, Mother, tell me now."

"Well, if you insist. Yes. Okay." I heard Ida inhale deeply. "When Daddy went to pick up Bubbe, he found her on the floor. In her apartment. She was dead, Jody. Is dead. Passed away. I'm sorry to tell you this on the phone, but you insisted. I know how special she is...was...to you."

"No, no, it's not possible!" I felt my mind go white and full of something like static, and my whole body felt wobbly. I leaned on the glass around the phone and looked toward Hallie who had walked a few feet over to the movie promotion sign and was talking to the dog in the image. I

147

sucked harder on my bloody finger for a few seconds and stared blankly into the crowd of people mingling about the mall like everything was normal.

"You okay? Can you drive here safely or should I send a driver to come for you, or, or what do you want to do about coming here, and what about Hallie?"

Strangely, I didn't cry. Rationally, I knew Bubbe was nearly ninety three, yet her good health didn't mean she would live forever. But I wondered why I wasn't crying, thinking perhaps it was because I was in a public place, with Hallie, and talking to Ida who was being eerily warm and sensitive.

"Jody?"

"I'm here, Mom. I was lost in thought."

"Of course, dear. I understand." It was only about the fourth time in my life Ida had shown empathy. What was going on here? "Should I send someone to get you?" she asked again.

"No, I'm okay. I think I'll get Hallie something to eat and try to take her to a friend's house, and then I'll come over alone. If I'm not there in an hour, I'll call you. Don't worry, Ma. Tell me though, how long ago do they think she died?"

"Well, that's the hardest part. She was near her bed, but she was nude, not in her pajamas. So it might have been in the middle of the night, but she still had her false teeth on, and it's strange she had no clothes on, but maybe it happened daytime after a bath."

I gasped. All of it was too much to hear.

"Sorry, dear, but they think she was lying there dead at least one or two days—but probably died quickly. Uncle Nathan says she didn't answer when he made his usual call, but foolishly he never contacted us to check on her."

I pictured my grandmother, the dignified Bubbe, lying in her own body fluids, naked and decaying. I only hoped her death was instant, whatever it was. I couldn't bear to think of her suffering. I felt nauseous.

"I'm sorry, dear."

"Thanks, Ma. And, um, are you okay?"

"Okay?"

"Oh, nothing, just something different in your tone tonight."

"My tone?"

"Oh, never mind. Must be my imagination. Thanks. I'll see you soon. Bye." As I was hanging up, I heard Ida mumble to herself, "Well, she *is* finally out of my life."

Chapter Seventeen

What was it about black that could make it so sophisticated, sexy and powerful—or so somber and symbolic of death? Like a new black onyx jewel, or a black hole of emptiness. Like a black party dress adorned with sparkling applique, or funeral garb, plain and symbolic in its statement of sorrow and mourning.

Ida's A-line black wool dress, reeking from the pungent aroma of mothballs and mixed with her usual odoriferous breath, evoked a sense of what death must smell like: sour, musty, foul, like the fumes released upon opening the lid of a casserole long forgotten in the back of the refrigerator.

Off to the side of the sanctuary in the "family mourning room," all of our immediate family greeted one another in a flood of quiet black hugs. Only Cousin Ellen asked where Stewart was, and I moved away, somehow forgetting to have made a plan about this "problem." I sure wasn't going to think of that now.

Someone whose unfortunate job it was to make the environment comfortable for the family of the deceased had chosen a daisy motif wallpaper in an attempt to brighten up the small dark windowless space. The furniture was scarce: a few oak chairs with soft daisy cushions, and two tiny tables covered with yellow tablecloths, each containing a water pitcher and cups, and a box of tissues. The tissues boxes were couched in yellow-and-white striped fabric covers matching the tiny trash baskets. Everyone blew their noses repeatedly, sounding like a sour band, and they dried tears with soggy tissues or mascara-smudged handkerchiefs. I made sure not to lock eyes with anyone because, other than Ida, I was the only dry-eyed person in the room.

"Whenever you're ready, we're ready to begin," the funeral home director said as he entered the room and placed a hand on each brother's shoulder. They nodded in silence. The director opened the door and walked down the long hallway toward the sanctuary. Two-by-two, everyone dutifully followed, moving slowly as we trailed behind. I was alone, at the rear, my legs feeling heavy as they carried me forward toward the place where Bubbe's lonely casket awaited us. It was also where Sam would be seated among the other mourners—if his plane back from California had arrived on time early this morning. And Ruthie would surely be there—but would Stewart? Frankly, what did any of it matter now? I only had a few things on my mind. Losing my beloved Bubbe. Burying her. And feeling so emotionally cold and alone.

Head to toe, I felt numb, almost outside of my body. I figured this must be what people call an out-of-body experience, the body moving, the mind frozen, watching, removed, as though the frightful experience must be happening to someone else, couldn't possibly be real. But it was. Toward the now-open sanctuary door marched Harry and Ida, Uncle Nathan and Aunt Bernice, Rhonda and Alan, Cousin Barry and his wife Leslie, Cousin Ellen and her husband Robbie. Those of us with children had left them with sitters; they were all way too young to understand, although with Hallie the oldest, and so attached to her Bubbe, I had tried to explain using the stupid child-appropriate fish-in-the-day-care-dying explanation. I missed

Hallie and realized too late that, perhaps, I should have brought her for some sort of goodbye she might remember years later. I lagged behind the others, stopping just before the doorway, my heaviness exacerbated by being the only one without a partner.

I looked into the sanctuary, as colorful and cheery as the moment was dark. The early-morning sun filtered through the partially opened vertical blinds, the light shining in a brilliant streak toward the casket as though God were sending a final blessing to Bubbe. People of all ages lined the thirty or so rows left and right of the center aisle, which my family now walked down, but I couldn't move my legs. I knew I needed to catch up, but I wasn't even sure I could trust my legs to hold me up and carry me forward. I looked down at my black pumps. Maybe I could will my shoes to propel my feet into action.

Suddenly, a hand grasped my shoulder and held me back in the now-empty hallway. It was the unquestionable warmth and strength of the man I loved. He pulled me towards him and hugged me tightly until I felt the life in his body penetrate mine and shake me out of my inert state. He kissed my hair and stroked my cheek, and my body quivered, my composure about to implode, but Sam quickly guided me the few steps into the sanctuary and squared my shoulders toward the aisle. He slipped a tiny note into my hand and closed my fist around it, then whispered into my ear.

"Go, my sweet lady. I'll be with you all the time in your heart. It would be wrong for me to sit with you and your family when they don't know me yet. I'll be right here at the back of the room so you can turn and see me if you need me." He gave me a gentle push.

Gulping air and shaking as though the temperature had just dropped below zero, I moved ahead, grasping Sam's note so tightly my palm ached from my nails digging into my flesh. Cousin Ellen, who never missed a thing, had been glancing behind her. She raised her eyes, tilted her head and mouthed at me, "Who's that?" I ignored her, instantly shifting back to my stalwart defensive pose: body stiff, eyes locked at the casket, not even looking for Ruthie or Stewart. Nothing would impede my honoring my grandmother. I reached my seat and dropped down next to Rhonda, leaving just enough space to avoid feeling her body against mine. If I couldn't sit with Sam, I preferred grieving alone while holding onto Sam's note and replaying last night's conversation. He had reached me several hours before boarding the plane home on the red-eye.

When I answered, his voice was unsteady. "I know I'm probably waking you, but I just called home for my messages and heard your shocking news."

I sat up, pulled the covers around me and cried into the phone.

"Shh, sweetheart, I'm here. I'm heading home. I can't stop thinking of how totally healthy and vibrant Bubbe was just recently. Oh Jo, I'm missing you beyond belief and wish I could be there for you right now. But we'll be together soon."

"Sam, you are here for me, believe me, you are."

Trying not to let Rhonda notice, I uncurled Sam's note in my hand and then quickly dropped it into my purse, face up, before pulling out a tissue. As I blew my nose, I peeked inside my purse: "Bubbe lives on, Jo...she's inside of *you*. S." At last, the tears I'd contained flowed like a fountain.

Chapter Eighteen

"**S**am, this is Ruthie. Ruthie, Sam." We stood outside the funeral home in the parking lot and I finally introduced the two most important people in my life—other than my Hallie. Harry and Ida and Uncle Nathan and Aunt Bernice were about to climb into the limo transporting them to the airport, where they would fly to New Jersey to bury Bubbe beside Bert. The rest of us were staying behind, so we had no graveside to rush off to, nor a shiva, because the brothers had decided to hold a small shiva in New Jersey for Bubbe's few remaining friends, instead of one here, where she had kind neighbors, but no lifelong friends.

Ruthie extended her hand to Sam. "So nice to finally meet you," she said at the exact same moment as Sam. They laughed and hugged one another like long-lost best friends.

"I've been dying to meet you, but I didn't plan to meet you at a place like this, that's for sure," Ruth said.

"I know, I know, me, too. But look at it this way: We didn't have to go through the usual pre-meeting jitters, you know, wondering whether we'd each approve of the other." Sam winked.

"Oh, I already knew I adored you,"

"Likewise!"

"Are you two gonna start bowing toward one another right here in the parking lot?" I treasured them both even more right now for this wonderful banter at a critical time.

Sam leaned toward me and kissed me on my forehead, which felt damp from a combination of stress and a thick humidity making the unusually warm spring air heavy. Just then, Harry forced his way between us, his hands folded on his chest.

Looking Sam straight in the eye, Harry spoke to me. "This is your young man you wrote me about?" Harry continued to stare at Sam, who extended his hand to Harry, but my father didn't take it. Sam dropped it by his side without breaking the gaze between them.

"Mr. Horowitz, I'm so sorry about your mother," Sam said. Ruthie added, "Me too, Mr. Horowitz. She was a very special woman."

"Yes, yes," Harry said, clearing his throat but still looking only at Sam. "So this is your young man?" he asked again of me. I froze. I was too startled by Harry's uncommonly rude assertiveness to know what to expect next. He wouldn't dare make an uncharacteristic scene, right here, would he? And where was the usual scene-maker, Ida?

"Yes," I said. Ruthie cleared her throat loudly, and I took the hint, correcting my bad manners. "Sam Puricelli, this is my father, Harry Horowitz. Harry Horowitz, Sam Puricelli." In the background I heard my mother yelling, "Harry, leave it, not now!" What, was Harry her dog, and she his trainer? Harry glanced over his shoulder and saw the limousine, one door ajar, the others inside. He looked back at Sam. "You take care of my little girl, you hear me now?" he said and extended his hand to Sam, who took it and shook firmly but gently. I noticed Harry holding on to Sam's hand a little longer than a usual business-like shake.

"Oh, I will sir. I can promise you that."

"Good, good." Then he dropped Sam's hand, quickly embraced me with a slight trembling, and rushed off to the limo.

Sam, Ruthie and I, all with tears in our eyes, stood silently, staring off toward the limo, until Cousin Ellen startled us out of our daze. She pushed her way between us, clutching her Chanel purse under one arm and extending the other toward Sam.

"Hello, I'm Ellen Horowitz Kleimer." She spoke in a tone of voice that sounded like she was at work making a cold call, though it was her husband who was the high-level corporate guy; she'd never worked a day in her life.

Sam glanced quickly at me and then back to Ellen. He was about to shake her hand when Ruthie shifted her body behind Ellen. Ruthie pretended to scrape her finger across her neck in a slicing motion, making it clear to Sam that Ellen was trouble. Then the ever-brilliant RuRu turned and bumped Ellen in the shoulder.

"Oh, I'm so sorry...er, I'm so sorry about your grandmother. You may remember me; I'm Jody's best friend. I knew Bubbe well. She was a really special lady."

Ellen nodded and turned back toward Sam, but I had already moved him back a few steps, where many of my other friends and colleagues had moved over to hug me and offer condolences. I introduced Sam to everyone as "my partner," even though I knew some would wonder whether I meant personal or business, and since he was both at the moment, I wasn't dishonest. At the right time, which certainly was not then, I would clarify.

A few minutes later the sky darkened, and it began to shower. Everyone scurried off to their cars, so I never had to deal with introducing Sam to Cousin Barry and his wife. The out-of-town cousins piled into a limousine to take them back to the airport to catch planes home. Rhonda and Alan headed home without saying goodbye or coming over to meet Sam, although I had caught Rhonda's eyes checking him out. I said a quick goodbye to Ruthie. Then Sam and I drove off to stop briefly at his condo so he could clean up from his long trip before we went, together, to pick up Hallie from my always-helpful sister-in-law.

In the few minutes I had alone while he showered, I realized I had not seen Stewart at the funeral. But the thought left me quickly as this was my first visit to Sam's condo, and I took in every well-appointed, cozily-furnished, neat-for-a-guy inch of it, trying not to wonder how much of the décor was Shelley's, and whether I could truly adjust to all the photos still up of her—or when he might be ready to take them down.

Chapter Nineteen

"Tiffany, don't touch that!" Rhonda was yelling at her fifteen-month old for the third time, and I was wondering yet again why my sister had brought her. We had a massive job ahead of us, cleaning out and packing up the contents of Bubbe's drawers, closets and cabinets. Harry had requested we handle this together so we could decide what we wanted to keep, and what could be donated to charities.

"If you touch that again we're going to leave," Rhonda shouted, and I wondered if Rhonda had brought eleven-month-old Tiffany in the first place just so she could wiggle out of this difficult task, leaving it for me to complete alone. But I dismissed that idea. Rhonda would never let me make decisions about Bubbe's things, because it would be granting me far too much power. For the same reason, Rhonda would never listen to my concerns that she was treating Tiffany the same careless way Ida had treated us. I made a mental note to mail my sister an article on self-esteem and positive discipline—even though she would probably just toss it out with the junk mail.

I lifted the desk drawer from my lap and placed it on the coffee table.

"How about I find her some things to play with?

"Oh, yeah, sure, go ahead if you want," Rhonda moved her gaze toward Bubbe's jewelry box. *Aah, the jewelry. That's what Rhonda's interested in,* I thought. I didn't think there was much of any value except, perhaps, what Aunt Bernice might have given her for birthdays or Chanukah. All I really cared about was keeping a few items that would help me most remember my grandmother and help Hallie learn more about Bubbe when she was old enough to understand the importance she played in my life.

I went into the kitchen and gathered a few of Bubbe's smallest pots, spoons and spatulas and brought them into the living room. I placed them on the floor, then picked up Tiffany and sat her back against the side of the couch, demonstrating how to bang on the tiny pots and pans and plastic containers. She awkwardly sucked on some and finally made some sounds by dropping some onto others.

I began sorting through Bubbe's enormous file of things that gave her nachas about her family. Bubbe had saved every announcement of any kind about each son, daughter-in-law, grandchild and even great grandchild. She had accumulated countless birth and marriage announcements, report cards, business cards, newspaper clippings about honor roll lists or new jobs or promotions, and national newspaper and magazine articles with stories and photos of her famous son.

Tiffany giggled and banged and giggled and banged some more, and I nearly ran out of safe things to bring out from the kitchen to keep her occupied.

In a little while, Rhonda shouted, "That's enough noise!" She stood up from the corner of the room where she had laid out all of the jewelry.

"Which do you want?" She held out her hands to reveal two pairs of gold earrings, two thin silver bracelets, a pair of small diamond stud earrings, and a diamond stickpin.

"Me?" I was incredulous that my sister didn't insist on choosing first. I didn't recognize the jewelry, so it probably wasn't anything that mattered much to Bubbe. "I really don't care. You?"

"None of it is worth much anyway. Mostly cheap shit. Here. You take these gold rose earrings and the diamond stickpin. I don't wear things like this. I will take the gold hoops and give the little studs to Tif. It's time to change her gold baby ones anyway. And I'll send Ellen and Leslie the sterling silver bracelets. Sound okay?" She didn't wait for my answer before dropping the pin and earrings on the table. She leaned over her toddler, took the spoon out of her hand, and lifted her onto her lap. Tiffany cried. Rhonda bounced her on her lap. "Don't cry, Tiffy, here come your first pair of diamonds. A girl can't have too many, you know." She opened her hand to show her the earrings. "Mama's gonna make you even more boot-i-ful." She reached for Tiffany's ear. The baby screamed.

"You probably should take those home and clean them first anyway."

Rhonda didn't answer, but she set Tiffany back on the floor and dropped the earrings and bracelets near her purse. She went to Bubbe's drawer and pulled out Hallie's stash of coloring paper and crayons.

"Here, honey, you can color." She placed a crayon in Tiffany's flimsy grip and set the thick paper before her. "Don't worry about getting it on the rug, it's not Bubbe's problem anymore!" She chuckled with an annoying snort sound.

Tiffany mouthed at the crayon, as I expected she might at such a young age, so I removed it from her hand and showed her how to rip at the paper and try to drop it into a container.

"Rhonda, while she's distracted, you might as well put all those pots and things into the box for the donations; you and I don't need them and someone else might." I motioned to the sea of kitchen items behind Tiffany. I brought my sister a box, a damp cloth to wipe down the items, and then I sat back down. "You know, Rhonda, Ruthie lives only fifteen minutes away. Would you mind if I called and had her come by to watch the baby? We can only accomplish so much with her here."

"What, you've gotta rush back to that new boyfriend you still haven't told me anything about, though I did see him at the funeral—and I hear Dad and cousin Ellen met him? You're getting serious with him, huh? Gonna give out rosary beads as party favors at your wedding?" Rhonda snorted.

It had been going so well, no talk about anything difficult, just focusing on the tasks at hand, but now I wanted to scream. Her sarcasm was not funny! Ruthie had helped prep me to count to ten, breathe, and think of something to say that would shut my sister up cold. "Just picture Alan-the-Doctor suggesting yet a new treatment to try to rid her of her stretch marks," Ruthie had suggested. "Or say it out loud! She could use a taste of her own medicine."

I picked up the diamond stickpin from the table and ran my finger along the small chips. "No comment, Rhonda, unless you also want to talk about where Alan is today instead of helping watch Tiffany?" I hated to lower myself to Rhonda's level, but enough was enough.

"What? He's on call."

"On call on a Sunday for plastic surgery?"

"He still has to cover in the ER now and then, you know."

"Um, I see." I suspected Alan probably refused to take Tiffany so he could go for a long run or bike ride, but Rhonda needed to keep up the image of having the perfect, loving husband. Besides, if he really were in the office on a Sunday, I suspected that a nurse or his office manager probably was, too, with the doors carefully locked behind them. How could I not think that way about him after the lewd comment he had once made toward me?

I wanted to focus on our packing, so I decided to drop the topic of Ruthie. The two never saw eye-to-eye anyway.

I changed the subject completely. "You know, Rhonda, I'd like the costume jewelry. I bet Hallie would love to play with some at home and I'd like to donate the rest to the day care center if you don't mind. I could take some of it back for Tif when she's older."

"After it's been at the day care center? No way!"

"So, I can take it all?" I kept to myself that the jewelry box was what I really wanted. I'd watched my grandmother open its worn hinges so many times to find just the right item for each outfit.

"Yeah, I'll just keep a few things." Rhonda walked over to where she had left the jewelry in a clump on the floor. She put a mock pearl necklace and a few clip earrings into her box of things to keep. Tiffany, bored with the paper tearing, cried. Rhonda sighed and quickly gathered the rest of the jewelry into a ball and tossed it into the jewelry box. She thrust the box at me and grabbed for her bag to find something to distract Tiffany.

When I opened the lid of the jewelry box, I immediately spotted Bubbe's heart-shaped drop earrings, which were worthless to Rhonda, but priceless to me; then I also noticed Rhonda had overlooked the heart-shaped locket Bubbe always wore, the one with her and Bert's picture in it. They had forgotten to bury her with it, as Bubbe had desired.

I stood, knocking the diamond stickpin to the floor. I bent to pick it up, and then placed it on the table, careful not to reveal the locket in my other hand.

"Ug, got my period," I said, in case Rhonda saw me pick up my purse before heading into the bathroom. With the door safely closed, I took the locket in my hand, ran my thumb over it, and let the tears slide down my face. I carefully slipped it into my purse. I would ask Harry later, in private, if I could keep it. Harry knew I was the sentimental one of the grandchildren; he'd surely say okay. I flushed the toilet so Rhonda wouldn't be suspicious, and then I opened a corner cabinet in the bathroom to find a washcloth to dab at my tears and fix my mascara. Stalling, I shouted out to Rhonda, "I might as well empty this room out while I'm here."

I couldn't find any washcloths in the cabinet I'd clearly never opened before; it was so unlike Bubbe to save worthless items. I found wads of well-past-their-prime hotel soaps and bobby pins and old aspirin bottles and packages of Tums—crap like that, all with brown discoloring on the ancient cartons. No one would want any of it, except maybe a museum. I dropped each into the garbage pail, taking a minute to dab my eyes with a tissue to fix the smudged mascara.

Next, I opened the bathroom door to allow room to bend down to look under the sink and gauge how long it might take to finish clearing the room. Behind a few rolls of toilet paper and square tissue boxes, something pale pink poked out between the wall and the bottom of the radiator, a cloth of some kind. I reached in, managed to grasp it and pulled it out. I shook off the coating of dust and opened it up, laying it flat on the pale blue rug. Suddenly, I felt four years old again, and Bubbe was coming to my rescue; it was Bubbe's handkerchief, the one with her initials, SFH, for Sadie Fine Horowitz, the one she used to dry my tears the long ago day when I had wanted to pick up my baby cousin Ellen, and Ida refused to help me after Rhonda had blocked my way; I fled to another room and cried until Bubbe found me. The painful memory was forever etched in my brain. I kissed the cloth and then quickly covered my mouth as I released a loud sob.

"What, what'd you find?"

"Uh, nothing, I, er, caught my hand on a sharp edge under the cabinet. Bleeding."

"Oh, shit!" Rhonda said as a symphony of pots and pans clanked again, and Tiffany giggled. For a split second I'd thought Rhonda had found an empathic moment toward my fake injury. I tucked the handkerchief into my bra and peeked out the door. Tiffany had dumped over the packed box of kitchen things.

As I turned back around, I spotted a small bottle of Aramis under the sink, a plastic bag beside it. With my back to the door, I dumped the bag's contents onto the rug and out fell a pair of green and blue paisley boxer shorts and a blue silk nighty.

"You okay in there?"

"Uh, I'm, I'm going to find a Band-Aid for my, uh, bloody finger, then I really think you should just take Tif home and we can finish this another day."

I tried to picture the man toward the front of the funeral home who was crying when I walked passed him. He had looked familiar and I tried to place him but couldn't. I had forgotten all about him. Until now. Until the Aramis and the memory of that man carrying up Bubbe's bundles just a few months before, and his teasing about wanting her to allow him inside. Then I remembered Bubbe was found not in her usual flannel pajamas, but nude. *No way!* At least there were no signs of foul play; my father had made that clear.

I touched the silky garments. Did elderly couples wear sexy things like this? Or *do* things like that? My mind raced to all the possible scenarios that night, or day, she had died, but I forced myself to stop my bizarre thoughts. *Bubbe, I'm shocked. It's like waking up and finding out I live on an entirely different planet than I did the day before. But I'll keep your secret, whatever it is. I'm glad you had company in the end, if that's what this is about.*

I shoved everything back under the counter for now and opened the bathroom door. I took a deep breath.

"You know, I'm not too busy with work this week. And I live closer of course. I'll put Hallie in day care and come back by myself, or with Ruthie. I don't mind. I really only have the bedroom left to do." *The bedroom...my God, what else might I find in there?*

"Fine. Good. Let's just get the hell out of here. It's too much to handle."

"Indeed."

Chapter Twenty

Morning had never been my strong suit. But with the sun shining in my window, and the day crisp and clear, I wanted nothing more than to arrive at Sam's nice and early. I was eager to enjoy our three-day getaway to Maine. We had carved out this precious time we needed to rejuvenate—me from the funeral and finishing up cleaning Bubbe's apartment—which thankfully held no other surprises—and he from his intensive trip to California and all of the photo editing he had tackled since. Yes, a break from life—together this time as a united couple—was exactly what we both needed. I planned to tell Sam about my pathetic night with Stewart, because we hadn't yet had a chance, and I felt confident he would understand. I also would ask, finally, out in the open, why he never took our lovemaking past passionate kissing. Maybe this weekend he would?

For a change, I had no distractions. I had safely settled Hallie and Ringo at Suzy's the night before. She was kind enough to make Hallie's transfer back and forth to Stewart while I was away so he could see his daughter. It would only be Hallie's second time seeing her father since "the episode." The first was while I was in California, and Suzy had made the transfers then, too. I was so grateful; I refused to speak to Stewart, or see him, until we met with our lawyers in less than a week. All Suzy knew was we'd had an argument, and she was glad to help me however she could. She even admitted she was never particularly fond of her brother. I had long suspected it.

I filled a cooler with iced tea, apple slices and some peanut butter sandwiches. Then I loaded up my Subaru and went about setting the bike rack tightly onto the back. Finally, I hoisted my old Schwinn onto the rack, locked it and secured it with a bungee cord, then went back into the house to lock up. All before seven in the morning; Sam didn't expect me until nine. *Pretty impressive. Sam is going to be so surprised.*

~~~

Finding a parking spot on Union Park Street in the South End of Boston was no easy task. Even the "residents only" spots were still filled because it was pretty early in the morning. Joggers and folks walking dogs dotted the area, making it difficult to navigate the narrow roads. I drove in circles for a few streets, past Aunt Sadie's Candlestix and the Infinity Gallery and Studio, both still closed; around the corner past the Pet Shop Girls, where people were dropping off their dogs for day care; back around on Shawmut Ave. and Tremont Street, where the trendy On the Park and Tremont 647 already had crowds waiting for breakfast. I hoped one day to go for breakfast at Tremont 647 when I finally woke up in Sam's bed one day soon.

As I turned back to his street, I saw a car pulling out of a "residents only" spot in front of his condo. I sped up to catch it. I would have to risk it. We'd only be inside 'til Sam was ready to leave for Maine. Just then I noticed a bright yellow placard with the word "GUEST" resting on the dash of the car pulling out. Just what I needed; maybe he'd let me have it, or maybe Sam could give me a guest-parking pass until we were ready to go. Distracted by these thoughts, I didn't realize the man behind the wheel had pulled back into the space and had rolled down his window. He was motioning to me. I rolled down my passenger window.

"If y'all need this spot, y'all're going to have to hang on a few minutes," he said, climbing out of his car but keeping it running. He was holding the "GUEST" pass. "Forgot to return this here thang."

I nodded, but before I could suggest I borrow it and return it, he had scuttled away. I killed the time thinking of the combination of his Southern drawl, effeminate tone, and interesting way of dressing. He wore a black corduroy blazer with what appeared to be an orange collar and matching buttons over a pair of jeans, and while lowering his window I had noticed what looked like bangle bracelets on his wrist. The South End certainly was known for its gay population. Sam loved living there because it also overflowed with art galleries and good food. Not to mention friendly neighbors who'd lived there for many years, as he had, first alone while teaching at the Museum School at the Museum of Fine Arts, and later with Shelley.

Through the years, I had known gay men at work who were sensitive, funny, and honest people. Hardly suspected they were gay. But I'd never had a gay friend. I turned on the radio and tapped at the steering wheel, looking for other spots but trying to stay patient for this one. I was so excited to park the car and rush into Sam's place. Fortunately, I knew where he hid the extra key; I would find it and sneak into the apartment and slide into his bed if he wasn't up yet. Or if he was already showering, I'd make him some coffee.

A few drivers looking for parking spots slowed down and peered at me quizzically, but I waved them on. I leaned forward to see if I could see into Sam's unit, the top floor, and noticed a light go on in his bedroom. Darn, he was getting up. Wait—what?!—I saw the man whose car was running next to mine enter the now-lit living room! I swallowed hard and scratched the side of my brow as I considered whether I had the wrong unit, but just then Sam walked into view. I could only see his back, but he appeared to be naked, at least the parts I could see from my angle, and the man, the most likely *gay* man's hands were now resting on Sam's back as he hugged him. *This couldn't be happening!* I took a big gulp of air, trying to stay calm, composed and focused on the two of them. Yet when I looked back, the embrace already had ended, and they were laughing. I blinked, hoping my eyes were tricking me at this early hour and I hadn't just seen a man hugging what I previously had feared was my possibly bisexual boyfriend, which in the last few weeks I had totally dismissed as ridiculous.

I held my face between both ice cold hands. My shoulders curled forward, jaw slightly ajar, and stayed that way until the man honked his car horn. He startled me back to what we earlier expected—me to move my car so he could pull out, me to take the spot and go into Sam's condo earlier than expected to surprise him. I hit the gas pedal hard and took off, tires squealing. Surprise *him*? Ha! Big joke on me instead! With my head pounding, I made the few turns leading to the highway, even passing through a yellow light just as it turned red, making a car in the intersection slam on its brakes, but I just kept on driving through my tears and nausea. I could not eradicate the image of a man embracing my man...my *naked* man! I played this over and over like a video clip until I was way out of Boston, well onto route 95, well past Kennebunkport, past Portland, and even past the exit for Freeport, where Sam and I had planned to stop at LL Bean. I was on the bridge in Bath, *look, a new bridge,* I noticed, and that's what startled me back from my 160-mile stupor. I glanced at my watch: It was nearly ten thirty and I was in the final hour of my drive to Boothbay.

~~~

I made it as far as Wiscasset before pulling over to sort things out. I parked on the side street in front of Red's Eats, climbed out of my car, and ordered an iced tea. "That all?" asked a lady behind the tiny street-front stand I remembered from when my family had once spent a week here one summer when I was in junior high school.

"You look like you could use a good Down East meal," the lady said, but I wasn't really listening. I tried to smile as I paid for my iced tea. Despite the reasonable spring air and bright sunshine, I noticed I was shivering. I walked back to my car to grab a sweatshirt, and then found a picnic table near the shoreline. I sat with my untouched iced tea, snuggling my body into a ball. I watched small waves joyously rolling over themselves and then suddenly disappearing into flat stillness, the process continuing in inconsistent patterns.

I sat mesmerized for a while, and although I considered calling Ruthie, I decided against it. No, I couldn't even explain to Ruthie how betrayed and stupid I felt. Shouldn't I have read the signs better that he was bisexual? Just because he had loved and married Shelley, it didn't mean he couldn't also love a man.

The spring after Stewart left, I had attended a memoir writing workshop to try my hand at creative writing—and failed; maybe just not the right time in my life yet. But I remembered a bisexual woman in it had revealed in a chapter she read to us that she had sexual yearnings for both genders and chose her partners opportunistically. I'd never before understood that could happen, always thinking people were this way, or that. But Sam should have told me! Although I loved him, I sure didn't want to be with a man who not only made love with other men, but who betrayed me and kept this secret from me.

Suddenly, next to all this, my secret about having sex with Stewart was inconsequential. That was a good sign; I

170

could sort of laugh at the absurdity of it all. I wanted so badly to call Ruthie, but, I wouldn't let myself. I had to sort this through alone.

I finished my iced tea and walked back to the car. I removed my new cell phone from my glove box. I wanted to listen to the messages Sam had no doubt left me, worrying about where I was. Even in my distress, I still felt pangs for him, but maybe it was pity. How could he be so two-faced? Besides, he had showed me such sweet sensitivity and tenderly helped me out of so many difficult circumstances— even if those were some of the very traits that had made me question his sexuality in the first place. *I should at least let him know I'm safe*, I thought. I would have to use some dumb excuse, though; I was not prepared to discuss what I learned.

Oddly, there were no messages on my cell phone. Maybe he never planned to keep his promise about this trip after all. Maybe he was going to leave the condo before I even arrived that morning. Maybe Lover Boy was going out to buy them breakfast, then would come back and scoop Sam up and out before his rival, Big Bad Jody, could move in on his territory, *his* Sam. Maybe just that morning Sam had made his choice.

I followed signs toward the Chamber of Commerce Visitor Center to get information on the place Sam had reserved for us. All I remembered him saying was the inn took only a few guests, was new and came highly recommended. It would be weird staying there alone, but it was all paid for and, besides, I could hear Ruthie saying I might as well have the second nervous breakdown of my life somewhere nice.

"Ah, you want the Great Bay B&B. Danny's new place," said the nice older gentleman staffing the quaint two-room Chamber of Commerce office. Colorful brochures and pamphlets packed the room; I would have collected them with zest had I been with Sam. Now, I had zero interest. "East Boothbay, nice and quiet there. Y'up."

I was so suspicious of everyone and everything at that moment that I even wondered about "Danny's place," about the "quiet" side of Boothbay. I'd never been homophobic before, but suddenly I wasn't sure whether to take the place, find another, or just make myself drive back home. No, I couldn't head home; how could I be a mother to my little girl until I sorted this out, and grieved everything I'd lost that month—my values, my grandmother, and now Sam. Oh God, how would he and I finish the stupid project? I needed this escape even more now. I wouldn't change anything; I would go ahead with the plans just the way they were, without him, no matter what.

"Danny and his wife did quite a job on that place. You'll just love it there," the man was now saying, as he drew a heavy black line on the map to take me from the Chamber to the inn. Danny and *his wife*. I felt stupid and rude about my homophobia, but I didn't fault myself. It wasn't exactly any ol' day.

I left the Visitor's Center and pulled into the parking lot of the Shop n Save nearby. I parked off to the side and climbed into the back seat, next to my cooler. I was starting to feel hungry, a good sign that maybe I wasn't going to break down again. This was just a man, for God's sake. It wasn't cancer, death, or something wrong with Hallie. I could find a way to finish the project with or without him and pick up my life; Sam had only been a brief piece of it. Albeit one of the best pieces. I hugged my legs into my body in the back seat and munched a peanut butter and jelly sandwich, glancing again at my cell. Still no messages.

~~~

"Just head up, heah," Danny, the innkeeper was now saying in his thick Maine accent as he pointed up the road. He had been so welcoming when I first arrived that I instantly felt guilty for my earlier idiotic thoughts. He was a retired fireman, short with a bald-headed, sweet face and broad, strong-looking torso. And his two friendly kitties rubbed against my legs like I was mama come home—all of which could make this stressed-out guest feel better. And his wife, though she was away for a few days, had decorated my magnificent private bedroom suite so perfectly. It had a four-post white wicker king bed set, hand-painted lampshades, ocean sketches on the walls, and tiny little seashell knickknacks placed just so. It all helped to take my thoughts far, far away from my troubles.

"Aftah a mile or so, bear right toward Ocean Point Inn, and keep going thata way a few more miles."

I straddled my bike and then tightened my helmet under my chin. "Is it very hilly?"

"Somewhat, just go slowly. Stop whenever ya needta. There's plenty of scenic vistas and galleries. Hey, if you wanna see some good aht and a special vista point, follow the signs to Premiere Gallery on your way back. It's all downhill aftah that, and by then I'll have fresh baked brownies and lemonade out in the common room."

"Brownies! Now you're talking my language. Great, thanks so much, Danny."

"And when Sam comes, I'll let him into the room."

I nodded, but nervously changed the subject away from the lie I'd created about Sam coming later. "I'm not a big biker, so I'll probably be back pretty soon. But I'm pretty fit, and I'm rather gutsy, so who knows how long I'll be gone."

"Just take time ta smell the flowers—and there ah plenty of them down at Ocean Point Inn."

~~~

An hour or so later, my legs wanting a break from those tough hills, I pulled over to look at the scenery at Ocean Point Inn. Danny was right. It offered a spectacular view of the ocean, and with its plethora of brightly colored flowers, it looked as colorful as if created by a painter's palette. I had been enjoying the biking and, surprisingly, I not only hadn't thought of Sam at all, but being alone was fine. My legs had held up okay so far, and the Maine folks I had encountered at a few roadside farm stands were so friendly. Maybe I needed this time alone even more than time with a man. I walked a few minutes on the beach, watching the tide coming in and picking up a few shells and stones. It was cool out, though fortunately sunny, and not too windy. I didn't want my legs to stiffen, so I straightened my bike from where I'd left it leaning against a post. I hopped back on for the long ride around the loop, back toward the B&B. But not far along, I noticed a small stone chapel. I braked and climbed off my bike. I rested it on the ground, laying my helmet down, too. Outside the chapel, a plaque explained that a Mr. Lewis Wilson had built it in 1917 in memory of his devoted late wife, Janet. I sauntered in and stood in the back of the small, empty church. I imagined Mr. Wilson standing there, taking it all in when it was finally completed. I walked up front and gazed at the well-preserved carved wood at the altar and the handful of lit votive candles. I felt blanketed in love as I imagined Mr. Wilson bending over to light a candle, his head hanging low with sorrow as he moved to sit in the front pew on the hand-carved benches he had helped create. I thought of him sitting there once each day, for the rest of his life, missing his beloved Janet.

"The man built a whole fucking chapel to honor his wife?" I could imagine Ruthie saying. "That's something Sam might have done for Shelley," I would reply. I exited the no-longer peaceful church.

Snapping on my helmet, I climbed onto my bike and pedaled hard. I went round a large bend and up a hill, then up some more hills. I focused only on the road, keeping my thoughts empty while my legs pedaled me forward and I lifted my body slightly off the seat to help me climb the never-ending hills. A few cars passed by now and then, and most of the drivers waved or honked a hello. What a friendly place! Atop the final slope, I saw a sign pointing to the Premiere Gallery. Remembering Danny's suggestion, I decided to visit before heading back. I could feel the muscles in my legs rebelling, but I kept pedaling, even up the last of the hills to the gallery. Finally, I reached what looked like a magical spot with a stone path and perennial gardens behind a wrought-iron gate, but the gate at the foot of the driveway was closed, and a sign read, "Sorry, but an emergency has taken us away. Will return Monday."

Despite my disappointment, I recalled Danny saying the ride back would be downhill, so I rode upward more quickly and soon began the descent. I kept my legs resting on the pedals now, unless they needed to do some work. A little pedaling, a lot of gliding. I kept up with this easy pace, feeling myself finally relaxing again, letting go of the tension in my neck and my heart, so loose now. Nothing much mattered anymore but the tree-lined roads and the fresh air, and my own strength. And when I began to pick up speed, I didn't bother to hold back, didn't brake, didn't hug the right side of the road the way Harry had taught me when I was five—like I'd be teaching Hallie one day. And I didn't think about anything but the freedom of speeding downhill fast, feeling free, because even though Sam was a traitor, Maine was purifying. So I sped up some more and then I cut the turn a little too quickly, a lot too wide, and went around a blind spot heading right toward an oncoming truck.

~~~

"Why don't you come in for a minute?" A woman of at least eighty was standing several yards from me. She spoke quietly and dangled her keys in her hand. Apparently, she had just parked her car, though I hadn't noticed. I was sitting off to the side of the road in front of the woman's house, crying. I had managed to miss the truck by about two yards, but not before forcing the stunned driver to slam on his brakes and veer to his right. My errant ways nearly caused his truck to stumble down a steep embankment. I had known enough to lean my body far to the right and cut away from the truck, but with my downhill momentum, all I could do was wave back at the driver to thank him for his quick reaction. But I couldn't even apologize. Somehow, I managed to be unscathed physically, but I needed to calm down. How unthinkable it would have been if this man had crashed his truck because of me. Or killed me and taken the blame for what was totally and unequivocally my careless cycling.

"Come in. You should come in," the woman with the kind eyes was saying.

I couldn't speak. I felt so ashamed. I managed to look the woman in the eye and smile politely, but I wanted to be alone. Then, as though God were writing me a prescription, I heard a dog bark in the distance.

"You, uh, have a dog?" I dug into my jeans pocket for a tissue, pulled it out, and blew my nose.

"Oh, yes, that's just Sunbeam. She won't hurt you. Come. Come in. Have some lemonade." She tucked her key into the pocket of her flowered housedress.

"Sunbeam, yes, thank you, I could use a ray of sunlight right about now. And some lemonade. I'm Jody. Staying up the road at the inn. From the Boston area."

"Annie Burke, nice to meet you."

The woman opened the unlocked front door of her small ranch home as though she were bringing in a friend or a daughter, certainly not a complete stranger she found curled in a ball on the edge of her lawn.

"Sunbeam, it's okay." I spoke in a soft voice to the barking white fur ball that jumped onto my lap the minute I sat down in one of Annie's comfortable armchairs. I scratched the dog behind the ears, and she settled into my lap and practically purred. All around me, I observed items reminding me of some I'd seen in Sam's mother's home, but in far more abundance here. Just about every surface was filled with knickknacks, including the floor, with its orange shag rug. Annie collected dried flower baskets and porcelain dogs and stained glass birds and small statues of Jesus Christ. And in between these items, wherever they could be squeezed in, a hundred photos of what appeared to be her many children, grandchildren, and great grandchildren warmed the home.

"You Catholic?" Annie asked after she and I had sat and talked for nearly an hour, mostly about my near accident, Annie's asthma, her husband's sudden death decades earlier, her children, and Maine.

"No, I'm not, but, my, er, boyfriend is, was. Well, he's still Catholic, but no longer my boyfriend as of yesterday."

"I'm sorry, dear. Perhaps that's adding to your distress today? Well let me show you something special I got from the Pope, I want you to have it." As though Stella Puricelli had intervened by calling her friend up in Maine, Annie Burke lifted herself off her chair and walked to the end table near me. She pulled open a drawer. "My niece, she worked for the Pope once. This is a special pendant." She opened the case and I saw a beautiful necklace of Jesus Christ on the cross. Annie closed it into my hand.

"I can't, no, please, it's too special to you."

"My kids, they don't need it. Sounds like you do. And now, you go in peace, and I will take my afternoon nap."

Annie and Sunbeam walked me to my bike. I stretched out my hand to thank her, but she ignored the hand and hugged me. I choked up, not only for the sympathy I was receiving, but for the experience of hugging what—I was convinced—was an angel on earth.

~~~

177

"If you're looking for a great meal tonight, eat at the Lobsterman's Wharf," Danny was saying. After napping soundly in the big bed in my room, I came downstairs for one of Danny's brownies and ended up devouring three. I gave him the short version of my day—omitting the near-accident.

"After that long ride and great nap, the Wharf'll be perfect. The other guests ah still out at the wedding. Hopefully Sam will come soon and join you at the Wharf."

"Uh, no, Danny, he called me, he can't come." I looked at my feet as I spoke. "Problems with his work. It's just me these next two days."

"Whatever, I'll still look for him. Been in the business enough to know sometimes these guys just show up."

~~~

Lobsterman's Wharf was indeed perfect. A little cool to sit outside, but I preferred the chill air to the bustling restaurant inside. So I bundled myself up in an extra sweatshirt I found in my trunk and settled into a table on the ocean-view deck. I absentmindedly watched the waves break against the shoreline while eating a lobster dinner brought out promptly by a pleasant waitress with gray-blond hair and a heavily-lined face. I was grateful for her quiet but efficient service. While struggling to break open my lobster with the awkward metal claw-cracker, piece by delicious piece, I distracted myself from thinking of Sam by observing the other diners: a large group of friends toasting to a special occasion; couples leaning close as they shared steamers and corn on the cob; a family with a sullen teenage son who kept replying with one-word answers to his parents' questions. It made me sad to be the only one alone. One couple bickered, and while it was unpleasant to watch, at least they had someone to bicker with. And one school-aged child dining alone with an older man, her grandpa maybe, made me miss my little girl, even though I knew I needed time to recover here on my own before returning to her.

When I wasn't studying the other diners, I entertained myself by trying to will the sun to emerge to the foreground of the clouds. And I caught myself fascinated by the crazy seagulls diving in and out of view, stealing an occasional tidbit from a table. One seagull scored an entire dinner roll, managing to fly away with it in his expansive beak. Another one carried off a wad of French fries, only to spill them on the ground as it flew off with a booby prize—the empty red-and-white checkered paper basket. The other seagulls appeared to laugh as they flew by trying to claim a piece of the tumbling prize. The one who lost his fries didn't give up, trying again for anything he could get away with, eventually sneaking off with an onion ring the size of a large hoop earring.

When the waitress had returned with the bill and cleaned up the table, I asked her what kind of seagulls they were. I'd never seen any like those before.

"They're smaller than the ones I've seen in California," I said. "But they're funny, persistent fellas. And so captivating. I love their black-hooded heads, white tails and belly, and their gray back and wings."

"Yeah, those ah laughing gulls. You've gotta hold onto your belongings around those characters."

"So funny, I heard their laughter and watched them steal stuff. Fortunately, nothing of mine."

"Yeah, they're nuts. But I like 'em, too. They're full 'a life, and they've got a lesson in them, too." She wiped up the crumbs from my cornbread.

"Excuse me?"

"Y'up. At my ripe old age, with all I seen in my day, I call 'em healthy seagulls." She looked me squarely in the eye, and paused, as though to ask if I wanted more of her philosophy, or should she leave with my empty plates?

"Please, tell me more."

She leaned on the table with one hand. "Y'up, they're healthy seagulls 'cause their very bodies carry a billboard of wisdom. Things ahren't always black or white, right? We humans usually have our messier gray sides, now don't we?"

I nodded.

"Wish more people would realize that about themselves. We gotta accept each other's middle ground, not just expect everything to be either perfect or, well, fucked." She threw back her head and laughed.

"Go on. This intrigues me. A lot."

"Well, think about it, you can't just embrace the people in your life when they're showing their good sides, can you? We're all a little fucked up now and then, or deep down in our bones, yet don't we need to accept everyone's flaws, too? If we don't, do we deserve 'em when they're at their best, bein' generous with their time, love, money, wisdom— whatever, ya know?"

I nodded again, my eyes and ears wanting to take in more of this, like a school kid eager to learn on her first day of philosophy class. "How'd you get this wise?"

"Me? Ha. Not wise, just lived a long time, been through a lot. Haven't we all? When I was growing up, my granddad was a drunk—disappointing my grandma and my ma left and right. He'd disappear for days on end, loving the bottle more than them. But he never said or did a bad thing to me, though I did hafta step over him now and then to change the channels on the TV." She threw back her head and snickered, then scowled, perhaps recalling his dark side.

"But ya know, I learned everything I know about the ocean and stormy weather and reading people's natures from him, God rest his soul in peace. And those laughing gulls, oh how he loved those intelligent, humorous little rascals. Mostly how they were successful risk-takers! We'd sit around this very bay and place bets with those sitting around us to pick which gull would score first! Darn if Granddad didn't walk away with more dollar bills stashed in his pockets than the other playahs. He had a way of just picking' out the gulls with either his instincts or, well, his bahls."

I stared at her, my mouth open, wondering if Maine made only weird perceptive and open people, free to speak their minds and share their wisdom. I felt captivated by her story-telling, and her ability to accept and clearly love someone who most likely had damaged her whole family, for generations. I opened my mouth to ask more questions, unsure quite why this all fascinated me so, but before I could think of what else to ask, she hummed some unknown tune and walked off with my debris. She left me alone to ponder her simple joyousness, and to scrutinize the gray middles of the little birds. Soon the clouds parted and the sky briefly lit up in shades of deep orange and vivid pinks just before the sun set below the horizon.

~~~

After evening turned to night, and the waitress had brought me a complimentary Amaretto on the rocks after I had tipped her nearly half the bill, I dug out my cell phone from my purse and lifted the top. I pressed the speed dial for "Home," but before it rang, I noticed the red light come on, indicating I had a message. I hung up and dialed my cell phone number and then my code to retrieve it. The successive beeps indicated I actually had five messages. Probably junk or hang ups.

I waited to hear the replay and froze as I listened—all were from Sam. He sounded curious at first, and then increasingly more agitated, asking me to please contact him, he was so terribly worried. The calls had started at nine twenty in the morning. Damn these new-fangled phones with inconsistent reception. Trembling, my head no longer clear, I called home. Nine more messages. Sam. Sam. Sam. Ruthie.

Sam. One from Hallie. Two more from Ruthie. The last was from the local police chief.

Other than a message from Hallie saying, "Hi, Mommy! I'm having fun!" all were increasingly more frantic messages asking where I was, if I was all right, and could I please let *someone* know of my whereabouts? Even Ruthie was serious for a change, no joking around.

How stupid I've been to think he wasn't concerned. Of course he's looking for me. Why wouldn't he be? He doesn't know I caught him.

~~~

The phone rang only once in Sam's condo.

"Hello?"

"Sam, it's me, I'm fine." I spoke into my cell phone in a businesslike tone while sitting at my empty table on the restaurant deck in near darkness. "Look, I'm sorry you've been worried, but--"

"What? You're all right? Oh, thank God. Wait, then where are you? Ruthie's here. We're out of our minds with worry!"

"Ruthie's there?" I moved the phone away from my ear and looked at it incredulously, then put it back to my ear.

"Tell me where you are! You're sure you're safe?!"

"Maybe I'd better explain to Ruthie."

"Jody, damn it all, talk to me! Remember *me*, the same man who three weeks ago said he wanted to be your husband for good or for bad, in sickness and in health?! If this is another bout of your damn fear of getting close, I'm starting to have just about enough, frankly. Do you have a clue how I've spent my entire day? You just disappear like that? I was petrified you were dead, lying in a field somewhere, kidnapped or something. Can you even try to imagine how terrified I've been of losing you, and now you sound so, so callous?"

Ruthie grabbed the phone. "Jody, where the f--."

"No, you're not dealing with Ruthie this time. You're going to have to face me!"

"*I'm* going to have to face *you*? *You*?!" I screamed back. "*You,* who has never more than kissed me but hugged that man naked, *naked* in your living room this morning?" I caught myself shouting out of control, so I quickly left the restaurant, hoping no one had heard me.

I listened closely to hear him explain, but he said nothing. Caught. After a bit, I said out loud, "Shit, did I lose them?"

"Jody, no you did not lose us." Sam sounded annoyed at first, and then laughed, sort of. It was the kind of exasperated laugh you might make after spilling an entire batch of pancake batter on the stove, as you watch it ooze into all the wrong places. "Oh, you idiot girl," he said. I pushed the phone closer to my ear. "You saw Ricky in my apartment? My *cousin* Ricky? That is what this whole missing person thing is all about? Jesus, Jo." He paused. Took a deep breath. Exhaled slowly. "He was up from Texas for the night. Had an appointment to show his work at a gallery today."

I heard Ruthie in the background asking, "What? What?"

"Sam, no, I saw him hug you. You were naked. I'm not gonna buy this story so easily, your 'cousin Ricky' that I've never even heard of?"

"You think I've given you my entire genealogy, for Christ's sake? He's my father's cousin's son, lives in Texas, called yesterday morning about this last-minute opportunity he had in Boston and could he stay with me for one night? Frankly, I never thought I had to, uh, ask your damn permission!" He paused a second, and when he continued his voice was less tense, just matter-of-fact. "Sorry, I'm just so sick of this craziness. Ricky left early this morning, and I jumped into the shower, but then I heard someone in my apartment and came out of the shower to see if maybe it was you coming early, as I had hoped. Jo, I was wearing a towel around my waist. And where the hell were you, anyway, that you couldn't see that?"

"Just go on. Please." With my free hand, I rubbed my temple where it was starting to throb above one eye.

"Ricky had forgotten to give me back the guest parking card I had given him for his windshield, so he came back up with it, threw it on my dresser and was leaving when I popped into the living room. In fact, when he hugged me goodbye, I slapped him on the rear end and made a joke that he'd better head out of there before my girl sees me hugging a gay dude."

I cleared my throat. Couldn't find any words. I heard Ruthie asking again, "What? What?"

"Say something, Jody. Anything! Stop testing me to death. You're either gonna kill me or drive me to drink!" He whispered to Ruthie, "She thought I had a gay lover."

"Oh fuck her," I heard Ruthie shout.

"Oh, Sam, I'm so stupid, so thoroughly unequivocally untrusting and stupid. It's a long story, but I sort of met your cousin when I was parking, and then I saw him in your building. Thought I saw 'everything' through that big window you have, but of course it was just my fear and imagination. Will you ever forgive me?"

"Only if you finally tell me where the hell you are. If Ruthie hadn't explained some more of your family background, honest, I think I might have just given up on you this time."

"I deserve that," I said, and then I shocked him by telling him I went to the Great Bay B&B.

"Damn, why the hell didn't I think to check up there?"

He asked how the B&B was, and I told him briefly about my unusual day. While listening to my sordid tale, his uneven breathing and occasional gasps on the other end of the phone hinted at his genuine concern. When I reached the part about meeting Annie and the whole Catholic discussion, he was as shocked as I.

"Wow, this whole crazy thing was meant to be?" He was silent a moment, and then he shared their nerve-wracking day trying to track me down. They were almost ready to call my parents. Thank God they stopped short of that.

When we were done swapping horror stories, he suggested I go back to the B&B, take a bath and go to sleep. He would call my town police, straighten everything out and drive up first thing in the morning. I just listened, taking specific directions and precise orders, doing anything and everything he said. Never even talked to Ruthie, who somehow respected this one was just between me and Sam.

Just before saying goodbye, I asked him why he always accepts me, no matter what I've thrown at him, and why even though he was angry, he never gave up on me. He paused.

"When you've lost someone the way I have, you learn to accept whatever time you have with someone you love. You learn to let go of the stupid stuff, Jo."

I sobbed, releasing deep feelings that I wasn't worth loving. No one had ever spoken to me with such wisdom and tolerance. This was so new and so full of acceptance and forgiveness. I'd rarely encountered such unconditional love.

"Go back to the inn and relax. Wish I could dry your tears from here, but I will soon," he said. "It's the end of tears and worries for us both. Please? And when I see you tomorrow, it's time we talk about why I haven't made love to you—yet."

Chapter Twenty-One

Eleven thirty, right on schedule. It was another beautifully sunny day, unusually warm for spring in Maine. I approached the turn into the parking lot of Freda's Fried Fish, the famous Boothbay fish 'n chip restaurant cooked and served out of a truck, which Sam had long told me about. I grinned like the Cheshire Cat as Sam approached from the opposite direction, about to turn in right then, too. We followed one another into the lot and he pulled in next to me in his silver Camry, his bike attached to the rear. We grinned at each other after pulling up our emergency brakes at the same second, lurching our cars forward slightly.

I had barely shut the ignition when Sam raced from his car, grabbed my door handle and practically wrenched it off its hinges. Wordlessly, he helped me climb out of my seat and pulled me toward him, squeezing me in such a tight hug that I felt it was where I always belonged, as though we had long been connected to each other's bodies. He smothered my hair with kisses before resting his head on my shoulder. I hoped he could smell the rose soap I had rubbed between my neck and my breasts that morning. No sooner had I released that thought when Sam nuzzled my neck. He breathed deeply and then exhaled hard, relaxing his body completely onto mine. No doubt he was letting go of the tension I'd

186

thrust on him the day before. If he were to let go of me, we both would have fallen to the ground, as my body was so limp too, leaning into his. My nose pressed into his neck, and I smelled his pine-scented soap mixed with a sweet-yet-spicy natural smell, like a mild cinnamon. The combined scents created a combination of pheromones that seeped into my senses, firing up my hormones. I also felt his new beard stubbles already pushing through. I pressed my cheek next to his as close as I could until I felt the roughness of his face against mine. It was a masculine sensation I didn't want to ever lose again.

"Yo, Samuele, *Sammy*! Yoo hoo!" The sound broke through our soundless worship of each other. But Sam didn't let go. He lifted his head and yelled, "Freda, I love ya, but I'm in the middle of reclaiming something I thought I lost, so hang on, love." Then he buried his head back in my hair and nuzzled me more.

"You two lovahs need ta pitch a tent right heah in my yahd or sumthin?" Freda shouted back with her strong Maine accent, then added, "Atta boy Sam!"

"Sam?" I whispered into his neck, where I stayed glued, frozen to the man I now knew I truly loved. "I trust you now, believe me, but please tell me who the hell knows you here? Another cousin, dear?"

He took my hand and led me toward Freda's truck.

"Freda, this is my Jody, and if you cook her a really good fish fry, I think she might agree to go steady with me."

Freda was practically leaning her entire body out the truck's window to squeeze Sam's face between her thick oven-gloved hands. She planted a wet kiss on his cheek, first on one side, then the other. Sam pretended to wipe off grease from his cheeks where the much-soiled gloves had just grasped them.

"This girl hasta be magical if she's brought you not only back ta life, but back heah ta Maine." Freda spoke with a throaty, deep voice

"You betcha." Then he whispered to me, "*Black* magic," as he pretended to jab his elbow into my ribs.

"Hi, I'm Jody, glad to meet you." I extended my hand toward Freda. She peeled off a glove and shook my hand, then held it a second before letting go.

"And glad to meet ya, too! I haven't seen this fella smile in over a year, and so fah as I can see, you're a miracle workah. Here, you two lovahs, fish 'n chips on the house." Freda leaned over to her fryer and pulled out crispy fried fish and slapped it on two paper plates. She covered them with hand-cut fries and placed it all on a giant tray beside two cups of water.

"You're in for a real down-east treat, Jo." Sam thanked his friend, agreeing they'd catch up in a while, and he carried our tray toward a picnic table behind the van. When we reached the empty table, he put down our tray, and I expected we'd sit. But Sam stayed standing. I stood and faced him, raising my eyebrows and tilting my head, as if to say, "What's up?"

"I asked you to meet me here for exactly the reason Freda's trying to tell you: I used to come up here with Shelley, and before that with my mom, and before that with my mom and dad. I just hadn't felt like coming here again until I met you, you bouncy-headed gal. Why don't you have any idea how patient and supportive and smart you are inside that insecure soul of yours? Not to mention what an amazing and intuitive mother you are." He pushed my chin up with two fingers and looked into my eyes. I made sure not to lower my gaze, which I usually couldn't control when a compliment came my way. Sam stared at me another second, then pulled me toward him and kissed me, gently at first, then passionately, more passionately than he ever had before, as though we were deep in the middle of love-making, private in our own world. I felt my body warming up beyond belief, right there in a public place yet I couldn't fight the feeling; I wanted to rush off together into the woods, strip him naked, and feel his body against mine.

"You skeptical girl, you, thinking I'm gay because I haven't made love to you. Let me make this perfectly clear: I want nothing more, *nothing*, than to rip off your clothes and pull you into those woods over there."

My entire body flushed, as though he had peeked into my thoughts.

"You think I don't *want* that?" He looked into my eyes then pulled me tightly to him again. I felt his erection pressing into my body just before he turned me slightly sideways and lifted his head, looking straight into my eyes again. "I have not made love to you for one simple reason: Because I want to make sure you, Jody Horowitz, know I am making love to *you*, to *all* of you! To your feisty spirit, your rich soul, not just to the curly-haired woman that waltzed into my life after I ate a magical box of fortune cookies! And when that time comes, when we *both* know, what I already know, that I want us to be together, always, then that genuine love-making moment will arrive."

I opened my mouth to speak, feeling so astonished that he was definitely the last romantic and self-controlled heterosexual male on the planet, but I didn't know what to say, and before I could release any utterance at all, he put his fingers over my mouth.

"Shhh, this is my time to explain, and I should have done so a long, long time ago so you knew how much I want you. All those nights I pulled myself away from you, forced myself to go home instead of sleeping over, the nights in the hotel when I would only kiss you for a while, then suggest we sleep? Whoa, I was suffering. Felt like an adolescent boy, holding back like that! But it just can't be intimacy for the wrong reasons. Jo, I will make love to you, *with* you, eagerly, happily, slowly, quickly, however you, *we,* want, when we know, for sure, you are ready to say, 'I do!' I don't want to risk loving you and then you're gone...again; I can't handle that. Can't lose someone I love again."

Still looking into the blue eyes that carry me off to faraway places, I bit my lower lip to keep from releasing happy sobs. His eyes were wet now, too, matching mine, and he took one finger to wipe my tear drop, then he whispered into my ear, "But tonight it's time we explore more, yes?"

"Oh, yes, *yes,* and Sam, I love you so much, too. And one more thing, yes, I'd like to go steady with you," I said, laughing.

While we held each other close, being open and raw, I needed to finally spill my secret. I whispered, "I do need to tell you something that happened not too long ago that you have a right to know about." I looked away from him, but he pushed my face back toward his.

"Don't find this rude, but I don't give a shit about your past anymore. Not to be callous, but maybe some things from 'before' just don't matter anymore? We're here to relax together, reconnect and move forward, not to keep looking backwards. Besides, if there's a past to talk about here in Boothbay, it's mine." He looked at me with his mouth set firmly closed.

I nodded, my heart beating quickly.

"That's right, girl, my past: I'm going to start by making you bike the roads I used to bike with my dad, then I'll show you my favorite butterfly collection exhibit at the Southport Library, then I'm making you eat a sandwich at the oldest bowling alley-turned-sandwich shop in the world....get the point, Jo? Let's stop being so bogged down in muck and start living again, having more fun together."

Before I could speak, two of those meshugenah laughing gulls swooped down to our tray, squawked, and then I swear one of them winked at me as it flew off with several of Freda's chips. We laughed so hard I had to catch my breath.

Then we sat to eat what tasted like the most delicious meal either of us had ever consumed.

MINDY POLLACK-FUSI

PART THREE

MINDY POLLACK-FUSI

Chapter Twenty-Two

"*Hey, girl, call me.*" Ruthie apparently had left a message on my answering machine Friday night after she had left Sam's condo and returned home. *"I've gotta hear what happened once your personal Pope met you in Boothbay. You've become one pain in the ass. I've definitely decided if you don't want him, I do. Not that he'd want me. Call me."*

I tucked Hallie into bed and climbed into my own. I would shut the light early to catch up on the sleep I delightfully had lost the night before in the B&B after a thrilling and exhausting day with Sam, and an equally thrilling and exhausting night. Every minute of all of it was still fresh and exciting in my mind. But before going off to sleep I wanted to call Ruthie back and share some highlights.

"Your nickel," Ruthie's answering machine said before it released a loud beep that indicated I could speak for as long as I wanted, since it wasn't clogged with other messages, as usual. So I did.

"Hey, Ruthie, I'm bummed you're not there. I needed to thank you and apologize for ruining your life Friday over what was my mishegas yet again. I deserve your calling me a pain in the ass, I really do. And you're not too far off about Sam: he is my guiding light, that's for sure. We had a

wonderful, incredible day-and-a-half together, and this time it got way more intimate, yes! It wasn't the 'real deal' yet, but I'll spare your machine the R-rated details. Let's just leave it at the fact that he, very definitely, is not gay or bi, and his wife definitely died happy, that's for sure! Hey: What's your schedule this week? I've got the big meeting with Stewart and the divorce lawyers out your way Thursday morning. If it doesn't go too late, maybe I can take you to lunch? I owe you. I know I'm rambling on your machine, sorry, but I thought maybe you'd pick up if I blabbed long enough. I wonder where you are at this hour? Still training for the marathon? Is it safe to run at night? Or maybe you're out to a movie with a friend? Whatever, call me, but not past nine-thirty tonight as I'm gonna crash early. Tomorrow, Suzy's dropping Hallie and Ringo off early, and I'm spending the whole day with Hallie, probably going to the Science Museum, or whatever she wants. Oh, let's make sure the next time we talk we work out a meeting place at the end of the marathon so Sam, Hallie and I can find you and hug you to death, sweaty and all. Who else will be there? Your brother or parents coming in? I'm psyched for you and I know you can do it. And it's definitely my turn to support you on your big day! Sorry for this looonnng message. Hope I didn't use up space for Mr. Right to call and whisper sweet nothings to you. Bye."

I switched off the phone ringer and answering machine volume, and within minutes I was fast asleep. Didn't even hear the phone ring twenty minutes later, didn't even know Ruthie had left a message until I woke up to pee at 2 a.m and saw the red light blinking, so when I returned from the bathroom, I listened to the message: *"Oh well, you're not answering, yet again. And funny joke, but there is no Mr. Right, never will be I guess. Thanks for the lunch offer, but I can't get together this week or next. Mental training week for the Big Race. As for who's coming to watch me die after my twenty-sixth mile, there's no one but you. No one from work's taking the day off apparently. My big shot brother is too busy to fly in, he now says, and my parents need to, I don't know, play Mahjong or do laundry or something like that, so you just let me know wherever in this grand city you and your beloveds want to meet."*

I wondered why she sounded so blue. We'd been through too much together for her to be angry at me, or no? Before I could think more about any of this, I fell right back to a deep sleep.

The next morning, Suzie unlocked the side door early with her key, as planned, and Hallie rushed into bed with me. Ringo joined us, pouncing on us both. I woke up smiling at my daughter's happy face, and my dog's kisses, and also because I had had a dream in which I found the key to a glass door where happy couples were wandering around a garden. But then I frowned, remembering that in the dream, Ruthie remained outside the glass door, crying. Nothing Sam or I tried to do could help Ruthie get into the happy garden.

Chapter Twenty-Three

What does one wear to face an ex-husband across a law firm's boardroom table, with scads of divorce papers spread out for both parties to examine before signing? I had this thought as I glanced into my closet, chose my black power suit, and pulled on black stockings. Next I chose a white silk shirt and buttoned it up, leaving the last two buttons undone.

"You look bootiful, Mommy."

"Thanks, honey, and I think you're always beautiful, too, inside and out." I lifted Hallie into my arms. The heck with the silk shirt: If Hallie dirtied it I would still wear it proudly. Let Stewart see Hallie's smudge marks on my shirt. After all, that's what he had done to Hallie's mother's heart. Twice.

~~~

I reached the office building early. But I didn't take the elevator up to Stewart's attorney's offices until a few minutes past the appointed time. And even then I remained outside the smoked-glass entrance door for a few minutes to gather my thoughts. I wanted to be sure to enter last, forcing Stewart's eyes toward me. I didn't want to be the one waiting in the boardroom for him. I'd waited long enough the past year for him to start the divorce process, which of course he hadn't, he had left it up to me. After I had finally forced the issue, and he sent his financial documents, my attorney worked out the details with the other side. Stewart had not contested anything I had proposed, which was no surprise to me. Guilt had a way of making a man sign away rights he otherwise might have fought for. Besides, my attorney had told me that I was unusual compared to most women, in that I wasn't asking for much from him except to keep what was mine before the marriage. That included my bank account and the house, which we had bought with my money. And I requested a modest amount in child support for Hallie, but no alimony. In return, I insisted I have full legal authority for her, with Stewart limited to visitation rights. He'd keep her physically safe, I trusted that, but I wanted legal control since I couldn't totally guarantee that Hallie would be shielded from hearing—or walking in on—adults shtupping. I shuddered at that thought.

The receptionist opened the door, interrupting my thoughts, and motioned toward the boardroom. "They are all waiting for you, go right on in." I stepped over the threshold, then paused and glanced toward the glass-enclosed space just ten yards away, while she took a phone call. The fawn-colored curtains shaded viewers from seeing into the boardroom, but those curtains couldn't camouflage the serious tension within. This would be the first time Stewart and I faced each other since that night—we hadn't even spoken, using email for brief parental planning. And we relied on Suzy and day care for transfers. Despite my anger toward him, he was the man I was once devoted to, and he did, after all, help create the greatest gift I'd ever known, my little girl. Thinking of the three of us as the happy family we pretended to be that night at the Ninety-Nine restaurant, I felt certain that, ultimately, Stewart had given me a gift by screwing me yet again. It forced me to finally control the reins of my life, no longer leaving that up to others.

The phone rang at the reception desk. I hadn't moved from the few feet inside the front door. While answering, the receptionist motioned again toward the boardroom. I lifted my eyes to look at the large, rectangular waiting room, its outer walls framed with oak-paneling. I stepped forward past the two formal tufted brown leather couches and the ornate side tables displaying the day's Wall Street Journal and Boston Globe. The well-appointed décor, mixed with the smell of leather, was intimidating. It reminded me of how I was raised—that money and power go hand-in-hand, and they're not mutually exclusive. I knew that my lawyer, Attorney Beatrice Caplan, known for successfully, and fairly, representing women in divorce, could present that way—hard-ass and totally in charge, although she had been direct, but gentle, with me. And her office, in her home, was hardly intimidating, despite the stately Tudor on a hill in a plush Boston suburb.

The receptionist hung up the phone. "Would you like me to walk you into the boardroom?"

"Oh, no, sorry, I'm all set." I pulled back my shoulders and stood tall, saying to myself, "You can do this."

"I'm sorry about Bubbe," Stewart was saying as I shook hands with both attorneys and took my place beside Attorney Caplan, quietly apologizing to her for being even later than we had planned.

"I'm sorry about Bubbe," I heard him repeat.

I nodded without looking at him. Instead, I gazed out the boardroom window at the striking view of Boston Harbor. Stewart and I had once taken a dinner cruise around that harbor, and we had been dancing close on the ship's deck, the moonlight crisp and bright, the air clear and warm, when he whispered how much he loved me. I had frozen that moment in my mind, because it was the same night we had conceived Hallie. Yet it was one of the last times he'd ever said those words, replacing them with three less endearing words that answered my repeated question of what was wrong, why he was working such long hours and acting disinterested in the pregnancy. "I don't know," he would answer. Now, in the boardroom, I contrasted that memory with the dark character that sat before me daring to mention Bubbe in this cold environment.

"I know it is not typical procedure, but my client has requested a few minutes alone with your client before we begin," Stewart's attorney said. "With your permission, I'd like to allow them five private minutes in this boardroom, Beatrice."

Attorney Caplan glared at him for a moment. Then I watched as her eyes glanced toward Stewart, at her watch, and finally at me. I shook my head. No! I was not going to allow him to turn this business meeting into a forum for either sympathy for Bubbe or an apology.

"My client declines," she said, taking a cup of coffee from the tray on the table and placing it before her. "Mr. Wolfman had plenty of time to contact Ms. Horowitz prior to this meeting. There was no judgment filed against it." She surveyed the room as she ripped open a sugar packet, poured it into her coffee, picked up her spoon and stirred. I looked straight ahead, focusing on a seagull soaring outside the window.

"My client would like to make it clear that this is a deeply personal matter that he was unable to speak to his wife about until this morning, and that he terribly regrets waiting this long." Attorney Matthews tapped the end of his pen on the desk and looked over at Beatrice, sitting silently. I noticed his eyes widen in subtle exasperation at his client's last-minute request. I stared down at my folded hands resting atop my notebook, glad they weren't trembling like my insides. The coffee smelled soothing and I wanted some, yet

I was afraid to take a cup for fear I'd spill it all over the legal papers on the table.

"Jody, I really need a moment with you."

I finally looked over at Stewart. Tears were welling up in his eyes, his lips quivering. He swiped at his nose with one finger and cleared his throat. I looked away.

"If you still want to sign the divorce agreement after what I have to say to you, I promise I'll sign."

"Yes, we are all prepared to sign, as you know, we agree to the terms," Stewart's attorney said, leaning back in his chair, his arms folded behind his head, his olive-colored suit jacket pulling backwards from the tension. "But I think my client deserves a chance to be heard."

"Deserves a chance to be heard?" I whispered too loudly.

Attorney Caplan was on this: She lifted her bottom up off her seat and leaned forward, both forearms supporting her weight as she pressed into the table and spoke sternly to her colleague. "Ms. Horowitz made it clear to me that she does not want time alone with Mr. Wolfman. If he has something to say, he had better say it before all of us."

She sat back down, paused, and then with the room quiet, she rose from her seat again, leaned forward, and slapped the divorce agreement down before Stewart, glaring directly at him. "If my client thinks nothing remains to be discussed, Mr. Wolfman, perhaps you are ready to sign?"

I looked over at Hallie's father and, this time, didn't look away. He looked like a child sitting in the principal's office, his body bent forward, his mouth contorted. His wrinkled gray suit looking nothing like the professional suits I had bought for him before. He was ringing his hands in his lap.

"Jody, my wife, mother of my Hallie." He sniffled and swiped again at his nose with one finger, "I, I...." He buried his head in his hands and sobbed. His attorney reached behind him to the counter, grabbed a box of tissues, and thrust them in front of his client.

Below the table, Beatrice put her hand on my knee and held it firmly, steadying me. I watched this man, who had rarely shown weakness, falling apart. I understood the term a "heart of steel," because I felt nothing for him but pity, no matter what he had to say. I remained stiff, my back straight and tall, my fingers tightly clenched on the table.

Suddenly, as though he hadn't just been sobbing like a baby in this sophisticated boardroom, Stewart stood up, dabbed a tissue at his face, and came around the table, kneeling on the floor. Both attorneys were poised to leave their chairs, but I motioned to them and turned slightly toward him. My silk shirt was sticking to my damp armpits under my jacket.

"Jody, I know you probably pity me right now, I don't look like much of a man." He made a gurgling sound in the back of his throat. "But you see, I've made a grave mistake, and, well, I want you back. Would you *please* stay married to me, Jody? We can all be a family again." He reached toward my hand, but I pulled it away from him and grabbed my attorney's hand under the table. I looked right into Stewart's eyes.

"I've done my best to listen respectfully, and I've also been in this same place of desperate feelings, as I'm sure you recall. You'll certainly recover in time. So go sit back in your place, and let's get on with this divorce—and on with our individual lives."

He blinked hard, then stood slowly and turned toward his seat. But I reached for his closest hand, and as he faced back toward me, a smile emerging on his lips, I clasped his hand between both of mine. I took a risk: "*Stewie*, I'm so, so sorry that Brooke broke up with you. You know, shit happens." Then I dropped his hand.

His mouth opened in classic jaw-dropping surprise. "How…how did you know?"

"Do you really think I don't know you by now? You've shown your true stripes one too many times." I took a deep breath and exhaled. So did both attorneys.

Attorney Matthews slipped a pen into his client's hand and, page by page, Stewart signed at the yellow-tagged spots, initialed every page, and then I signed. When we were done, Stewart silently left the room like a man whose boss had just given him the axe.

Chapter Twenty-Four

That evening, of all events to be "commemorating" my divorce, I was expected at Ida and Harry's for Passover. So Sam and I met for an early lunch at the Copley Plaza Oak Room right after I left the law firm, and we both agreed that even a simple iced tea and tuna melt tasted better than ever before. Despite the sad reality of a marriage obliterated, I felt free to put the distress with Stewart behind me to lead my own life, make my own choices, and be with Sam without restraints. All we had to do was wait out the ninety days until the court made our divorce official. But I had to get through Passover first—and since it was the first one without Bubbe to help cushion my always-mixed feelings around the holiday table with my family, I decided to keep my news secret for now. Ida and I had barely talked since the funeral. This was becoming our regular routine. And I preferred the silence to her words, as either way I had no support from my mother.

Since then, Ida and Harry had dug into their work even deeper, especially with the massive Museum of Fine Arts project looming closer. It kept Ida occupied—and off my back. And as for the reunion coming up in less than three months despite its main honoree now in the great beyond, Ida had kept mum, perhaps not wanting to hear that I intended to bring Sam. Or, I wondered, had my father, after meeting Sam, finally told Ida to just stop her nonsense. Doubtful, since he didn't speak up to her very often, although I liked to think he stuck up for me now and then.

Meantime, Sam had his own emotional weight: his second Passover at his in-laws without Shelley, and because he was close to Shelley's brother and sister and their families, it made it almost tougher for him to be there just with his mother, missing a wife and family of his own. We agreed that next year we would do Passover together. We might even try to get both families in the same room, but that sounded ludicrous, like putting Hillary and Monica around the same dinner table. We had plenty of time to solve that one.

Outside the Oak Room, Sam and I kissed goodbye and shared a long, supportive hug, and I drove home to gather up Hallie from day care and let Ringo out. It was a not-so-ordinary day that felt ever so extraordinary, sort of like the sun shined not only above, but it also hugged my sides, encasing me in a warm, cozy cocoon that hinted at a new life ahead.

~~~

That evening, I was stuck sitting beside Alan-the-Doctor at Ida's Passover Seder table, and other than polite greetings, we hardly talked much at first. Seating me there was probably Ida's cruel way of telling me my preferences no longer matter—if hers don't to me.

Harry led the Seder, as was traditional for the lead male in the home. As we began to read the Haggadah to reenact the story of Passover, commemorating the Jews Exodus from Egypt, I felt happy that my Hallie was by my side. Fortunately, Ida, in her controlling way of deciding where to seat everyone at every occasion, hadn't plucked my girl away from her Mom. Hallie was old enough to learn about Passover, and we had prepared her to recite the part assigned to the youngest around the table, since it was way too soon for Tiffany.

Until it was Hallie's turn to recite, she asked me at least five times—"Mommy is it time yet?" Finally it was. She recited her part in a confident, singsong voice. When she was done, she received loud applause. I loved watching Hallie's grin form way wider than ever before. Wow, she already understood how self pride felt; it had taken me a lifetime.

During her singing of the words "Why is this night different from all other nights?" I couldn't help thinking that I had my own secret answer, not just the true Passover meaning about all of the special rituals performed on Passover. This was a challenging yet important day for me, yet Hallie had no clue that her parents were never getting back together. Did it really matter to her? She had hardly known it any other way. Time would tell, but I was sure that Stewart and I could do the hard work to keep Hallie emotionally healthy, and close to her family.

At that moment, I realized the irony: here I was enjoying my family for a change because they were supportive of my daughter. And the few neighbors around the table formed an important buffer from regular tensions. Ironic, since usually I felt like an outsider. Could Hallie be a bridge of some sort?

As the Seder continued, the Haggadah called for participants to read portions of the Torah that speak of four sons.

Rhonda grabbed the part of the wise one, and Ida, as usual, selected me to recite the role of the "wicked" one. Big, fat, ongoing joke in our family. No more would I read it feeling teased and annoyed! This time, I read with an edgy Cruella De Vil accent that made Hallie laugh and Ida smile. Rhonda even looked impressed with my acting ability.

Next, out of character, Ida assigned Alan the "simple one," and then she read the role of the "one who does not know how to ask." As Ida read, I thanked God that maybe she had finally taken that seriously, just once in her life, because she had neither mentioned Sam nor Stewart's names all evening.

We all missed Bubbe, and at a bathroom break in the Seder, we told funny stories about her from past Passovers. The time she didn't hear herself fart during the reading of the ten plagues, so she looked perplexed about our giggling during the solemn dripping of wine for each plague God sent down upon the Egyptians who had enslaved the Jews. Then there was the time she forgot to add the eggs when making her usually flawless and delicious matzo balls, and they were so hard her false teeth came out in her lap. And the crazy time, after the Seder, when she lifted Harry's cigar from the ashtray and took a few puffs herself, laughing and shocking everyone.

Perhaps this talk about Bubbe had set a warm tone for our entire family, even Ida. Because throughout the night, especially when Hallie asked to sit in Zayde's lap to drip the wine on the plate for the plagues, and later as we devoured Rhonda's matzo balls and chicken soup she'd made using Bubbe's recipes for the first time, I felt calm around my family. I was even proud of my sister for trying her hand at cooking. Perhaps it was simply because I was en route to a divorce and to a life with a far better life partner. And with improved self-esteem and independence. And that the following week Sam and I planned to take Hallie to a Tot Shabbat at my temple. I was ready to march my Italian Catholic lover into the daylight. Even at the family reunion.

Chapter Twenty-Five

What a gorgeous day for the Boston Marathon! Hallie climbed into my bed that morning, and after hugs and giggles, we looked out the window: Partly cloudy skies and just a bit windy. Good, there'd be a slight breeze for the runners, but sunny enough for the viewers who would line all twenty-six miles of the race from Hopkinton to Boston, offering up cups of water, pieces of banana or juicy oranges, and endless supplies of encouragement and applause.

Ruthie and I watched the marathon together most years, beginning when we first covered it for one of our early jobs at Beth Israel Hospital. I was an employee newsletter writer, and I helped Ruthie get a gig as a freelance photographer for the hospital. Every April for three years, we'd cheer on employees at a spot in Coolidge Corner. Each year after that we watched from the same spot, but while Ruthie never missed a year, I dropped out on cold or damp days, particularly after I was married to Stewart.

Now it was Ruthie's first attempt to run it, and I was prepared to go in any weather, yet what a relief that it was a beautiful day. Armed with huge bags of cut-up oranges, a camera, and flowers to present to Ruthie at the finish line, Hallie and I headed in to the Alewife parking garage in Cambridge and traveled the rest of the way by train. We were meeting Sam at the race. What a glorious day lay ahead!

By the time we met up with Sam, the sun had emerged brightly in a cloudless sky. This made it better weather for onlookers than racers, with the temperature hovering in the low seventies. Hallie handed out oranges to runners, standing a bit too far into the street. Every once in a while the policeman on patrol would push the crowds back onto the sidewalk to make more room in the street for the runners. The street boomed with excitement as the wheelchair racers whooshed by, followed by the top competitors and the noisy sirens of their police motorcade escorts. The crowd went wild applauding for the father-son team, the Hoyts, who do the race every year, the father pushing his disabled son in a racing seat. Sam lifted up Hallie for a better view of the Hoyts, and I hid my tears of joy and sadness into my little girl's curls, not only for the Hoyts challenges and achievements, but also for having Sam in our lives.

But by 4:15, the tone had changed. Runners and spectators were thinning out, and Ruthie had not emerged among the runners. She had calculated that she would make it to us between 3:45 and 4:15, with only the final two miles to go. There was still time, yet most of the red and blue Dana Farber team shirts had already passed by, so I was concerned. Ruthie was probably having a tough run in the sun.

By 4:45, we were all starving, and Hallie was bored, starting to pull at my shirt to drag me away. I wished I had thought to bring her something to do. I handed her the bouquet of flowers we had brought for Ruthie and let her pick off some of the tiny pieces of greenery around them and make a design in the street. Soon, Sam decided to buy us some pizza at the corner store and brought Hallie along to use the bathroom. I waited behind, but still no Ruthie. She and I hadn't talked all week, but we'd left messages with a plan: she'd run by the usual spot, stop quickly for a photo and hugs, then she'd run to the finish. The three of us would then hop on the train, parallel to the route, and find her at the end near the recovery tent.

But Ruthie was way behind her expected schedule. Something must have happened. Probably the heat slowed her down. Or maybe her colitis acted up and she had to find a bathroom. I tried my answering machine in case Ruthie had left a message. Nothing. When Sam and Hallie returned with the pizza, we sat on the curb. All the tossed water cups scattered on the street looked like a maze of pigeons in an abandoned city. We devoured the pizza and tried to have fun cheering on the few remaining racers, but in my gut I sensed something was wrong.

5:15. Still no Ruthie, and now the sun was lower in the sky, bringing on a chill. Beacon Street had cleared out but for the strewn paper cups and some orange peels that still littered the ground. Hallie sat playing with a nearby dog, asking every few minutes if we could leave. Sam put his arm around my shoulder, knowing I was concerned for my best friend. Unsure what to do, we decided to give Ruthie's home phone a try just for the heck of it. It took my cell phone a few tries to get service, but when I finally got through there was no answer, only the machine. It had the same quirky message she'd posted a few weeks earlier: "Your nickel." Where had her previously cheerful messages gone, the ones that started with a few seconds of music and ended with versions of "have a great day"?

I called "411" for the Dana Farber phone number, but once I finally got through and reached someone at the hospital, he had zero details on how to find out about a runner with their team. Frustrated, and with no one else to call, I suggested we head to the finish line and find someone on the staff that might have some information. As we walked to the train stop, dragging our weary bodies, with long faces and an aging bouquet of flowers, I wondered if I should ask Sam to take Hallie home while I looked for Ruthie. Maybe Ruthie couldn't handle Heartbreak Hill and ended up, ironically, in the same emergency room that we had worked for way back when. Just then, the train pulled up and we all climbed aboard before I could change any plans.

~~~

"Ruthie Rosenthal? Uh, hmm, she never picked up her number."

"That's impossible. Check again. She's been training all year. You sure you spelled it right? Please try again, Rosenthal, R-O-S-E-N-T-H-A-L," I rambled at the young, skinny girl staffing an info table at the finish line. We had reached her after fighting our way to her table via a crowd as packed as Times Square at New Year's Eve. The flowers I had carried for Ruthie had been crushed in the crowd.

The girl kept shaking her head and twirling a hoop earring while scanning her list. The place was still a madhouse of media, runners wrapped in post-run metallic blankets to help keep their body's warm until they cooled down, and their friends and family surrounding them. The air smelled like a mix of sweat, deodorant, and roses. Several health care workers in the medic tents were still treating a few late-finishing runners, but the info table was staffed at this late time of day only by this one bored young girl who chomped on her gum and picked at her nail polish and refused to look for Ruthie's name a third time.

A few other people pushed their way toward the table now. Sam took me by the arm and pulled me aside, Hallie clinging to his other hand. I dug out my cell phone and tried Ruthie's number again. Still nothing.

"You know her better than I, but something seems wrong, Jo. Maybe we should head out of here and go look for her somewhere?"

"Look for her somewhere? Where? Like in the middle of a million people?" I discarded the crushed flowers in a massive wastebasket overflowing with cans, bottles, the metallic wrappers, and other debris that represented the end of a long, long day for so many people.

"Sweetie, I understand you're anxious, but let's figure this out together somehow. Do you want to go to her condo? We can ask her neighbors if they've seen her? Why don't we do that?" Sam put his arm around me.

I nodded. Yes, we could do that. We turned toward the subway entrance when I decided one of us should stay there just in case Ruthie was looking for us, too. He agreed to stay and to keep Hallie with him so I could look for Ruthie unencumbered. We'd meet up later in the lobby of the Copley Plaza Hotel, and he'd call my cell or I'd leave a message on his home phone if either one found Ruthie, and otherwise—

Just then an emergency vehicle forced its way through the crowd, opening up the area like the parting of the Red Sea. The loud siren meant Sam and I could no longer hear each other, and then as people jockeyed around the vehicles, we three became separated by a rush of people following the ambulance. But we had a plan in place…didn't we? And Sam had long been holding Hallie's hand, yes? As I bolted to the subway and headed for an outbound train, sticking to our plan, my heart raced and my mind went to my worst fear. I had to trust that Sam was still holding Hallie's hand. Or should I go back? What to do? What to do? I jumped on the outbound train. I had to trust him. He didn't carry a phone and, besides, I was unable to get service on the train. I'd call his home phone at my stop, and leave a message, although I was sure he had taken charge of Hallie.

~~~

Shit. I emerged from the subway at my stop and discovered that my phone was dead. It was meant only for

213

emergencies, and I foolishly had attempted to dial Ruthie that whole train ride despite no cell service. Between my useless phone, my fear over Ruthie's mysterious disappearance and whether Hallie was safe, I felt like the abandoned debris I saw all over the street. Sam had no cell, but I would figure out who to call from Ruthie's. I ran the quarter-mile from the train to her house, peeling off my fleece jacket when sweat and heat overwhelmed me.

Crocus poked up their little heads outside Ruthie's brownstone, but I focused straight ahead to the outside door and the double row of buzzers lined up inside the tiny vestibule. I practically leaned my entire body on buzzer number six. No answer. So she wasn't there. Now what? I figured I'd go up and pee, then check out the place; maybe Ruthie had left some sign of her whereabouts. She never locked her door, but how to get past the vestibule? I tried buzzing a random unit. Within seconds, a woman answered in what I assumed was Russian. I figured she didn't speak much English, like many of the families in the building, so it would be tough to explain why I needed entry. So I muttered "excuse me" and skimmed names on the buzzers to find an American one. But the door clicked. I grabbed the handle and pulled...unlocked! I looked at the ceiling and thought, "There is a God." Suddenly remembering the one word of Russian Bubbe had taught me long ago, I shouted as joyfully as if I'd just found Ruthie and Hallie both right there in the hallway: "Spasibo!" Then I climbed all three floors, two steps at a time.

~~~

"Oh my God! Say something, Ru, it's Jody, talk to me!" I darted to Ruthie's phone. Dialed 911. Aggressively shook my friend, who lay in bed under a thick down comforter that I pulled down. She wore pajamas. Was neither awake nor asleep but in some kind of semi-comatose stupor.

I shouted into the phone. "Yes, she's breathing!"

214

Her skin was a scary grayish hue. Her black and silver-streaked long hair hung about her like Morticia Addams. I pulled a clump.

"No, she's not responsive!"

Ruthie's crazy red tabby cat, Red Baron, rubbed against me and meowed in that ear-piercing tone that meant only one thing: He hadn't been fed for hours. I shouted in Ru's ear, "SHOULD I FEED THE BARON?"

"No, she can't speak!"

Next to the bed was a drained glass of something, soda? Wine? Juice? It was slightly pinkish. And Ruthie's running clothes were neatly stacked on the floor beneath the nightstand, her Adidas shoes beside them.

I tapped my foot, paced in little circles, and then dropped the phone. I flew to the bathroom to wet a few cloths like the calm lady on the phone suggested. And as I wondered how the fuck those 911 people stay calm, I scoured the medicine cabinet and then looked under the kitchen sink. No ammonia.

The stupid cat followed me everywhere, meowing like he was about to deliver sextuplets. I was petrified to trip on him.

"Yes, I placed them on her forehead and wrists but she's STILL NOT MOVING! Yes, yes, I'll go unlock the door of the building," I shouted at the dispatcher. "WHAT? And gather up any meds? Lock up any pets?" I repeated her commands out loud. I doubted I could manage that last one without getting my arm shredded. "YES, YES."

The next ten minutes became a blur of blue- and white-uniformed EMTs and paramedics rushing into the lobby and up to the apartment. As they noisily approached her door, I pounced on the Red Baron and threw him in the hall closet so maniacally he never saw it coming!

Within minutes, the obviously highly-skilled EMTs and paramedics determined Ruthie was massively dehydrated, might have overdosed on some of the pills I'd gathered up—and the liquid was indeed alcohol, but she had a stable pulse! The second round of EMTs wound their way up the narrow stairway with multiple pieces of equipment I'd never seen before, including a scary stretcher. Downstairs, a cluster of mostly Russian-speaking tenants kept shouting so many questions from the echoing stairway it sounded like a subway station at rush hour.

After they had placed some contraption over her face and started an I.V., they managed to carry her out on the stretcher, leaving me behind to deal with a screaming cat clawing the door. His raw sounds echoed how my heart and gut felt. I released him from his jail and threw food into his bowl. I quickly peed and then ran out of the apartment and out onto the street. I didn't stop running until I'd completed the mile-and-a-half to the Beth Israel Emergency room. By then it was nearly dark out. In my desperate fear, I'd forgotten to call Sam's answering machine, or mine, to be sure that he and Hallie were together.

Chapter Twenty-Six

Ruthie was "sitting up and taking nourishment," as she called it. I was so grateful her eyes were open, her color had returned and the mouth was flapping again! She had one tube going into her nose and another into her veins, and at least two drip bags hanging off those metal bars. I gazed at her, remaining stone quiet. She knew the question I was asking with only my eyes and turned down mouth.

She shook her head. But I wanted to be sure, so I asked it outright as only best friends could.

"No, no, no and no again. I guess I'm self-destructive as crap—I can't believe I missed the goddamn marathon after all that fucking training—but I'm *not* suicidal."

"Thank God" was all I could say. I kissed her cheek.

Ironically, she wore the blue Johnnies adorned with the Beth Israel logo—the very logo I had helped redesign when I worked in the public relations department.

"We're back," Ruthie joked when she saw me examining her Johnny. I tried to laugh, but the chaos of the emergency room, and my deep concerns about Ruthie and Hallie, kept me focused and somber.

Ruthie turned serious, too, telling me the story. Turns out she'd had a bad bout of diarrhea from her colitis at bedtime last night. So she figured the marathon might be out, but she decided to wait until morning to decide. When she couldn't fall asleep, she drank some wine, and then when still awake well past midnight, she swallowed "a couple" of antihistamines to try to dose off. When she awoke again "sometime later," she took "a couple" of Tylenol PM with the rest of the bottle of wine, not realizing the Tylenol had antihistamines in them, too. When the alarm went off early in the morning, she had such a bad migraine she knew she'd never make it to the marathon, so she took "a couple" of her migraine pills. The combination cocktail over the seven hours or so from the first glass of wine apparently was too much for her petite, one-hundred-and-five-pound body to handle, particularly after the earlier diarrhea. The doctor had explained she probably developed a serious state of dehydration and fell into a deep sleep lasting all day.

"Well that explains why I don't think I even got up to pee all night or day," Ruthie quipped. "Shit, what about the Red Baron...I didn't feed him this morning."

"All set."

Just then the doctor returned. He told Ruthie she was lucky I had found her when I did. He had serious concerns regarding her state of mind and possible depression. And although she may not have consciously attempted suicide, what she did was dangerously close, so he was not comfortable releasing her until the on-call psychiatrist met with her.

"No fucking way. I'll be fine!"

As much as I wanted to flee to the Copley Plaza meeting place to find Sam and—I prayed—Hallie, I asked her to see the psychiatrist immediately—for me if not for herself. She conceded.

We suspected it would be a long wait for the psychiatrist to show up, so I located some ginger ale from the ER fridge, poured it into plastic cups, and handed one to Ruthie. She nudged over in bed and I lay by her side, leaning on her pillow. We both sipped through our tiny straws, trying to unwind from the last hour's tension. I apologized for not recognizing she had probably been depressed for quite a while.

"I was too preoccupied with myself for so long, I didn't grasp the signs. I'm so sorry."

"Hey, you and I have taken turns supporting each other our whole lives. This was your turn to have some fun after all you've been through. I never felt you'd abandoned me. I just let myself get too closed in for too long. Became a workaholic instead of getting out and *living*. This sucks, but it's a wakeup call I guess."

We leaned our heads together and sat quietly until the psychiatrist surprised us sooner than expected.

"Had another call here in the ER, so I'm fitting you in, too. What's going on?" He lifted his clipboard, ready to take notes.

When his evaluation was over, he concluded she was no harm to herself right now, but he suggested she start seeing a therapist immediately, possibly get on some meds. He scribbled a few psychiatrists' names on a prescription pad. Ru promised she'd make the call the next day. I believed her.

Finally, Ruthie was ready to be released after signing gobs of paperwork. I was beyond eager by then to take her home and rush to the Copley Plaza. My stomach had been in knots for hours. It was only after the final nurse left that I told Ruthie the situation.

Without hesitation, she jumped out of bed and climbed into the red and white flannel cat pajamas she'd been wearing when I found her. In my haste, I'd forgotten to bring her any clothes.

"Let's get outta here!" she announced.

I pushed her outside in the required wheelchair, and as the Beth Israel volunteer helped us toward our taxi, I couldn't believe it: Thomas's Taxi was the next cab in line!

"Cute pjs" he said to Ruthie, as she climbed into the back seat and I sat in the front. "So I see you two have traded nutcase roles since the last time I've seen ya, eh?"

Tom let me use his cab phone to check the messages on my dead cell phone. The first message was from Sam about twenty minutes after we parted, sounding more agitated than I'd ever heard him, which confirmed my worst fears. I was so petrified to keep listening that I pressed the speaker phone button right in the middle: "…. because she was right beside me holding my hand one second, gone a second later in the rush of people." I gasped and covered my mouth; I turned as pale as Ruthie had been earlier and started to hyperventilate. Ruthie leaned forward to grab my shoulder, and at the same time, Tom raised the volume so we could all listen to the rest of the messages, each one loud and booming as though the world were coming to an end:

"Jody, I wish I could reach you, wherever you are, but since I can't, I'm proceeding as though you do not have Hallie, and an Officer Donahue from the Boston police force is helping me locate her, so if you get this and do have her, please call the Boston police at 619-220-1212. Try not to worry; we're doing everything we can, and she's a tough little girl…but I hope to God she's with you."

"Hello there, Madame single lady, this is your soon-to-be ex-husband wondering why the hell the Boston Police Department has called me after finding our daughter alone on the streets of Boston. Call me."

"Jody, me again; thank God Officer Donahue heard from another officer that they've located Hallie. She's fine, thankfully. She was petting a dog right next to the medic tent and someone noticed she was alone and reported it. Quite a kid you've raised; she wasn't even crying, just wondering where we were. I'm going now to meet them at the lobby of

the Four Seasons Hotel. Apparently they have a children's officer there today. A woman officer is hanging out with Hallie 'til I arrive. I'll stay as long as it takes. Meet us there whenever you can. Just ask for us at the front desk; I'll take care of whatever—I'll get Hallie some dinner and even get us a room to hang 'til you come, if we need. I sure hope you check your messages soon. And I hope Ruthie's all right; obviously I haven't spent any time looking for her."

"Well, you're not answering your cell and you're not home, so I'm going to head into town and retrieve our daughter. I sure hope you have a good explanation for this, because, well, I sure would like to have full custody if you're no longer fit for the job."

Tom swerved his taxi around and headed for The Four Seasons. Ruthie obviously couldn't come in her weak state, though she fought me when I told Tom to drive her home afterwards, and settle her into her apartment if he wouldn't mind.

In minutes, we were in front of the luxurious hotel, and Tom insisted the fare was on him. I hopped out. Ruthie tried to follow me in her cat pajamas, but I led her to the front seat and kissed the top of her head.

"Good luck, Jo, and if that fucker thinks he's going after you for custody after you saved my life today, he's got another thing coming."

~~~

As if the day hadn't already been a nightmare, I entered the posh Four Seasons, my hair a mess, my makeup smudged, and the bottom of my jeans and sneakers coated in dirt. The concierge directed me to Room 420, and with the high-end furnishings and art all color-coded in shades of maroon and taupe and a touch of gold—I felt I was headed to a wedding not an emotional trial. Inside the room, I nearly plotzed. There sat Stewart and Sam side-by-side on a velvet couch, deep in conversation. Before I could worry whether Stewart had revealed the secret of our night together, Hallie darted away from the officer who played with her in the corner. I squatted low, and Hallie jumped into my arms. I held her so close and cried fierce, rocking sobs. I felt utterly unable to contain myself.

"What's the matter, Mommy?" She patted my head. "Shh, shh, it'll be okay Mommy."

I smiled at her nurturing behavior and sucked in enough air to reply without scaring her. "These are happy tears, sweetie. I'm just so glad to see you!"

Sam rushed over to us, and I noticed he didn't embrace me as he might have, had Stewart not also been present. I turned toward him anyway and pulled him toward us. The three of us hugged tightly. I whispered into his ear how grateful I was he had acted quickly and called the police.

"So you're not mad at me for losing your little girl?" he whispered back, barely audibly.

"Oh my God, no, it wasn't your fault."

"Did you find anything out about Ruthie? What's up?"

"She's okay. It was awful, but could have been way worse. She's home now. We've both been in the ER the last couple of hours. Nothing to do with the marathon. I'll tell you what happened later."

He hugged me close. Hallie had already run back to play with the officer.

Next, I had to deal with Stewart. I turned to face him, but he was in the corner with the officer, too. I exhaled, relaxing as I recognized his insatiable appetite for a pretty woman. His body leaned in toward hers. Despite her bulky blue pantsuit labeled "Boston Police," she still looked curvaceous and sexy, her blond hair falling onto her shoulders from the bun I watched her release. Apparently, she was making it clear she liked his attention.

I approached them with a nod hello but no words. Stewart glanced at my grimy clothes and introduced me to Officer Andrews. "Hallie's mother, the vagabond."

I apologized for my appearance, looking only at the officer. I pulled out my driver's license and took the pen she extended to sign the police release she had placed before me. I held onto the side of the clipboard and wrote my signature just below Stewart's. With few words exchanged between us, and no disturbance, I knew Stewart would let me take our daughter, and he no longer planned to pursue custody. Before I even walked away, he was asking Officer Andrews out to dinner, and I heard her say in a flirty tone, "Sure, I'm officially off-duty now."

After such a long, long sickening day, I felt so relieved that I felt like giving him my credit card to treat her right there at the Four Seasons' fancy restaurant, Aujourd'hui.

~~~

Hallie and I walked across the hall to the bathroom, my daughter and I tightly holding hands. We laughed as I practically took an entire bath in the hotel sink, although there was little I could do for my clothing other than brush it off.

As soon as I was a tad more presentable, we three went outside into the fresh air, walking down Boylston Street toward the train holding hands. I didn't want to ruin the moment, but I assumed Stewart, in his annoyance, had told Sam about our pathetic night together, and I felt it was finally the right time to close that chapter. I asked Sam how long he and Stewart had been together in the hotel room. My quiet, quizzical voice must have revealed my concern.

"Jo, put it to rest. That ex-husband of yours, it turns out, likes me, even though I nearly lost his kid. Maybe it's because we talked sports for a bit and I knew almost as much as he did about Larry Bird." Then he paused, his face grim. "Although I hope to keep you far, far away from him in the future, except for Hallie's sake, because he did tell me what happened with you…"

"Uhhh," I gasped, but Sam ignored me.

"….and he actually admitted it was one thousand percent his fault, although I must say the lustful glint in his eye made me want to punch him. Wouldn't have been cool with an officer right there, ya think? It helped me keep control, plus my karate mental training came in handy. So I told him to back off, but restrained myself, because although I might not trust him on the topic of women, in this case, I believed him. Besides, it was during those months you were uncertain about my, shall I say, libido, and since his obviously is in overdrive, what can I say?"

"I'm so sorry, I…"

"Stop. It's over. I don't like it, but I blame him, not you. And I hope you and I never mention it again. That's in the rear view mirror. It's all gone. Let's only look ahead now."

He stopped walking and turned me toward him with his free arm, the other tightly holding onto Hallie. He pulled me against his chest and kissed me squarely on the mouth in a passionate embrace. Hallie stared up at us and a bunch of people walking by clapped.

Chapter Twenty-Seven

The surprising applause at the end of the Public Relations Association's Anniversary event, held at the Copley Plaza ballroom in June, carried on for five minutes, with a standing ovation. Sam and I later wondered if the crowd had been congratulating us not only for the gorgeous commemorative book and video, and the creative collaboration between two great Boston organizations, but our personal relationship. We had revealed this fact to our colleagues earlier in the month while completing the book and preparing the video together. Perhaps our warm body language had made it clear to the many other guests who knew of Sam's sad loss?

Sam and I also had made a shrewd decision the month before. We had brought Harry into the commemoration project and, later, when she relented, Ida joined us as we requested a printing bid from their firm. We four actually sat in the boardroom together, civilly—nothing short of a miracle. Fortunately, Ida kept to the topic at hand at our meetings without delving into Sam's personal life. And as I hoped, they gave us a reasonable price, including a large gift-in-kind donation. It met our budget, and Sam and I chose their bid.

The past few months had passed by so happily I hardly could believe it. Not only did Hallie, Sam and I start enjoying life as often as our schedules allowed, but it even worked out well that Stewart was now dating the cop, whom we liked and trusted, so we let them take Hallie together—though only during the day.

And the best shock and delight of all: Ruthie and Tom had become an item! Tom, it turned out, had never been married and always knew he'd find the right woman when she loved sports and could chow down a good meal without complaining of gaining weight. Bingo! That was Ruthie! He told her once a day he was nuts about her, and once posted it on the Fenway "jumbotron" at a Red Sox game! She'd not only found a true romantic, but, like Sam toward me, he nurtured her better than any past boyfriend.

Ruthie had seen the psychiatrist and decided to take Prozac. She felt great. She worked a bit less and even rode along with Tom on some of his gigs. She also gave up running; it was better for her health, and although she was starting to get a little plump in the middle, she was happy. Oddly, even her parents liked Tom. "He makes us laugh, and he adores you," her parents had said. "How can that bring anything but good?" Her asshole brother refused to meet "a cabbie," but Ruthie no longer gave a shit what he thought.

Sam and I had joined Ruthie and Tom for Mexican food one night recently, and after a pitcher of sangria and endless tostadas and tacos, I realized Sam and I, and Ruthie, hadn't laughed that much maybe ever. Tom was good for all of us!

And while Sam and I still hadn't had intercourse—waiting until closer to my official divorce when old-fashioned Sam had proof I could be his forever—I learned that not making love in the ultimate act actually made the sex more intimate and more intense. I was a happy woman.

And Hallie adored him, and vice versa. Enough said.

Just as amazing, I had created a slightly different relationship with my parents, which seemed to be working sufficiently. Instead of dealing with them less often, I called them regularly, leaving short upbeat messages, including telling them about the fabulous response to the commemorative book, and how Hallie was enjoying her first summer day camp experience where she helped groom alpacas, feed chickens and collect hen eggs, along with taking her first tennis lessons.

My mother even said she had run into Gossip-Is-My-Middle-Name Ethel Schwartz, who told her all about how everyone at the Temple loved meeting Sam at the Tot Shabbat a few months back. Instead of whining about my not telling her myself about Sam's successful temple debut, Ida bragged to me about how well the work for the MFA had gone. They'd even won a second exciting bid for the museum's newest exhibit.

And best of all: Ida called one evening to, matter of factly, announce she had reached my aunt and uncle to tell them about Stewart, and our divorce. And about Sam. While she had thought she'd let the cat out of the bag, it turned out they all knew, as Ellen had put two and two together at the funeral, asked Rhonda for details, and shared it with the others! I was relieved to hear it, as I had already made the decision to bring Sam to the reunion, and this made it easier.

I thanked Ida for coming around, but she clearly didn't want to spend another second talking about it.

"I have to go," she said, and hung up.

So what if she couldn't fully face what was happening in my life, or face talking about emotions; that was her problem. Yet I was relieved the print job had paved the way for acceptance of Sam. What was not to like about him?

The only thing I still avoided was *seeing* Ida, unless absolutely necessary. Most of the time, I claimed to be too busy catching up with my volunteer projects, now that the time-consuming work project had wrapped up. Some of that was true, of course, with visits to the elderly at Bubbe's former place with Ringo when Hallie was off with Stewart, and working my shifts at the soup kitchen. But mostly I spent any spare time with Sam at his place or mine. Once I even watched him teach a class at the South Boston karate studio he still taught at now and then. Wow. My guy was something else! And the rest of the time I savored whenever I could be with Hallie—either the two of us or with Sam, too. Whenever we three went to the zoo, the aquarium, the Museum of Science or whatnot, we felt like a true family. Hallie had even begun holding Sam's hand more than mine on these outings! It warmed my heart! And his. Yes, we were becoming a family.

We also visited sometimes with other members of Sam's family, mostly Shelley's siblings and their young children. Including an occasional Tot Shabbat at their temples. I adored them all and loved that my family was expanding incrementally.

Sam and I kept busy with everything that kept us all enjoying life as a soon-to-be-official family. We were happily closing in on that reality.

I still had a hurdle to tackle first, however: The Reunion! It would be the final event Sam and I needed to survive together before I would provide him with the long-awaited sign I was ready to commit to him for life. I needed him to spend the weekend with my family first. While I loved him as fully as my heart could bear, and was happier than ever before, what worried me most was whether he would feel the same way about me after being immersed in my family's mishegas for an entire weekend.

Though the reunion piece of things was only once a year, I knew it represented a monumental gap between us. Might my family's superficial values, lack of outward warmth and hyper-competitive ways scare him off? And would I ever be so shallow as to let the financial gap between Sam's family and mine seriously bother me, now or later—even if I were to lose my admissions ticket to future family fortunes? When he and I were together, we seemed to share equally modest spending habits, and we both cared more about life values than material items. But then there were our different religions. How would it be one day at Hallie's Bat Mitzvah if he weren't permitted to participate in some of the Jewish rituals, as a non-Jew? If we had a child together, which we hoped to, would he really be okay raising him or her as a Jew, as he promised Bubbe? And what if I ever leaned one way and he another regarding religion, like married Republicans and Democrats who say they don't care about the differences, but sometimes, around exasperating political times, they sleep in different rooms. Could we still get along if this happened regarding our religions, or would it fracture the relationship?

I knew this was all just my old nerves coming back. But the reunion weekend ahead seemed to be an essential telltale event, despite our planning for it with sensitivity and humor. And with back-up plans: we would take time away from the group—or exit completely—if anything occurred that was insurmountable for us—or a negative influence on Hallie.

Chapter Twenty-Eight

I grabbed Sam's hand as I steered my Outback onto the pebbled driveway of Uncle Nathan and Aunt Bernice's estate. I knew from so many prior visits that the electronic alarm system would be announcing our arrival with a shrill "ping." Sam was duly impressed. He also noted the landscaping was "aristocratic," bursting with gargantuan, rhododendrons, azaleas and exotic Japanese maple trees.

"Wait 'til you see the river-birch path to the tennis court."

He looked at me as though I were exaggerating, but realized I wasn't.

I maneuvered my car into a space between my sister's black Mercedes and what was probably Cousin Ellen's new black Porsche. Glancing farther down the driveway, I saw my parents' new coal-gray Jaguar and Cousin Barry's newest "midnight black" Lexus—the color he consistently chose for each new car.

"All that's missing is a hearse."

"Funny guy."

"Really, hon, shouldn't we trade in this green car by next summer? Time to lease on my biz, like them?"

"Ah, suddenly you're turning into a conformist? Shit, we must be the last ones here. That's never good, gonna be questions about what took us so long."

"I'll just tell 'em we stopped five times to have sex."

"Ya, with Hallie asleep in the back. Good one."

Actually, we weren't last. Uncle Nathan was busy round-the-clock handling the onslaught of media regarding the President and Monica Lewinsky, but he planned to sneak away from Washington later in the day. He'd never consider missing the annual family weekend to celebrate his cherished mother's birthday. Particularly this year, with her gone. Apparently, the President's helicopter would be dropping him off on his newly constructed helipad. This fact alone made Sam hopeful for an exciting weekend, while I just hoped nothing would go terribly wrong.

I pulled up the emergency brake with a sudden strong lurch, startling Hallie. She had dozed off an hour earlier after playing with her dolls in the back seat much of the drive.

"Yeah, we're here!" She scrambled out of the car when she noticed my dad standing by the pool gate.

"Go on to Zayde if you'd like, honey. We'll be in soon with your toys."

Hallie ran off, and I shouted a quick hello to my dad and informed him she had her suit on under her clothes. Sam and I each grabbed an overstuffed satchel containing our tennis racquets, tennis clothes, bathing suits and a couple of pool toys. With my other arm, I accepted the hand Sam offered. I felt like a child on my first day of school, my eyes wide open, a bit excited and a lot scared. While I had come a long way in the past few months, I still didn't know if I had the stamina or desire to withstand all the teasing and sarcastic putdowns. Sam was prepared to field what he could, as his wit was quicker than mine, and these strangers couldn't push his buttons as they could mine.

"Welcome to the Lion's Den, my love," I said to Sam as we pushed open the heavy steel front door, and I noted to myself this weighty obstacle was the least of what separated us from the others.

Fortunately, when we walked into the foyer, it was quiet. Everyone must have been out back around the pool or on the tennis court. We used the hall bathroom to change into our suits together, and lingered in there for a few sweet kisses. With Sam's fit physique, I hoped the customary Horowitz-one-upmanship might be hushed by his good looks, kindness and strength. And, most of all, by his warm, open, "no airs" demeanor.

We stood a moment by the sliding glass door to the outside, taking in what we could observe at poolside, but we only noticed a few people there. Perhaps the others were on the courts already. Good, we could ease in slowly. We began by walking over to Ida who was sitting in a chair in the shade, a closed hard-cover book turned upside down in her lap.

"Where've you been?" she asked, neither standing to hug us nor putting out her hand to shake Sam's. I shook my head and started to say we stopped a few times along the drive, but she cut me off. "No, not that. Hallie's been here five minutes already."

"Great suit," Sam said, commenting on Ida's blue and gold bathing suit with a wide skirt to hide her thighs, although her legs were still shapely, and one of the luckier genetic features Rhonda and I had both inherited. Although of course I was much taller than both of them, and with longer legs. "We were getting into our suits, too," he said. "Great to be here, it's a lovely setting."

Sam seemed surprisingly comfortable around her, which immediately calmed me down, as it diffused that first irritating non-hello by Ida.

We three continued to make small talk about the good weather, and then we excused ourselves to greet Aunt Bernice. She was approaching with arms outstretched, ready to hug us both. Her body looked trim in her form-fitted bathing suit.

"I've so wanted to meet you, welcome to our home! We'll talk more later, when Nathan arrives, but please, make yourself totally at home. Help yourself to anything all weekend."

Sam thanked her, and as we moved toward the pool, he whispered, "Thanks, I'll help myself to your niece." We quietly laughed. Just then, my father jumped out of the pool to shake Sam's hand, placing his other hand over Sam's and looking him in the eye a moment. Sam thanked him, and my father welcomed me with a kiss on the cheek, then hurried back into the pool where he and Hallie were already shooting hoops in the shallow end. I was glad no one else was around the pool at that moment, but even later when Sam met the others, introductions went smoothly, with everyone on their best behavior.

But an hour later, Sam was invited to play tennis with Alan, Cousin Barry and Cousin Ellen's husband Robbie, though Sam was not used to competitive tennis. He had only hit a half dozen times indoors with me and friends as he learned the rules of doubles. While he accepted the challenge and didn't seem to mind being far less skilled, I tensed, because I knew what lay ahead for him. Yet I sent him off with just an encouraging pat on his back, and I settled into an empty pool lounge chair near where my mother and sister were engrossed in books—the only topic of conversation we three had engaged in so far. A miracle.

From where I rested, I had a clear view of Hallie who was now in the pool with Aunt Bernice and Barry's wife, Leslie, who were all playing with Ellen's toddler, too. My headphones played comforting jazz and served a secondary purpose of keeping the others from talking to me. I was glad Ellen, the usual trouble maker, was nowhere in sight. Things actually felt pleasant.

I lay that way in the bright sun for a while, taking off my headphones once or twice to comment on some harmless conversations, but I popped them back over my ears before things could head into personal topics. Once, I went inside to check on baby Tiffany who was asleep in the den. I also took a minute to scrutinize my face in the bathroom mirror for any emerging sun spots. Fortunately none had surfaced. I had recently noticed my skin no longer seemed as sensitive. I went back outside and played a bit in the pool with Hallie, still avoiding adult conversation, other than minor kid talk. Eventually I dried off and lay back down, this time on my stomach. I must have dozed off, because I was awakened by Sam kneeling down, kissing my cheek. As my eyes opened and focused, the first thing I noticed was he wasn't as red-faced, or sweaty, as I had expected.

I sat up and slipped my bathing suit straps back onto my shoulders. I had wanted to watch his match but had decided against it in case I felt embarrassed. Better to not know.

"How'd it go, honey?"

"Not bad. I held my own, but I chose to sit out the last few rounds."

"The last few 'games,'" I said, immediately sorry I hadn't kept the correction to myself. But Ellen's voice interrupted before I could apologize.

"Hey, Jody, you picked another one who doesn't play tennis, eh?" Ellen yelled from the river-birch path that wound its way up from the courts below. "You sure are the black sheep of the family!"

I wanted to blast her. Didn't she have any regard for Sam's feelings, if not mine? So what if Sam, like Stewart, didn't play competitive tennis like the rest of the men? I knew how the other men—with their competitive personalities—treated their women, coming home from work most nights at eight, leaving at six the next morning, gone overnight often for business, and who knows what else. But how could I speak up while taking the high road? I turned toward Sam who had either chosen to ignore Ellen, or truly hadn't heard. He was busy putting his racquet back in its case.

You really are the black sheep, I played over in my head. Was this a reference to my choice in men, or just a reminder I was so different from them? I had promised myself not to let this shit bother me this year, but it was so ingrained in me, how could I not?

I glanced toward my cousin who had climbed the hill and walked right past us, swinging her wide hips with a little extra wiggle. Ellen's hair was wild, bushy, her makeup caked on her face. The outdated blue eye shadow painted onto each eyelid looked out of place by the pool, like a party dress at a funeral. I took a deep breath, still undecided if I should respond at all, but I was trying not to repeat past years' patterns. If I replied at all, I had to say something noticeably different....

"Why thank you, Ellen, that's actually a compliment in this family," blurted out of me. I took Sam's welcoming hand as he pulled me off my lounge chair.

"Just ignore her, Jo. Come on, I'll help you cool off." He motioned toward the pool. So he had heard after all but had let it go. Maybe he could teach me how to do that?

Ellen muttered something under her breath as her son began to whine and tug on her shorts. Hallie, meanwhile, was in the pool playing basketball with Grandpa Harry and managed to get the ball into the four-foot-high basket for a dunk shot. "Atta girl, Hallie," roared out of Harry's mouth. Everyone in the pool cheered, too.

From across the pool deck, Rhonda lifted her head to peek at the commotion, and then rose to check on Tiffany.

Just then Ida boomed, "Jody, play tennis with me. Let Sam have a break from you."

"Not now, Mom, we're going into the pool."

"Well, in ten minutes then." She stood and headed toward the house. A navy blue tennis dress with gold buttons hung from her arm, and sneakers dangled from her hand.

"The admiral speaks," Sam whispered into my ear. "Go ahead and accept; it's a match I'd pay money to watch." Perhaps his levity allowed my mood to soften.

"In ten minutes, okay," I heard myself say. Then I whispered to Sam, "Truth is, I've never been able to beat her. But I'm sure gonna try today. I guess it'll be good exercise, either way." He and I both knew I was lying that the outcome of this match didn't really matter.

~~~

Nearly forty minutes into the game, Ida was ahead, five games to four. I had managed to keep the games tightly competitive but hadn't taken the lead yet. In two tight games, I had won the deuce point and turned the game to my advantage, yet Ida went on to win the next point and bring us back to deuce. We went back and forth this way in those two games until she unfortunately won both games with a drop shot. Despite her little bit of wobbly flesh, my mother moved around the court like a much younger person! Even more so than usual.

Throughout the match, I pushed my body so hard, and although I felt drenched in sweat I remained hyper-focused. A few times, her first serve missed the service box by inches, giving me a chance to do something fierce with her lighter second serve.

This time, with Ida up by one game, and me leading in this one, I was extra ready for her second serve, on my toes, watching the yellow orb leave Ida's racquet as it traveled toward me...right into the net. How unusual: She double faulted! Just the edge I needed. We were now tied. I could take the lead with this next game!

As I approached the net to get the tennis balls from Ida, to start my service game, I wondered if she might blame the double fault on being tired—and want to stop playing.

"Oh, these clay courts, let's finish up," she said, even though I could easily win a debate about the court having nothing to do with a serve into the net!

The two of us returned to our proper places for the final game. We had agreed earlier that the first to win six games would be the winner. It was too hot to keep going.

I concentrated hard. I used a slice on my first serve, popping it short into the service box, a shot I hadn't perfected well, but when it worked, my mother couldn't run fast enough to catch it. It worked! Fifteen to love. I stayed focused for the next point, choosing a hard serve this time, and it landed deep in the court to her backhand, just where I wanted it! Shit. She not only returned my serve well, but my ground stroke return back wasn't deep enough. Ida rushed to it, hit it cross court toward the sideline in front of me at a sharp angle, and although I moved forward to grab it as a forehand, it suddenly switched directions through the air as a slice. I couldn't change direction quickly enough to catch its curve as a backhand before it landed—right on the line.

Fifteen to fifteen.

My next serve landed where I wanted it, deep in the center of the court, and the point lasted a while, with each of us returning well, strong, hard, but no one finding an opportunity to put the ball away. Finally, Ida scored the point on my error, a shot that hit the net, balanced a second on top, then dropped onto my side. *So the net gods gave her that point; ok, I'm going straight on to win the next point*, I said to myself, and I quickly tossed the ball and propelled my racquet, arm and body forward and down on it to serve a strong shot to her backhand that she couldn't pull her racquet back for in time and it sailed past her. Yes!

Thirty to fifteen. *Two more points and I've succeeded. Self-talk, self-talk, keep this going.* I dared not glance up toward Sam, who I knew was watching from the cliff beside the pool, high up above the courts, but this thought must have distracted my focus because I lost that point, hitting a shot well past the baseline.

"Home run! Too far, my dear," Ida said, yet she hadn't said a word when my great shot had sailed by her before.

I ignored her comment and announced the score, thirty to thirty. I decided to use my slice serve again, but it hit the net and landed wide. Bummer, why did I risk that? I concentrated hard and popped the next serve in, a bit too lightly but in the corner of the box at Ida's backhand, well placed. But Ida was ready and sliced it back, barely making it over the net—but it did, rolling down my side of the net, so I rushed forward, and although my mother had turned away thinking she'd scored the point, I scooped it up and managed to lift it until it dropped right back over the net on Ida's side. The net gods had helped me out this time!

"Forty-thirty," I announced, just as Ida realized what had happened. Another opponent would have praised my lucky shot, but no, not good ol' Ida. I let the thought go, excited I could win with this next point.

"You know, tennis is a head game, Jody," Ida said, startling me as I was about to toss the ball for what I hoped would be my final serve. "Age and experience is bound to beat youth and brawn, dear." I dug down deeper than I knew I could to hold myself together, although I wanted to wallop the ball straight at her. *Who says things like this at a set point?* "But you've really improved, dear. You just need to work some more on your backhand." *I need to work on my backhand? My backhand? She needs to kill her backhanded comments. Tennis is a head game? Life is a head game with you, lady.*

I needed to shake my mother's ill-timed, cutting intrusion from my mind and focus on the game. *Self-talk. Positive self-talk only.* No more Jody taking Ida's bait. Anywhere. Anytime. Done with that shit! This would be the last game despite her trying to psych me out and manipulate me once again. While I was determined to change this habitual dance between the two of us, I needed an excuse to stall and compose myself. I feigned a cough.

"Oh, have some water and let this be over with. It's brutally hot"

"Thanks, Ma, but I'm all set now."

Still forty-thirty, my lead. Match point.

I returned to the service line. The sun was so powerful, the humidity thickening. I wanted to leave the heat, but I wanted to do so triumphant. *Take a risk,* I thought. *Break the pattern. Go for my toughest serve.* I readied myself in position, bounced the ball in my left hand several times to loosen up until I felt my concentration was completely back on the court. I tossed the ball high. Shit. A lousy toss, too far left, and before I could stop myself from hitting it, I'd swung. The ball went straight into the net. *How could I choke like this?* Ida, meanwhile, looked bored.

Do I go for the hard second serve or pop this one in? Back to deuce if I lose. From somewhere deep inside of me I knew I had to risk the killer serve again. Ida would never suspect another hard serve. So what if my father had taught me when I played on the high school tennis team not to do a risky tough serve on a second serve? Especially at a set point…*hmmm, what to do?*

I looked right through Ida. I bounced, bounced, bounced the ball, preparing to put my entire body into the upward motion of the serve, and then power forward and down with a final pop of my wrist. *Take the risk, Jody!*

The force of energy rocked me hard, and while moving forward in anticipation of an effective deep shot, I was surprised to see my powerful serve landed far shorter than I had planned. It landed in the front corner of the service box—a tough backhand serve for Ida to reach and hit with any force. I hoped there'd be no return, so this would be over. But it all happened so quickly, of course, and Ida connected the tip of her racquet to the ball, and although it was a miss-hit, the ball arced up instead of straight, because Ida, rarely able to lob, had aimed it high enough into the air to sail over my head. I stretched my racquet as high as I could, nearly wrenching my arm from my shoulder, but I couldn't reach it, nor could I shuffle sideways fast enough to grab it. Back to deuce. At least two more points to go to win—or lose. "Goddamn it," I said, hoping my mother didn't hear.

But Sam was up above clapping and shouting, and Ida was busy yelling, "I'm famished, let's eat!" because, apparently, the ball had some spin on it and landed wide, outside of the sideline, which I noticed as I turned to watch it roll into the fence. I had won!

"Come eat!" Ida said as she turned to walk off the court, leaving me to collect the balls.

"No thanks, I'm really quite full right now," I muttered under my breath.

Sam must have flown down the hill, because he nearly knocked Ida over as she exited the court. He bounded over to me. "Babe, I saw that. You were terrific." He pulled me toward him and hugged me tightly.

Despite my sweat and the flame-like heat, I rested my entire weight onto his chest. Tears of amazement and relief filled my eyes.

"I really did it."

"You did! Man am I impressed!" He rubbed his hand along my cheek in that magical way. He always made me feel as though I were a precious shell he had found on a beach and forever kept in his pocket, close to his heart. My fears of his liking me less around my family were ill-founded. I choked back tears. *"Yes, Bubbe,"* I said to myself, *"this man of mine has good character."* I touched the front of the gold locket he'd presented me the night before. I'd teared up when he said it reminded him of the one Bubbe had always worn. Inside, he had placed a photo of me and Sam on one side, and on the other side he had engraved the words, "Forever, Sam." Joy overcame me then, and now.

"Honey, it's time for a break from this place, no?" I motioned toward the pool, where the others no doubt were nibbling on the mid-afternoon fruit and veggie platter Aunt Bernice always set out. "I know we were looking forward to seeing Uncle Nathan arrive in Marine Two but, honestly, I'd rather check into the hotel with you and wash up. I need a shower and maybe even a nap. My dad won't mind looking after Hallie. We can come back dinnertime. What d'ya say?"

"Hmmm, watching a helicopter landing with absurd wind to lift all the girls' skirts, or time alone with you, happy, clean and naked? Tough one."

~~~

I was too mentally exhausted, and way too gross, to drive. I dropped my car keys into Sam's hand and sank into the passenger seat. It was still a beautiful day, but the sun was uncomfortable through the windshield, so I lowered my visor. As I directed him toward the hotel, we exchanged observations about the day's line-up of characters. Sam teased that I had most of them pegged so perfectly, I should create a sit-com. Or write a novel.

I laughed. "No one would want to watch it or read it, at least in my mind, 'cause it's been my whole life. But I guess if you're one step removed, it's all pretty laughable." I then launched into an ideal scene for the sit-com: "While I was showering during one reunion, Ellen had taken my clothes

241

off the hook outside the small poolside cabana. Afterward, I was stuck in the cabana, naked, with only my soaking wet bathing suit and a towel, but I knew exactly who'd done it. So instead of taking the bait and freaking out, I wordlessly tiptoed out of the cabana stark naked, not even wrapping in my towel, and came up behind Ellen's chaise lounge. 'Hand me my clothes please,' is all I said. She startled and screamed. I acted as though nothing was unusual. Just a cousin asking a favor. Ellen pretended she had no clue what I was talking about. And then I noticed my shirt sticking out a tad from under a towel beside her chair. 'You never ever wear pink.' I said to her, pointing to her balled-up towel with my hot-pink shirt poking out. 'Weird, those are yours? Wonder who put 'em there,' she said. She handed me the clothes, and I silently marched back to the cabana. Neither one of us ever mentioned the episode again.

"Perfect sit-com material! That really happened, just like that?"

"Ya, but only 'cause I suspected everyone else had gone inside and she would be the only one left at the pool, which fortunately was true. I knew she'd hand 'em over without a fuss—or I'd take her clothes next time!"

Sam and I both hooted over this crazy memory. Approaching the hotel, I pointed up ahead to the long, windy driveway.

"By the way, were there any 'characters' I didn't perfectly peg?" I asked.

"Well, Aunt Bernice was sweet, and your dad was charming, what little we talked; mostly we just played in the pool with Hallie. He didn't ask anything important. And Rhonda just watched me all day, her eyes practically disrobing me." He threw his head back and laughed. "I said as little to her as I could, though she hardly asked me a thing either. Let's see: Ida was benign-enough and then mostly busy with you on the court. I was pleasantly surprised by

Barry. And his wife. They seemed down-to-earth, genuine. Barry kept asking questions about my line of work, quite interested in all of it—my photo calendars, the graphic design, we even talked about my karate stuff. He genuinely seemed curious, and so did Leslie. And she's quite a looker, like you said—even though those big boobs and snow-white teeth are clearly the result of some skilled practitioners— even the blonde hair that clashes with her black brows!"

I told Sam Alan-the-Doctor had done Leslie's boob job. One big, happy, intimate family.

"Whoa, that's really weird. But you know, overall, they've all been pretty welcoming, except Alan, well, your cousin Ellen and her husband, too.

"Yeah, Robbie's a bit odd, but they all pick on him so it can't be easy. What bothered you about those three?"

"Other than talking only about themselves? Let's see, I learned about beach houses, ski condos, business accolades, travels to celebrity resorts, and so on. Geez, you'd think they were applying for application to a posh golf club, not just talking with your boyfriend!" He let out a hearty carefree laugh I especially loved right then, because I knew these braggy people weren't getting to him the way they had to Stewart, who felt he was supposed to offer that lifestyle to me, too, even though he knew it wasn't my preferred way of life.

"Yup, you got a good solid dose of them, dear. Watch out. You're new to this crowd; there's usually something up their sleeves with a newcomer. It's sad really. Why can't they just be genuinely interested in one another instead of competing all the time?"

"Hey, what's it matter? You aptly warned me, so I let them ramble on all full of themselves about the stars they've mingled with and so on. Some of it was really cool." Sam eased the car into a parking spot and leaned over to kiss my cheek. "By the way, I suggested Barry and Leslie invite us to their ski chalet in Utah this winter. Can't wait!"

I playfully swatted him. Sam didn't even ski.

We parked in the lot, bypassing the valet—preferring to use our well-working sets of legs, and arms strong-enough to carry in our own bags.

While Sam checked us into the hotel, I went into the gift shop. My triumph over winning the match, and Sam's admirable overall performance, deserved a chocolate bar reward, but the cards I walked by drew my interest instead. One in particular struck me. I quickly bought it, stuffing it into my purse. The chocolate, in fact, had lost its appeal. I had other rewards on my mind.

Chapter Twenty-Nine

We settled into the room, with its king-sized bed and fancy but comfy décor. I suggested Sam shower first, testing his reply. It would be new for us to shower together.

"You sure?"

"Well, I oughta stretch a tad first."

"Yeah, all right."

He sounded disappointed we wouldn't be showering together. *Good.* "Uh, just let me pee first," I added.

Without him noticing, I grabbed my purse and brought it into the bathroom. I retrieved the card I had just bought and dug out a pen and a tube of bright red lipstick. I signed it, "I do." Then I applied the lipstick to my lips and kissed the inside panel of the card repeatedly, leaving sensuous trails where my lips had grazed the paper. Quietly, I placed the card in its envelope and set it in the corner of the shower, slightly hidden behind the soap and tiny bottles of complimentary shampoo and conditioner, trying hard not to knock it all over and create a commotion. There, it worked; the card was noticeable but mostly hidden. I flushed the toilet and left the room, first swishing with mouthwash.

A few minutes later, when Sam went into the bathroom, I stripped off my sweaty things and tucked them in a bag in my suitcase. I heard him start the water flowing, and a tad

245

later he flushed the toilet. *Ten-nine-eight-seven-six-five...* Stark naked, except for my new gold locket, I stood between the bed and the bathroom and thought about his nude body. His long, lean, powerful legs would now be stepping over the edge of the tub and into the shower, his upper body relaxing as the stream of hot water pours over his muscular chest, his thighs and buttocks tightening as he leans over to pick up the soap...and notices my card.

The cover of the card displayed an image of a curvy woman, and printed below her nude bottom were the words: "You trying to take advantage of me?" Inside, the card shifts an overlay to show the woman winking as she unbuttons her blouse: "Or am I just hoping you will?"

Of course, in our case, it wasn't "taking advantage," it was finally agreeing to make love, fully and completely, and it seemed the perfect time now that I felt reassured I could love him unconditionally even around my family, and, best of all, he could tolerate them. My heart swelled with love for him and dreams for our future, with Hallie. No question about it; we both knew we were ready to commit to each other for life, and it was time to let go of any last restraints. I was ready to take the risk. I hoped he still felt the same way.

I quietly opened the bathroom door and pulled the curtain back a mere inch or two. Sam stood there, deliciously naked, the card in one hand and the bar of soap in the other, and though I had felt his erection many times, I gasped, feeling not only aroused but so satisfied he was reacting exactly the way I wanted him to. It was time; he knew it, too.

I looked up at his face, and although he was smirking and looking at me with a sexy intensity I'd never seen before, I thought I also noticed tears mixed in with the water splashing out of the faucet. I moved to step over the tub edge to join him in the shower, but I hesitated, not wanting to ruin what we'd been savoring all these months; was this okay, or did he have a different plan, or place, in mind? I tilted my head and raised my eyebrows, as though to ask, "Okay?" Then just for effect, I also touched the locket, as though to say, "Isn't that what this meant?"

He answered by leaning toward me, dropping the card onto the floor, and helping me step over the tub, the bar of soap still in his other hand. Gently, slowly, he pulled me close, and pressed against me as he kissed me passionately, but only for a second, long enough for both of us to be boiling with desire. Then he pulled back from me slightly and rubbed the bar of soap slowly down my neck, onto one breast and then the other, his other hand braced behind my back, just barely grazing my bottom, his fingers gently tickling me with the soap. I wet my fingers, gathered some of the soap from my breasts, and closed my slippery fingers around him, releasing a deep moan from Sam. He ran the soap down my belly slowly, ever so slowly, and although I wanted him so badly, I held back, letting go of his flesh, letting him take control. Just then, he pulled the curtain wide and tossed the bar of soap behind me. He climbed over the tub edge, and soapy and soaked, he managed to lift me up, carry me out of the bathroom, and place me on the bed.

I melted into the moment, into him, as we both said, "I love you" and I added, "I do, Sam, I do."

~~~

When I opened my eyes, I still felt the warmth from beautiful love-making. How did I get this lucky to find someone emotional, honest, and giving—both in life and in the bedroom? I rolled over to cuddle into Sam's naked body…but he wasn't there. I sat up and peered around the corner toward the bathroom: all quiet, the door wide open. I thought I knew everything about Sam by then, but of course I didn't know his post-coital habits and hoped he didn't do something weird after making love, like go for a run or do something strange, leaving me alone, feeling abandoned. Perplexed, I went into the bathroom, peed, and then wrapped the white fluffy hotel robe about my body. I sat on the edge of the bed, unsure what to do next. I glanced at the clock, relieved we had an hour before needing to return to the house for dinner. I looked around for a note. Nothing. My old, familiar anxiety resurfaced, but I calmed myself by assuming Sam didn't want to wake me and would be right back. I decided to sit on the balcony and wait it out. I slid open the curtain to unlock the latch. There, with his head in his hands, sat Sam, naked except for gym shorts.

I opened the sliding glass door. He straightened up and wiped his eyes with the side of his hand, and then patted his thigh for me to sit. I lowered myself onto his lap, facing sideways. He silently leaned his forehead onto the side of my face. I took his hand in mine and massaged it so slowly it suddenly brought me back to Grandpa's shiva when I was a child and Bubbe had held my hand and massaged it whenever she needed comfort. This time, nothing was childlike; this was real adult life, real adult issues. We sat that way for several minutes, feeling each other's breath and hearing only quiet rustling of trees and birds chirping in the distance. I trusted that when he was ready, he would share what he could. I imagined this must be painful for him: How do you make love to another woman when your beloved wife, whose body you knew as intimately as your own, is gone forever? I knew I hadn't disappointed him; whatever Shelley's skin had felt like to him, whatever Shelley had done while they made love—her movements, her sighs, her mouth on his body—I knew the two of us had also begun creating patterns of our own, love-making that heightened my senses like never before, our hands and mouths gently groping to find and caress every part of each other, his warm lips tickling their way down my body, as exciting and stimulating and loving as anything I'd ever experienced.

Finally, he spoke in broken words, as though it was all he had the emotional stamina to reveal: "Beautiful. Intense.

Real." Then he paused, moved his forehead from mine, and we locked warm, sad eyes: "Jody, we waited so long, and it was great. Really great. So powerful it brought me to a place I didn't realize I was headed. I'm sorry...being with you like this made me miss Shelley, I have to admit it. Yet I felt so deeply happy, knowing I couldn't feel anything this intense if you weren't right for me. I had known it, but I didn't expect this reaction. And at the same time, I know she would approve of us being together."

I remained quiet, lifting my hand to the back of his head, stroking the tiny curve at the base of his neck.

"I guess the only reason Shelley rushed back to me like this is because of how good this is," he added, and I nodded my head and pulled him to me. The two of us hugged gently in silence for a long time. Eventually, instinctively, we both sensed it was time to get up, shower again, and get ready for dinner. We stood, holding hands, and walked into the room, locking the door behind us and pulling the curtain closed. Then Sam led me to the bed and patted it, asking me to sit beside him.

"There's one more thing I need to share with you," he said, this time taking my hands in his. I continued to trust him. I had no idea what to expect. Did he want us to have a child together? I would definitely consider that. Did he want to make sure we had no more children? I might consider that, too, although I would be disappointed. Did he want to tell me his condo rent was increasing and he wanted to move in with me? That might be fine, or maybe we should move to a place of our own. Whatever it was, I could handle it.

"Jody, I've lied to you." Hearing the word "lie," I wasn't sure I could stay composed, but I tried. I sat up tall, my head tucked toward my shoulder, like Ringo did when he was curious about a strange sound. I rubbed the lowest part of my neck, my hand resting on my throat until he continued.

"I wanted to make sure you loved me for who I am, not for what my father has left me," he said. Despite my wrinkled brow and half frown on my face, I managed to stay focused and trusting, wondering where this was headed. "You know my condo? Well, I not only own it, but, well, my mother and I own the entire building and two others like it in Boston. I help oversee them all. My dad was not just a successful graphic designer, but he also dabbled in real estate, and so do I, although mostly just managing a few managers these days."

I looked right through the man I love, studying the ugly squiggly wallpaper behind him. Then I glanced down toward my lap, confused, but he cupped my chin in his hand and turned my face back up toward his.

"I'm the same person with the exact same values I've always had. Money isn't what drives me. Nor does stepping on others to acquire assets. Nor bragging about it. Nor do I have as much as your family I assume, but I'm happily comfortable."

My mind raced through all the times he had said "no problem" when I offered to pay, including the trip to the fancy La Valencia Hotel, and the extravagant dress in La Jolla I'd turned down, and his expensive wool jackets that hung so well on his fit body, and his beautifully decorated office and condo and—

"I'm just like my dad, Jo: pursuing my life full of joy and desire, humbly, though it was time I come clean with you before presenting you with this." He stood up and asked if I was all right with his news, as though asking my permission to continue with his plans. I nodded, yes, and it was true; I was stunned, but it all made sense now. And it took pressure off of future finances if we were to merge our lives together. *When* we were to merge our lives together.

Sam walked the few feet to his suitcase as I continued to digest all of this, and once I truly grasped it, I felt a huge sense of relief that money no longer remained an imbalance between us, though it wouldn't change either of us much, only provide more comfort and security.

The sound of the suitcase zipper drew me out of my reverie. My pulse quickened and I watched as he pulled out a small wrapped item. He placed the gold box, tied with red velvet ribbon, onto my lap. "And no, it's not perfume, nor another locket."

I wasn't speechless often, but this whole shock certainly took my voice away. I giggled inwardly, curious if his exquisite lovemaking had made me mute. But I remained quiet, fumbling with the ribbon and recalling the day he had handed me the special box on that early date, and how I had worried back then that it might contain jewelry, but of course it was perfume. Shelley's perfume litmus test. This time I knew what it was for sure: Sam had, after all, asked me to marry him months before and was still waiting for my affirmative reply, which I had granted informally just hours before. As I untied the last of the ribbon, Sam went down on one knee, his smirk reminiscent of the day he burst into his office late for a meeting and encountered me, the fortune cookie lady. I never forgot that look, and here it was again.

"I must do this traditionally," he said. He looked adorably silly in his red gym shorts, one knee on the brown tweed hotel carpet. I didn't know whether to look at him or the glistening ring that now revealed itself in its red velvet nest. It appeared to be a one carat, or so, solitaire diamond tastefully set between two smaller, brilliant rubies on a simple white-gold band. It made me catch my breath, learning for the first time what that cliché truly meant. I lifted my eyes to his.

"My dearest, loving Jody, who has brought me back to life—despite months of, well, unusual antics," he paused, smiling, "would you please forgive my lying to you for the sake of knowing you truly loved me for me, and not for my money and my great sexual talents—and yours equally so I might add?" We both laughed. "And would you, forever and ever, promise to be my wife?" He lifted the ring out of its holder, slid it onto the tip of my finger, and waited for my response.

I leaned forward and grabbed the back of his head with my right hand, sending the box and ribbon flying. I buried my face in his neck while shouting yes, yes, yes over and over again until the ring settled just right onto my finger. Sam placed his arms around my neck, and the two of us fell onto the bed and held each other close. No words, no kisses. Just quiet, peaceful comfort knowing we'd lived through so many of life's tests in less than a year, and we were now stronger together than apart.

~~~

Our second shower in just a few hours was far less sensual than the first, with both of us spending more time looking at my ring than much of anything else. I wanted to know how he'd figured out my size (stole my silver ring from my jewelry case, but since put it back). And he wanted to know if I had figured out why the two rubies.

"I just figured you were bragging about how much money you've really got," I said, playfully kicking him in the butt as we toweled off.

"Well, one is for Hallie, it's her birthstone."

"Of course, how sweet!" I said, studying the ring yet again. Hallie's fourth birthday was just weeks away. She'd love this present!

"The other's more complicated, but I think you can handle it."

No more surprises, please. "Huh?"

"Well, for now, if it's all right with you, I'd like to think the other stone symbolizes Shelley, because without losing her, I wouldn't have found you. But that may just be for now. Maybe there's another 'Hallie' in our future, too, who knows?"

We both stopped drying off and turned to face each other.

I touched his cheek. "Either one is acceptable to me. All I know is I trust your love fully and love you back with all my heart."

Chapter Thirty

Sam, my fiancé—a word I would easily become used to—couldn't have looked more charming. He wore a black short-sleeved shirt tucked into dark gray slacks, his straight posture and toned chest and arms adding to my attraction. His late-in-the-day stubble made him look even sexier.

Back home, I had struggled over what I might feel like wearing to the dinner, so I brought along a few outfits. Sam suggested I wear the sleeveless red cotton dress, because it had a higher neckline than I usually wore. We had agreed to hang the new ring on the same chain as the gold heart, and I would wear it inside my dress until—*if*—we were ready to share our news.

When we arrived, Aunt Bernice welcomed us back. She motioned downstairs to where the three children were settled into a lower-level den eating early dinner with Ellen and Robbie's nanny. Apparently, Uncle Nathan had made his grand entrance from Marine Two not long after we had left, and Hallie couldn't stop talking about the wind Uncle Nathan brought with him. The nanny said everyone pretended they were in a windstorm and Nathan was James Bond, hopping out onto the roof. Feeling all giddy after that experience, everyone went straight for the drinks and hors d'oeuvres, not even bothering to shower or change, she explained.

Sure enough, we went back upstairs and peeked into the living room through the artwork that doubled as a room divider. Everyone was in a bathing suit, cover-up or tennis clothes, their tuchuses settled on towels on the taupe suede couches and chairs. My red cotton dress suddenly felt out of place, as did Sam's dress pants, but at least Uncle Nathan, shoe-and-tie-less, still wore his suit pants and dress shirt, though he had opened his shirt collar to the third button. We heard everyone drilling Uncle Nathan.

"Did he really do it with 'that woman, Monica Lewinsky'?" Ellen's husband, Robbie, was shouting, and soon the room echoed with "Did he? Did he? Come on Nathan, did he?" Nathan sat on his throne—his special oversized chair—and clamped his mouth into a forced smirk. He sipped his drink now and then during breaks from the Rubik's cube he was busy twisting with determination. Everyone knew he was the cat who ate the cream, and yet I knew he would reveal bupkis. Nathan never disclosed anything about his clients. We had to learn the usual way— the media. But this time Sam and I had entered a circus, as they were pushing harder for answers to the country's biggest pastime. And from the look of those charcoal-colored circles under my uncle's eyes, I suspected new facts might well be emerging in the media soon.

I sometimes wondered if my uncle was on the right side of the President's messy case—had Clinton truly crossed a line with a young, innocent intern, or had it been fabricated by those who leaked it? If she did participate, what might her motivations have been? Yet what did it matter? *He* needed to know right from wrong! Not only was he married, but he was forty-nine and she was twenty-two! The truth would come to the fore eventually.

As sober latecomers to this rowdy party, Sam and I decided to hold back in the foyer a while, observing the goings-on in the living room through the artful lattice slats. The first odd thing we noticed was Robbie and Alan using the others as a decoy of some sort to distract Uncle Nathan. My sister and Cousin Barry and his wife totally surrounded Nathan. Aah, Robbie and Alan went about adding more vodka to Nathan's drink resting on the end table. We quickly pieced together their scheme to get Nathan drunk, yet I knew my uncle was too shrewd.

Sure enough, as we moved toward the room, Uncle Nathan jumped up. He rushed to hug me and shake Sam's hand firmly, meeting him for the first time with a warm welcome. Nathan apologized for the craziness inside the living room. He wanted us to know he'd caught on to the others' little game—and reversed it. He had switched the contents of the labeled bottles: The supposed tonic water bottle was now half-filled with vodka, and the vodka bottle contained water with just enough vodka to keep the taste. He also filled up a strong vodka tonic mix on ice in a crystal pitcher. Every time he'd get up for another stuffed mushroom or cracker with caviar, he'd offer the willing imbibers a bit more "vodka tonic mix" while Robbie sneakily poured more of what the schemers all assumed was "vodka" into Nathan's drink, back by his throne. Wise Uncle Nathan stayed rather sober while the others spoke with slurred words at deafening decibels, giggling nonstop.

Sam and I were glad my uncle had trusted us with his secret—and that he had poured us each a glass of chardonnay instead!

Fortunately, Bernice missed most of the chaos while supervising dinner with her hired kitchen helpers. I'd heard we were having lobster for the first time, since Bubbe had refused to eat shellfish, and now we were free to do so. Sam and I were starved and could hardly wait. And other than a quick hello to thank Ida for helping watch Hallie—noticing she had showered and put on a skirt and blouse—we didn't speak to her, as she was preoccupied with adjusting the table seating to her liking.

After a few Frank Sinatra songs blared through the stereo system with Nathan singing along trying to look a bit tipsy, and everyone still pumping him unsuccessfully, Bernice and company emerged into the dining room through the swinging kitchen door. The dining room flowed right into the living room. The open floor plan was divided only by half walls, furnishings or modern sculptures. All heads turned toward Aunt Bernice, who carried a steaming platter of lobsters piled so high her head looked like a big red ball hidden beneath clouds. She placed the platter down and ushered everyone to their chairs around the large oval table.

Ida, as always, played traffic cop. She assigned my sister to sit next to our father; Alan-the-Doctor next to Barry's wife, Leslie; Ellen's husband, Robbie, beside Aunt Bernice; Cousin Barry next to me, and so on, placing Sam between herself and Rhonda. As he found his way to his seat, Sam caught my attention and made a throat-slitting gesture. I laughed out loud…until I saw I was stuck between Barry and Robbie, not quite as bad a fate as Sam's, as Barry was usually harmless, but I never had anything to say to Robbie.

Glasses clanked and voices escalated as one-by-one we located our spots, pulled out the heavy chairs and plunked into them. Just as all the tuchuses finally hit the seats, as though on cue, the three servers burst through the kitchen door with several bowls of corn on the cob, dishes of gourmet coleslaw, buckets full of clams on the half shell, and corn bread chunks the size of cobblestones. They placed it all on the serving table and then walked about tying red and white plastic lobster bibs on everyone. It looked like a table full of toddlers ready for dinner. Ida nudged her server away, but somehow the petite server managed to tie the bib over my mother's navy blue blouse, the gold shoulder epaulets barely peeking out of the sides of the bib. Finally, the servers plunked a lobster on everyone's plate and went about serving the rest of the food until everyone's plate was full.

Uncle Nathan stood, and everyone pulled themselves together with all eyes on him.

"Raise your glasses to the reason we first came together every summer for our reunion weekend: To Bubbe, our beloved matriarch who brought us all this." He swept his hand around the table toward the family, then leaned over to Harry. As he clinked his brother's glass, the tough public relations man choked up as he said, "To Mom."

"To Bubbe!" Everyone clinked glasses with whatever they held. Nathan sat. And Rhonda immediately stood. I was surprised, as my sister rarely did anything bold. I sensed she was continuing the scheme to get Nathan to squeal.

"Let's lighten things up a little," Rhonda began, giggling and slurring her words. "Shince we're eating lobster for da first time, let's shtart some other new traditions and play the 'I Reveal' game." Everyone looked askance at her. "Okay, so here's the deal: Ya eat everyting on your plate 'cept your lobster. Don't crack your 'lobby' 'til it's your turn ta tell the others some personal secret." She sat down, swaying a tad in her seat, then stood right back up: "And make it sometin' juiceee." Then she sunk down in her seat again.

Ida, who never drank alcohol, made a loud huffing sound and looked at her older daughter like she'd suddenly turned into some low-class stranger who didn't belong at our dinner table. Bernice, who also never drank, looked down at her lap, as though Rhonda and this game were going to totally ruin her fabulous meal. But neither dissuaded Rhonda. Harry, too, looked questionably at his daughter's odd behavior, but just took another sip of his drink. Nathan smirked; clearly, they were still trying to trip him up. The

258

others just laughed at Rhonda's drunken state and nibbled at their meal.

I twisted my hands in my lap, certain this odd game could never work with this unimaginative crowd. I looked at Sam. He was scowling at me. But all I could do was shrug and send him a pained glance, hoping he assumed this was atypical and we did not have to join in this stupid game.

My sister stood again. "You sissies, I'll shtart," she said, but before she did, she motioned for the servers to pour her some of the merlot they were now pouring Nathan. "In fact, wine fa evevvyone," Rhonda said, lifting her glass of vodka tonic into the air and taking a few more gulps.

I watched my mother's face contort as she leaned past Sam and shouted, "Haven't you had more than enough, young lady?" Her voice was drowned out by everyone's laughter, as Rhonda held up her lobster, with her hand under its tail, like she was a puppeteer about to perform. In her other hand, she held a thick red nutcracker. Suddenly, Rhonda leaned her lobster so close to Sam's face, it looked as though she might gouge him in the eyes with its legs.

"I reveal that I find this new boyfriend of my sister's to be…" she nearly stumbled onto Sam's chest, and he had to put his hands out to steady her, "to be simply deee-lisshhhh-us." Then she sat down, failed at an attempt to crack her lobster, and the table went silent as she leaned her head onto Sam's shoulder. Sam managed an awkward smile and said, "Sorry, Rhonda, I'm taken." Ida grabbed Rhonda's hair and tilted her head back. I put my hands in my face and frowned at Sam, letting him know this was idiotic, and new to me, too. We'd planned for so many things, so many ways we could excuse ourselves if things weren't going well, but we never could have planned for something absurd like this.

Alan-the-Doctor stood up. "Well, two can play this game, dear one. He leaned his face inches from Leslie's enhanced breasts—which, of course, he, the plastic surgeon, had augmented himself. "I reveal that I've always wanted to play motor boat in here! Brrrrrrrr!" he said, as Leslie pushed him back into his seat, covering her breasts, which practically flopped out of her bathing suit cover. She faked a seated bow, as though she were flattered.

Barry shouted, "Hey, Alan, keep your horny thoughts to yourself, will ya?!"

Alan lifted his lobster from his plate and clamped his teeth into the tail, dangling the entire lobster from his mouth. Then he bowed, and sat.

"Now, now," Harry said, standing, a bit off balance. "A little decorum please."

Nathan piped in, "Yeah, let's just enjoy this special meal everyone. Please. Enough of this silliness."

But now Ida joined in. "Hey Harry, you're standing. Go ahead, what's your big secret? You wish you would have run away with Maria, right? Right?"

"Ida, stop."

"I should stop? Why don't you ever start? Without me you'd be nothing much."

I felt so ashamed of how this night was unfolding. I thought about grabbing Sam and Hallie and fleeing. But it seemed everyone else among the younger generation was caught up in this stupid game, actually having fun.

"For God's sake!" Harry said, grabbing his lobster and pretending it was talking: "I reveal I wish Ida wasn't so headstrong and would just leave a fella alone sometimes— I'm not your narcissistic puppet!" The room went silent. He sat down, his head hanging down as though he were ashamed he had lost his temper. My father was never one to speak ill of others. Everyone had enormous respect for him. I felt proud of my dad for finally speaking up, though I knew it killed him to do so. Meanwhile, Ida pretended to pull on puppet strings and acted like it was all a big joke—though I knew it reached her.

"I need to follow that one!" Robbie said as he stood and grabbed a lobster. He wiggled it across the table toward his wife, Ellen. "Somehow you inherited your Aunt Ida's headstrong genes. Maybe she's really your mom!" He winked at Uncle Nathan, who through the years had warmed Robbie's pockets and probably still did. The room went silent again, this time out of annoyance. No one much liked him and his unscrupulous business practices, which he denied.

Robbie sat down. "Just teasing everyone, love ya honey!" Ellen stuck out her tongue and smiled whimsically, as though everything was all just one big joke.

Maybe to them it was, but to me, this game was going nowhere. And if this was supposed to be a way to get Nathan talking about the President, that certainly wasn't happening! It was as though everyone had forgotten about the topic obsessing them earlier. My mind raced, anxiety rising. I felt disgusted this was how the evening was unfolding instead of honoring Bubbe or helping Sam feel comfortable. I couldn't just sit there any longer and let this happen. But what could I do?

As though my body had control over me, my legs pushed me up, and without even looking at Sam, or lifting my lobster, I dove in: "I'm revealing that for a long, long time, probably my entire life, these reunions have made me feel like I'm adopted. Like I just don't belong here, and tonight I don't find any of this fun or funny, just absolutely absurd. And no way to honor Bubbe's memory or welcome my Sam. You may think it's all in good fun, but he and I don't. Believe me. This really needs to stop." As I dropped back into my seat, I felt my entire body tremble. I looked toward Sam, knowing he was miserable with this shit, too, yet he responded with an awkward half-smile half-frown and a "thumbs up." I felt numb.

"You mean you *weren't* adopted?" Rhonda blurted. She fell into a shrieking witchlike laugh. Several muffled snickers followed. I might have laughed had I not endured a lifetime of her inability to stay with real, difficult emotions. I said across the table to Sam, "Let's go," but he shocked me by standing next.

"I'm certainly the newcomer to this group, so maybe I should go last, or not at all," he said, and while a few nodded their heads, Alan-the-Doctor chanted, "Go Sam, go Sam, go Sam," and Ellen and Robbie joined in. "I just want to say, even though it seems this silly game is in good fun to most of you, it's difficult to observe everyone stinging everyone. It's just not my, or Jody's, idea of fun. I don't like judging you any more than I want you judging me, guys, yet what you may not know is my father died many years back, and I think you all know my wife died not long ago, and I'd give anything to have them both back—well, if my wife came back it certainly would ruin my chances with Jody, but you get my point. Man, we really need to love everyone while we're still here, foibles and all. Sarcasm's funny, but it also cuts deep. Thanks for hearing me out, not that you had a choice." He smiled awkwardly, and sat down.

I was dazzled Sam had spoken up right when it mattered most. And, somehow, he'd managed to quiet the wild animals to such an extent the room went silent again, and all we heard were Aunt Bernice's multiple clocks ticking in a multitude of tones. No one moved. I figured Sam was either a fun-buster, or a mensch, yet it wasn't clear yet which one they'd coin him. I didn't care; to me he was Mahatma Gandi.

Barry stood next, motioning to Leslie to stand up, too. Those who'd eaten already were licking their lips or wiping fingers with wet naps. Alan-the-Doctor seized the untouched food from Leslie's plate and began consuming it.

"We just want to welcome Sam to the family and hope he joins us officially soon," Barry began, looking at me.

Leslie smiled like Dolly Parton winning another Grammy. "He might not be able to kick our butts on the tennis court, but apparently he can anywhere else, he's a third-degree black belt and aside from being one of the best photographers and designers in Bahston, he owns some city real estate." And with that, Barry winked at Sam and added, "Let's talk soon. Tax shelter opps?"

I couldn't see Sam's reaction from my angle. But I had warned him Barry's kindness was usually loaded. Sure enough, he'd done his research on Sam and wanted to pull him into his corner. Thank God I wasn't learning the news about Sam this way!

"Jody, why did you keep the real estate piece from me all this time?" Ida asked. "So he's got money, huh?"

"And when has that ever been one of my key values, Mother? Are you telling me money buys happiness--"

"Oh, it can't, yet it can sure disguise unhappiness. But more important, you need inner strength," she said, and then turned toward Sam. "And you know, while I could not understand my Jody wanting to be with you at first, Sam, I now get it. It takes balls to stand there in front of all of us and point out we are being utterly wretched...and I guess it's your balls that finally gave Jody some confidence." She sat, while many around the table giggled, but she quickly rose again, her bib bobbing over her bosoms: "As long as I'm on a roll, Nathan, say what you want about my being too strong-willed, but here is the honest truth for this stupid game tonight: I grew up tough after becoming a six-year-old with a dead mother. I'm a survivor, and I'd be damned if I raised girls who were shrinking violets. End of story." She glanced toward Bernice as she planted her bottom back down and drained her glass of wine.

We all looked from one to the other, mouths agape, and many heads turned toward Harry, who wore a quiet, glazed look. But before he could get this under control—

somehow—a chair pushed back with a thump, and all eyes went to Bernice, who stood up.

"I reveal I nearly had an affair with Nathan's limo driver," she said, her eyebrow twitching as she spurted out her words so run-on they sounded like one gigantic word: "I mean, after all, Gregg is available far more than Nathan, but in the end I did not do it. I love my husband and my family too much. And, and, I am no shrinking violet, I just keep to myself!"

Bernice stomped toward the kitchen, and over her shoulder added, "And Nathan knows all about it, so don't think you've got the scoop before he does." She pushed the kitchen door open hurriedly, and it flapped repeatedly, in out, in out. The high-pitched hinges squeaked like bedsprings.

Ellen's eyes widened like she'd just seen a murder. "With Gregg, the schvartze? My mother?! Shit, makes my thoughts of having an affair acceptable now." She darted after Bernice. Robbie chased after Ellen.

All nine remaining heads turned toward Nathan. Uncharacteristically, he hid his head in his hands. Suddenly, a chair made a scraping sound on the hardwood floor, and Sam stood and walked behind the table, edging his way in the tight squeeze past Rhonda and Harry and Ellen's chair, all the way around to me. He helped me the rest of the way out of my seat. We both knew we were going downstairs to claim Hallie. And leave.

"No, please stay." Uncle Nathan stood and spoke in a bold voice. "I am terribly embarrassed by my family's behavior tonight, and I am actually rather responsible, as you know, Sam." Nathan pushed away from his chair and walked over to me and Sam. In the open marble foyer, the massive mirrors on both sides created an effect of dozens and dozens of Jodys, Sams and Nathans. Uncle Nathan placed one arm around Sam's shoulders. Nathan announced to the others that he had figured out their little game with the vodka, so he switched things up, like a dumb teenager.

"Once everyone got drunk and out of control, it was too late to turn back the joke," he said. "So this is entirely my fault. Please sit back down, Sam. Let's all return to some normalcy. I suspect with all the pressure I have been under, and losing Mom, I am just not myself tonight either." He glanced at Harry for help.

"Let's not let this reunion shatter us just because Bubbe's no longer here," Harry said. Then his eyes froze, locked on me. He rose and walked over to where I stood, leaning onto Sam. My father stopped directly in front of me. With all the nervous tension, I had absentmindedly slipped my hand under my dress, pulled out my locket and engagement ring, and I was fondling both. I quickly let go and they dangled on my chest. Sam noticed what was happening and angled his tall frame toward Harry. Harry stood squarely in front of us. He looked from me to Sam, and then back to me, studying us closely. My bottom lip trembled. The others had no idea what was happening but remained quiet, the family patriarch clearly up to something important.

Sam managed to mutter, "This may not be the proper time and place, but despite your crazy family, I still intend to marry your daughter. May I please have your daughter's hand in marriage, sir, well, after she's officially divorced...soon."

Harry, squealing like a child, took Sam's hand in his, hugged us, and shouted like his team had just won the championship. "Yes. Yes. We needed some good news tonight! Mazel tov!" To Sam, he warmly said, "You're a good man. I'm so ashamed about tonight." He leaned over and kissed my cheek.

Ida marched over and stared at the dangling ring. She lifted it between her fingers and practically pushed her nose into it, inspecting the stones as though she were head jeweler emerging with a magnifying loupe. I stood motionless.

"Oy, vey iz mir!" Mother shouted, but I couldn't decipher her tone. Thrilled? Or disappointed that the stones, while beautiful, were hardly her ostentatious style?

"So he's *really* not just after her money!" Ida shouted.

Ah, so that was it all this time? No one could love me unless they were after money?

"Uh, you forgetting he is Cath-o-lic, Mother?"

Sam tapped my side. It meant: "Let it go." He was right. Striving all these years for my mother's approval had proved to be detrimental to my self-worth and identity. It was time to stop reacting to her. I had to leave her be—and change myself instead. Fortunately, Stella, Isaac, Debra and the rest of Sam's entire family were to be my new, loving mishpucha. I'd figure out what to do about my own family with time.

"Do you think the world would truly be as interesting if we were all Jewish?" Ida said. "To Jody and Sam! My new son-in-law!"

What had she been smoking: a joint, or a peace pipe? Who was this woman before us? Certainly not the mother I'd known for nearly thirty-four years. But her little speech had excavated invaluable treasures—even made some sense out of her narcissistic ways—so I clamped my mouth shut, glanced at Sam and rolled my eyes. He placed his arm around my shoulder and pulled me close. I knew Ida smelled money and could change her tune—but not her stripes. Sam and I had the next move on the chess board of life. We needed to decide immediately whether to stay and give this another chance—without rose-colored glasses—or still leave, now that our news, as well as our disgust for the last half hour's events, were out in the open.

But before Sam or I could speak, Nathan appeared out of nowhere and pushed the five of us into a football huddle of an embrace. The others rose from the table, clamoring toward the foyer.

Rhonda rushed over to be first to inspect my ring. "Not bad, sis, not bad at all." She sounded less inebriated now, but still stood too close to Sam, who hugged her briefly and backed away.

The others pushed toward me, nearly knocking me over. Reflecting into the giant mirrors surrounding us, we looked like a TV scene from Times Square on New Year's Eve— with thousands upon thousands of people squeezed in way too tightly. And everyone shouting in annoyingly high decibels.

Leslie edged her way toward me. She tugged the chain too close to her face. I steadied myself on Sam's arm.

"Oh, you'd rather wear it around your neck, honey?" she asked, then without waiting for an answer asked, "Is it the real thing?"

Barry pushed his way in. "Of course it is, Les," he said. "Mazel tov, future cousin, I'll go get you my biz card!"

Leslie kissed my cheek, saying into my ear, "By the way, it's okay, I was adopted, too!" Barry whisked her away.

The rest of the family lined up near us, forming what felt like a receiving line. Even Robbie returned to the room despite the bomb Ellen had dropped on him. Maybe her near-affair was to counter one he had had? This was all too bizarre. Had I fallen asleep and woken up in a Woody Allen movie?

The children entered the room with the nanny to see what the commotion was about, just as the kitchen door swung open and Bernice and Ellen appeared with a platter piled high with Ellen's famous chocolate chip butterscotch brownies. The servers brought out trays of éclairs and ice cream bonbons and placed them on the living room buffet beside cups and saucers and coffee.

Rhonda lifted Tiffany into her arms, and Hallie raced toward me. Sam bent down and picked her up.

"Mommy and I are going to be married, what do you think of that?"

"Does that mean I can have a little brother or sister?"

"Maybe," I answered, "but there's plenty of time to talk about it."

"Only if the child is Jewish," Ida bellowed. Ah, my mother was showing her true colors again; so much for her diversity speech.

Sam defrayed the moment by bending down to ruffle Ida's hair. Although she attempted to reach up to the top of his head, the tips of her fingers barely met his chin. He lifted her up off the ground, and she mussed his hair. I knew Sam brought out the best in me, but what a nice surprise that he could turn a lion into a kitty cat. At least for one evening.

"Dessert anyone?" Bernice shouted. Then she came over to hug me and Sam. Ellen followed, examining the ring wordlessly then heading back to the buffet. Bernice motioned us into the living room where everyone was settling in, then headed in herself.

Barry and Leslie sat squished together in one armchair feeding each other dessert. Alan spread his body across an entire couch, nodding off to sleep. Robbie sat nearby in a big chair, looking like a little boy. My parents sat on the other couch, my father accepting an after-dinner brandy and a cigar from Nathan—but he kept it unlit for now. Nathan plopped into his throne with his crystal brandy glass in one hand and a lit cigar in the other. Bernice was placing an overflowing plate of pastries beside him.

Sam and I remained between the foyer and the living room, whispering platitudes that life was not going to go on happily ever after with this crew and us, but we could handle it for now. While we couldn't expect to ever change them, they were family: bonded by blood and memories, messy and obnoxious, rude but mostly harmless, and, in truth, not that different from most meshugenah families. Moving forward, we must decide what to participate in, set limits on, and say an outright "no" to.

I took Hallie's hand and walked her over to where Ellen and Rhonda had hoisted up their little ones to the buffet to choose their desserts. I observed as the next generation reached for the biggest brownies and fattest éclairs and plumpest chocolate rugelach—which Rhonda had made in Bubbe's memory, much to my shock and delight.

As joyous chatter echoed up into the rafters, my first thought was after all these sweets, there'd probably be lots of high-energy, belly aching kids—and adults—later. But for now, let them have their fun. And for the first time, instead of my seeing "competition" and "one-upmanship" of all kinds, I saw, simply, an imperfect—but loving-in-their-own way—family. I saw them just as they are: People who were being themselves, for good and for bad, and struggling with desires for love and recognition, and grappling with demons. I no longer needed to judge and control *them* in order to change *myself*. And I could finally move on with my life, following my own path and values, no matter how different from theirs. I had a choice, and I could choose to reject them, sure—or I could accept them as they are, couldn't I? Just like I had come to accept myself, finally, in the way Bubbe and my best friend, Ruthie, and Sam and his mother and so many others had for so long—but I never could before. I, too, was human: imperfect, delicate and a good bit neurotic, but kind, loving and, most important, feeling loveable.

Sam filled a plate of goodies for both of us, and we walked to the couch hand-in-hand—right beside Hallie, who stood tall and proud as she carried her own plate.

The End

***Glossary of Yiddish Words / Jewish Terms
Used in This Novel***

Borscht Belt: A group of resorts in the Catskills in New York, once a major vacation destination for American Jews from the 1920s to the 1960s.

Bubbe: Grandmother

Bupkis: Nothing

Challah: Egg-rich, leavened bread braided and made into shapes, traditionally eaten by Jews on the Sabbath and holidays.

Daven: To recite prayers.

Gefilte fish: The flesh of a fish ground up with ingredients such as eggs, spices, onions and carrots. It is handmade by some, but more often it is purchased in jars.

Goy/Goyim: A derogatory word for non-Jewish person/persons.

Hamantaschen: A triangular, filled cookie/pastry associated with the Jewish holiday of Purim.

Kaput: Finished/dead

Kosher: Appropriate food to be eaten or dishes/serving items used, according to dietary laws.

Lokshen kugel (also called noodle kugel): A sweet or savory casserole served as a side dish on Shabbat or other holidays or commemorations.

Macher: An important person; someone who makes things happen.

Mazel tov: A Jewish phrase meaning "congratulations" or "good luck."

Mensch: A highly honorable and decent person.

Meshugenah: Crazy

Mishpucha: Family, including in-laws

Mishegas: Crazy/ludicrous

Nachas: Pride

Oneg Shabbat: A Jewish celebration of the Sabbath, which ends with refreshments.

Oy, vey iz mir!: Woe is me!

Plotz: To faint or collapse in shock.

Rugelach: A crescent-shaped cookie-like dessert traditionally filled with walnuts, raisins and cinnamon.

Schlepping: Carrying, as in something heavy.

Secular: Jews who maintain their Jewish identity with little participation in Judaism beliefs and practices.

Shiksa: Derogatory word for a non-Jewish woman.

Shtupping: Having sexual intercourse with someone.

Schvartze: Derogatory word for a black person.

Shiva: A mourning period held after a death during which close relatives/friends visit the bereaved; the ritual is referred to as "sitting shiva." Food is usually served.

Tot Shabbat: Jewish Sabbath service for young children and their families, with festive activities.

Treif: Non-Kosher food; any food not in accordance with Jewish laws.

Tuchus: Rear-end/buttocks

Yenta: A woman who is a gossip or busybody.

Zaftig: A woman with a full figure, usually including large breasts and shapely wide bottom.

Zayde: Grandfather

Acknowledgements

Thank you to my parents, Sandy and Herb Pollack, for being role models for living a fruitful life, and for their pride in my writing accomplishments through the years.

A hearty thank you to my early supporters, as I began this book nearly two decades ago: Author Michael G. Levin, for lighting my fictional fire; sisters Sue Hall Place and the greatly missed Nancy Hall Young for their delight in my first drafts; Gladys Drohan for loving the Bubbe character way back; Heather Pullen, for incessantly pushing me to finish this novel; Phyllis Giller, for superb, early editorial input and lifetime friendship; my daughter Melissa Serotkin for reading chapters at a time and always encouraging me to publish; my sister Jill Kutchin for pointing out my many run-on sentences in early chapters; author Michelle Hoover at GrubStreet for critical novel-writing lessons that redirected me; and fellow writer Adam Olenn for keeping me motivated when he said this book won't be for every reader, but those who like it will love it. I'd also like to recognize my cousins Sheila Bender and Wendy Pollack Isaacs for perpetuating the "Fine" creative writing gene. And special thanks to Louise S. Andrews for introducing me to so many spiritual adventures—which double as quiet time to create.

In the last few years, the following readers of completed drafts have been invaluable: Rabbi Susan Abramson, Judi Boviard, Dana Fine, Jean Duffy, my stepdaughter Gina Fusi, Judith Gray, Jennifer Klein, Stephanie Kriesberg PsyD, Judy Smith-Pfeffer, Marnie Pilachowski, Dori Pulizzi, Jill Tapper, Leslie Wittman, and Jim Young. Also, Irwin Mirsky for saying he loved my draft the day it was inches from the shredder. And thank you to William Ian Whitney, National Registry of Emergency Medical Technicians

Paramedic, for helping with my 911 scene, and to Rhona Barlevy for feedback and guidance on the language in the emergency room scene. And, above and beyond, to Debi Dulberg for eleventh hour eagle eyes.

A giant thank you to artist Patricia Kaegi for her amazing cover illustration; I found her the exact day I needed her. And to Molly McLaughlin, who completed her tribute CD to her mom, inspiring me to complete my goal, too!

Finally, this novel would not be possible without the never-ending love of my husband, Steve Fusi, who always supports my need for writing junkets and late-night editing. Thank you, too, to my former spouse, Paul, for being an ongoing fan of my writing—and nothing like this fictional ex-husband. Also, Gary and Anne Woonteiler and team for editing, marketing, and publishing advice—and friendship. And to Deb, a high school classmate who long ago asked me to create a short story about her breakup with her boyfriend for my creative writing class. Look where that propelled me, decades later!

Thank you all for your input, output, motivation and joy!

About the Author

Mindy Pollack-Fusi is an award-winning, lifelong writer, former public relations professional and veteran journalist and essayist for *The Boston Globe*. She founded The Place for Words in 2009 in Bedford, Mass. to teach creative writing to adults, and coach students on college application essays. She is the editor of "The Ice Cream Stand, Stories & Poems" by 21 writers that attended her workshops. The collection includes contributions by Mindy and poetry teacher Dianalee Velie.

Mindy earned a Bachelor of Science in Magazine Journalism from Syracuse University's S.I. Newhouse School of Communications and a Master of Science in Public Relations from Boston University's School of Public Communications.

Originally from Long Island, NY, and, later, Brookline, Mass., Mindy now divides her time between Bedford and Falmouth, Mass., where she lives with her husband, Steve, and rescue dog, Doogie Howser, M.D., The Doctor of Love! They have two adult children. This is Mindy's first novel, published by her indie imprint, The Place for Words Press.

MINDY POLLACK-FUSI

For More Information:

Contact Mindy via the inquiry form at:
www.MindyPollackFusi.com for:

- A copy of Book Club questions & commentary
- Scheduling Mindy for:
  - ✓ Book Club visits or Skype
  - ✓ Jewish organization talks or panels
  - ✓ Narcissist survivors' panels or Meetups;
  - ✓ Bookstore visits;
  - ✓ Blog or other media interviews/book reviews.

MINDY POLLACK-FUSI

THE NARCISSIST'S DAUGHTER

41173106R00165

Made in the USA
Middletown, DE
04 April 2019